Acclaim for Peter Ackroyd's

The Clerkenwell Tales

"Dreams, visions, and history are fused together to form a work of tremendous imaginative strangeness. . . . It is hard not to admire the boldness of this attempt to make the Middle Ages breathe again for the benefit of modern readers." —*The Boston Globe*

"Plumped with arcane, fascinating historical tidbits *[The Clerkenwell Tales]* assumes an immediacy and an intimacy that shrinks the gap between the centuries." —*The Orlando Sentinel*

"Marvelous. . . . An absorbing and twisted (in all senses) story of madness, intrigue and treason." —*Houston Chronicle*

"Captures a world that has seemingly vanished . . . historical details are woven seamlessly with the writer's artistic license. . . . An exhilarating panorama of London." —*The News & Observer*

"Ackroyd's learning is as impressive as his imagination. . . . Like Chaucer, Ackroyd sees literature and history as part of the same tradition." —*The Observer*

"A compellingly dark plot—more Ellroy's L.A. than Merrie England." —*Newsday*

D1016865

"Brilliant. . . . A tightly written and suspenseful novel. Peter Ackroyd is one of the best historical novelists and literary biographers writing today."   —*The Tennessean*

"A fascinating combination of fact and keenly imagined fiction."
—*Deseret News*

"Ackroyd's 'colour' is so curious, so rich and so variegated that there is something in almost every sentence to sharpen one's sense of late 14th-century London as squirmingly alive—and extremely pungent. . . . A cunning little intrigue."   —*The Spectator*

Peter Ackroyd

The Clerkenwell Tales

Peter Ackroyd is the author of biographies of Dickens, Blake, and Thomas More, and of the bestselling *London: The Biography*. His most recent book is *Albion: The Origins of the English Imagination*. He has won the Whitbread Book Award for Biography, the Royal Society of Literature's William Heinemann Award, the James Tait Black Memorial Prize, *The Guardian* Fiction prize, the Somerset Maugham Award, and the South Bank Award for Literature. He lives in London.

ALSO BY PETER ACKROYD

Fiction

The Great Fire of London
The Last Testament of Oscar Wilde
Hawksmoor
Chatterton
First Light
English Music
The House of Doctor Dee
Dan Leno and the Limehouse Golem
Milton in America
The Plato Papers

Nonfiction

Dressing Up: Transvestism and Drag: The History of an Obsession
London: The Biography
Albion: The Origins of the English Imagination

Biography

Ezra Pound and His World
T. S. Eliot
Dickens
Blake
The Life of Thomas More

Poetry

Ouch!
The Diversions of Purley and Other Poems

Criticism

Notes for a New Culture
The Collection: Journalism, Reviews, Essays, Short Stories, Lectures
(edited by Thomas Wright)

The Clerkenwell Tales

Peter Ackroyd

ANCHOR BOOKS

A DIVISION OF RANDOM HOUSE, INC.

NEW YORK

FIRST ANCHOR BOOKS EDITION, NOVEMBER 2005

Copyright © 2004 by Peter Ackroyd

All rights reserved. Published in the United States by Anchor Books, a division of Random House, Inc., New York. Originally published in hardcover in the United Kingdom by Chatto & Windus, London, in 2003, and subsequently in hardcover in the United States by Nan A. Talese, an imprint of Doubleday, a division of Random House, Inc., New York, in 2004.

Anchor Books and colophon are registered trademarks of Random House, Inc.

The Library of Congress has cataloged the Nan A. Talese/Doubleday edition
as follows:
Ackroyd, Peter, 1949–
The Clerkenwell tales / Peter Ackroyd.—1st U.S. ed.
p. cm.
1. Great Britain—History—Richard II, 1377–1399—Fiction.
2. London (England)—History—To 1500—Fiction.
3. Christian pilgrims and pilgrimages—Fiction.
4. Prophecies—Fiction. 5. Nuns—Fiction. I. Title.
PR6051.C64C55 2004
823'914—dc21
2004041211

Anchor ISBN-10: 1-4000-7595-5
Anchor ISBN-13: 978-1-4000-7595-9

www.anchorbooks.com

Printed in the United States of America
10 9 8 7 6 5 4 3 2 1

Contents

List of Characters

The reader may recall that many of the characters within this narrative are also to be found in *The Canterbury Tales* by Geoffrey Chaucer. As William Blake remarked, "the characters of Chaucer's pilgrims are the characters which compose all ages and nations: as one age falls, another rises, different to mortal sight, but to immortals only the same . . ."

Dame Agnes de Mordaunt, prioress
Dame Alice, procuratrix
Garret Barton, franklin
Coke Bateman, miller
Bogo, summoner
Henry Bolingbroke, claimant to the throne
Oliver Boteler, squire
Robert Braybroke, Bishop of London
Sister Bridget, second nun
Geoffrey de Calis, knight
Sister Clarice, nun
Drago, canon's yeoman
John Duckling, nun's priest
William Exmewe, Augustine friar
John Ferrour, parson
Hamo Fulberd, illuminator
Thomas Gunter, physician
Emnot Hallyng, clerk
Gabriel Hilton, jeweller

Janekin, apprentice
Jolland, monk
Oswald Koo, reeve
Dame Magga, hosteler
Gybon Maghfeld, squire
Richard Marrow, carpenter
Martin, man of law
Brank Mongorray, monk
Robert Rafu, manciple
Richard II, King of England
Gilbert Rosseler, shipman
Anne Strago, merchant's wife
Radulf Strago, merchant
William Swinderby, canon
Umbald of Arderne, pardoner
Miles Vavasour, sergeant-at-law
Roger Walden, Archbishop of Canterbury
Roger of Ware, cook

Chapter One

The Prioress's Tale

Dame Agnes de Mordaunt was sitting in the window of her chamber, looking out over the garden of the House of Mary at Clerkenwell. Her aunt had been prioress before her, and she assumed familial responsibility for the acres as well as the souls under her care. The garden was called "Forparadis," "Out of Paradise," but on this mild February morning it seemed blessed with the air of Eden itself. It was triangular in shape, in commemoration of the Blessed Trinity, and there was a triangular bed on each side. The three paths connecting them had been constructed with thirty-three flagstones; the three walls around the garden, each one of thirty-three feet, were built out of three layers of stone – pebble stone, flint and rag stone. Some lilies had been planted round a cherry tree in token of the Resurrection, and in the language of flowers might spell the words she knew by heart, "The just man will grow like the lily, and he will flourish in the sight of God." But then Dame Agnes sighed. Who could bring more unhappiness upon this house? Who can give more heat to the fire, or joy to heaven, or pain to hell?

In the open fields beyond the walled garden, stretching down to the river, she could see the malt-house with its dovecote, the familiar cart-house, and the turf-house beside the stables. On the western bank of the Fleet river stood the mill-house and, on the other side, a cottage of whitewashed walls and thatched roof which belonged to the bailiff of the convent. The miller and the bailiff were engaged in a protracted lawsuit over their rights to the river which flowed between them. They had often taken one of the Thames barges from the mouth of the Fleet to Westminster in order to press their cases with a judge or a sergeant-at-law, but nothing had been resolved; the boat costs two-pence, the bailiff had said to Agnes, but the law costs a man everything. The prioress had tried to intercede but had been told by her cellaress, among others, that she might as well spread honey among thorns.

She could smell the steam coming from the kitchen across the cloister, and could hear the clatter of brass plates being washed for bread and beef after prime. Would the world always run in this way until the day of doom? We are like drops of rain, falling slantwise to the earth. Her monkey, sensing her melancholy, clambered upon her shoulders and began to play with the gold ring suspended on a silken thread between her breasts. She sang to it a new French song, "Jay tout perdu mon temps et mon labour," and then played handy-dandy with a hazelnut.

She had entered the House of Mary while still a young girl, and had somehow maintained the dazed demureness of her childhood. But she could also be excitable and irascible, taking pride in her exalted position as a child might. Some of the younger nuns whispered that, on Innocents Day, she ought to couple with the Boy Bishop. Her chamber was hung with green cloths, together with curtains of green velvet. Green was the colour considered to be friendly to the underworld spirits. It were wise, she had said, not to wake the well. This clerk's well lay just beyond the stone wall of the convent, a few feet from the infirmary, and was deemed to be a sacred place.[1]

---

[1] For this and subsequent references, see Chapter Twenty-three, "The Author's Tale."

At this hour of the morning she drank either ypocras or claree, the sweet wine soothing her stomach made tender by the ordeals which she had recently endured. Rumours of the strange events within the convent had already reached as far as the cookshops of East Cheap and the fish-stalls of Friday Street; although Agnes had not been informed of these somewhat garbled reports, she was aware of a strange disquiet in the vicinity and felt uneasy. She dipped her finger into the wine and honey before giving it to her monkey to suck. "The first finger is the little man," she murmured to it in a childish voice which would have embarrassed her in company. "This is the leech finger, for it is the one that the physician uses. The next is called the long man. This one here is the toucher or lick-pot. Do you see? I touch your nose with it." There was a sharp rap upon the door, and she rose quickly from the window seat. "Who is knocking?"

"Idonea, ma dame."

"Enter in God's name, Idonea."

The sub-prioress, an elderly nun whose face was as raw and as pitted as over-salted meat, hardly waited for the invitation. She made a hurried pretence at bowing, but it was clear that she could not contain her excitement. "She has fallen into a fit. She is speaking in another voice than her own rightful voice."

Agnes looked with pity, as always, at the ill-favoured visage of Idonea. "She is fighting with God."

There was no need to explain who "she" was. The mad nun of Clerkenwell, Sister Clarice, had been conceived and born in the tunnels beneath the convent.

"Where is she now?"

"In the painted chamber."

There had been unhappiness before in the House of Mary. A great scandal had been provoked by certain nuns under the rule of Agnes's aunt, Joyeuse de Mordaunt, whose manifest infirmities prevented her from keeping control over her flock.

Two hundred yards from the convent stood the more celebrated priory of St. John of Jerusalem, the house of the Knights Hospitallers. A great congeries of stone buildings, chapels, orchards, gardens, fishponds, wooden dwellings and outhouses which stretched as far as Smithfield to the south and the Fleet river to the west, it was an ancient foundation, rendered more sacred by the relics which had been the gifts of several popes, among them a phial of milk from the breasts of the Virgin Mary, a piece of sail-cloth from St. Peter's boat, a feather from the wings of Gabriel and fragments from the multiplied loaves and fishes. Only recently the senses of a man, dumb and blind from birth, had been restored by a drop of the Blessed Mother's milk. The priory was a church and hostel for travellers, as well as a hospital and large working farm, but twenty years before it had also acquired a reputation for licentiousness. In the words of the cardinal legate who had been sent by the pope to investigate the matter, it had harboured "nervous and demoniacal merriment" together with "dances and lascivious games."

Everyone agreed that it had been the fault primarily of the young nuns. It was remarked how eager they had become to cross the green of Clerkenwell in order to confess to the priests attached to the priory, and it soon became clear that confession was not their main purpose. The cellarer of the priory had told the kitcheness of the convent that the nuns had been observed dancing and playing the lute; as he put it to her, "the devil was dancing on their heads." Some of the nuns had draped strings of small bells about their necks, which prompted the kitcheness to call them "the devil's cows." It was said that the mistress of the novices had thrown away her birch in sympathy, and had joined her charges in all this wantonness. It was also noted that several of the younger nuns were absent at vespers or at compline. Dame Joyeuse de Mordaunt suffered from the palsy, and could in no way be made to understand the seriousness of these reports.

But the disorder had grown so great that the prior of St. John felt obliged to seek an audience *secreto* with the Bishop of London. The bishop duly ordered a visitation, reminding the prior of the text "Evil shall have that evil will deserve," and in person interviewed every nun in the convent of St. Mary. In the report of these proceedings, it was revealed that there had indeed been much running and leaping and flying, much lifting up and discovering, among the monks and nuns. But there were other enormities. Certain of the nuns admitted to clandestine meetings with the male servants of the convent in the cart-house and in the bake-house; even the church itself had become a place of assignation. It was often said by the citizens that nuns were fond of ginger hot in the mouth, and now the popular aphorism had been decisively proved. A cook, a porter, a gardener and cowherd were as a result discharged, while the errant nuns were despatched to other convents in disgrace. By dispersing them it was hoped, according to the bishop, that all their heat would be turned to cold.

The most shocking discovery came last, however, when it was revealed by the infirmaress, Sister Eglantine, that there existed a series of passages running beneath the earth between the priory and the convent. Their construction pre-dated the foundation of both religious houses, and their original purpose could not be divined, but they had been employed in more recent years as a convenient gateway for those who did not wish to be seen above the ground. In the bishop's secret report, sent under seal to Rome, it was also disclosed that certain infants born of the illicit union between monk and nun were kept in these subterranean tunnels until they were of an age to join the life of the religious institutions without scandal. Such a child was Clarice, whose behaviour now so troubled the repose of Agnes de Mordaunt.

The vengeance of God had been swift. In the year of Clarice's birth, 1381, the ragged army of Wat Tyler had stormed and burned the priory of St. John; the prior himself had been beheaded on Clerkenwell Green. As the fire raged the nuns of the House of Mary brought Joyeuse de Mordaunt before the rebels as an emblem of their weakness and helplessness. "The Virgin protects us," they had called out to Tyler.

He had laughed and raised his hat in greeting; he had already dipped its feathers in the blood of the prior. The nuns had feared rape, but endured only a few loud and salacious remarks. The convent was spared but, three months later, the elderly prioress died of apoplexy. Her last words were, "The head was off before his hat was on."

Agnes de Mordaunt adjusted her veil and wimple in order to ensure that her forehead was covered before leading Sister Idonea out of the chamber; she tied her monkey with a long ribbon to the base of her close-stool and, taking up her crozier, proceeded down the stone stairway to the refectory. Before confronting Sister Clarice she wished to ensure that the others were quiet. She found them finishing their beef and bread. Sister Bona, the sub-chantress, was reading aloud from the *Vitis Mystica*, and was expounding the five wits of hearing, sight, smelling, feeling and chewing. When Agnes entered she stopped, and the others rose at the table.

The nuns of course observed the rule of silence, and employed their hands in sign language to receive salt or beer; to ask for salt, for example, it was necessary to put the right thumb over the left thumb. Agnes suspected, however, that there had been a slight murmur of words before her arrival, a little whisper of "sic" or "non" as Sister Bona had maintained her slow and steady reading of the treatise. If any nun had been caught she would have been compelled to eat in the convent cellar with the infirm and the feeble-minded but, under the gaze of Dame Agnes, each one preserved her decorum. The prioress passed through, acknowledging their reverence with the smallest bow of the head, but she could not resist a sidelong glance at Sister Beryl who was smiling broadly at her. It was no sin to smile, especially since the holy scriptures had taught that we would all be merry in heaven, but Beryl's expression angered Agnes; it was the anger of a child left out of the game.

Sister Idonea walked softly behind and, as they left through the side door of the refectory, she slipped upon the cobbles. "You should not walk wet-shod." Agnes could hardly keep her countenance and resist laughing. "The stones are treacherous."

They walked across the cloister to the painted chamber, a small room beside the chapter-house which was used by the treasuress as her office.

Sister Clarice was standing in a corner, her hands folded across her chest.

"Where be the gay robes and the soft sheets and the little monkey playing with a ring?" The prioress said nothing. "Agnes, you will conceive of a holy man and give birth to the fifth evangelist." Clarice was only eighteen years, but already her voice was possessed of an implacable authority.

Agnes could feel herself trembling. "Listen, cocatrice, I will send you to do penance among the lepers of St. Giles."

"And I shall teach them the words of Jesus the flower-maker."

"Not so. You are the devil's story-teller."

"Is it the devil who tells me of the king? Is it the devil who prophesies his undoing?"

"Ave Genetrix! Mother of lies!"

It had all begun with a dream, or a vision. Clarice had fallen into a fever three months before and, while confined to bed, had confided to the infirmaress that she had seen a demon in the shape of a deformed and very ancient manikin going around the dormitory and touching each of the nun's beds. He had then turned and said to Clarice, "Take careful note of each place, little sister, for they shall not be without a visit from me." In another dream, or vision, Clarice had fallen upon the demon and beaten him with her fists; he laughed and sprang out of her grasp, saying, "Yesterday I disturbed your sister the chantress much more, but she did not hit me." On hearing of this strange interview, the chantress herself had become very indignant and demanded that Agnes rebuke Clarice before the whole community in the chapter-house.

Instead Agnes had invited the young nun to her chamber. "You know," she began, "that there are three forms of dream. There is that of *somnium coeleste* or heavenly influence. Your wind does not blow from that corner."

Clarice laughed out loud. "Purge me with rhubarb, ma dame."

"Then there is the dream which springs from *somnium naturale* and your bodily humours. The third comes from *somnium animale* or dejection of spirits. Can you tell me, Clarice, which of these is yours?" The nun shook her head. "Do you know that your brain is filled with owls and apes?" Clarice still said nothing. "Do you dream of King Richard?"

"Yes. I dream of the damned."

Agnes ignored her dangerous answer. "A dream is sometimes called a meeting. What is it, then, that comes to you?"

"I am sister to the day and night. I am sister to the woods. They come to me."

"You are babbling like a child."

"Why, then, I should go to a dark place beneath the nunnery."

Dame Agnes walked across the chamber to her and slapped her face. Her monkey began to cry and chatter, and suddenly she felt an overwhelming need to sleep. "I pray that God gives me wisdom enough to reach true judgement. Now go."

That night Sister Clarice rose from her bed and wept, as if she were being berated by some unseen power. Resisting as much as she could, she seemed to be pushed from the dormitory and into the choir of the church. She lay down in one of the stalls, and began to speak in a low voice. Many of the nuns had now gathered in alarm, among them the infirmaress and the sub-prioress who repeated her words to Dame Agnes the next morning. "He shall awake the waster with water. Before five years are fulfilled such famine will arise through floods and foul weather that fruit shall fail. And so he has warned me. When you see the sun amiss, and two monks' heads, and a maid has the mastery, and multiply by eight. Then death will draw on and Davy the ditcher will die of despair." The plague or "death" had come only nine years before, and Clarice's prophecy was sufficiently alarming to send two nuns into a fit of weeping. The rest looked on, horrified, as Clarice trussed up her habit and in open view placed her hand within her queynte crying, "The first house of Sunday belongs to the sun, and the second to Venus." Then she fell into a faint, and was carried into the infirmary from which she did not emerge for six days.

The convent was in uproar. The prioress prostrated herself before the high altar, and remained in silent prayer for several hours; those in her charge crept into the chapter-house where in low voices they debated whether the sins of the community had brought down this visitation. The words whispered were fantasy, fancy, fantastic, phantasma – but others suggested that Sister Clarice was indeed divinely inspired and that her words were true prophecies.

Two evenings after the event in the choir stalls the prioress consulted the nun's priest, a young Benedictine by the name of John Duckling. He was acquainted with the art of surgery; by his own account, he was acquainted with the art of everything. "We may cut a vein in her forehead against frenzy," he was explaining to Dame Agnes.

"Not the temples?"

"They are good for the migraine only. The foremost ventricle of the brain, you see, is situate here." He tapped his own forehead, which was as smooth as any nun's. "It is the proper home of the imagination which receives things that contain fantasy. Did you know that the brain is white, like the canvas of a painter? Its colour allows it to be stained by reason and understanding."

"Is it not true that all veins have their beginning in the liver?"

"Of course yes." He seemed puzzled for a moment. "But we may not cut there. There is too much flesh, ma dame. Too much flesh."

Dame Agnes smiled. "But we will not find much matter in her brain, John."

"No indeed. Give the poor sister some toasted bread and wine before the letting. Then cut the vein with a golden instrument. That is the rule. After the blood has been taken wrap her in some blue cloth, and take care that all about her bed is blue also. Make sure that she sleeps on her right side, and that her nightcap has a hole in it through which the vapour may go out." Instead of remaining with his head bowed, and with his hands hidden in his sleeves, he was pacing up and down the prioress's chamber.

Agnes was determined to ignore his discourtesy, however, since this was a pressing matter. "And," she asked him, "if her humours rebel against it?"

"Sage is good for convulsions. Hence the sentence, why should a man die when sage grows in the garden? Give her sage, mixed with the excrements of a sparrow, of a child, and of a dog that eats only bones."

"I thought of hellebore to cleanse her."

"Oh no. Hellebore is a bitter and violent herb, so hot and dry that it should only be used warily. Why, I have seen men so heavy after hellebore that they might have been dead."

Dame Agnes asked these questions because she feared that Sister Clarice would refuse to be letted, and that she would need to be restrained. Any violence would cause clamour and excitement among the younger nuns. But, in fact, Clarice made not the slightest objection. She seemed entirely complaisant about the matter, as if she welcomed the chance of being the object of medical attention. No one in holy orders was permitted to spill blood and so the local leech, Hubert Jonkyns, was called to the convent. He was skilled in all the arts of blood and sat Clarice upon a moveable privy, her legs straddling it, before gently cutting the vein. She did not speak or move, but only smiled when he put the phial up to her forehead; he pressed gently against the vein, and she gazed at him tenderly while letting out a fart whose odour filled the chamber. He patted her on the head when his work was done.

"You may lose some of your remembrance with your blood," he told her. "Comb your hair each morning with an ivory comb, since nothing recreates the memory more. Walnuts are hurtful to the memory. And so are onions. Avoid them. Do not stay in the house of a red-haired or red-faced person."

"There is always Sister Idonea," she said.

The leech did not understand what she meant, and turned to the nun's priest who was standing in the corner. "Her white neck is the sign of lecherousness," he whispered. "Did you smell that fart?"

Despite all of Hubert Jonkyns' precautions, however, Clarice did not sleep well that night. She rose from her bed at the time of lauds and, in the sight of all those who had gathered in the choir, she began to sweep the nave of the church while prophesying the ravishment and ruin of the convent itself. She cried out, also, that all the churches of England would be wrecked and wiped clean.

Rumours of her prophecies soon spread beyond the walls of the convent and into the city where, in the turbulent time of a weak and wretched king, her admonitions were given credence. Some called her the mad nun of Clerkenwell, but many others revered her as the blessed maid of Clerkenwell. The bishop's exorcist conducted several interviews with her, but he found her distracted and contradictory. "The sweetness of Christ's Mother has pierced my heart," she told him on one occasion. "To me she came and bade me to sing, O Alma Redemptoris mater."

"But Dame Agnes tells me that you dream only of the damned. Or so you said to her."

"I can no more expound in this matter. I learn my song, but I have small grammar."

Then she called out for the Redeemer.

At another meeting she had foreseen fire and the sword, but then in the next moment had howled at the prospect of bliss. The exorcist could not fathom her words; his only remedy was to confine her to the convent and on no account allow her to walk abroad.

Three weeks after the sweeping of the church, another extra-ordinary event was being reported from street to street. The chantress had been heard to scream loudly and repeatedly. When others ran to the chapter-house, where she was standing, they found several nuns lying on the stone floor with their arms outstretched in the shape of the cross; around them was a circle of little wooden and stone images of the Virgin, with a burning candle between each of them. These nuns were intoning, in low voices, the antiphon "Media vita in morte sumus"; the chantress had thought that they were singing "Revelabunt celi iniquitatem ludi," which was used notoriously as a spell. That was why she had screamed. One nun then rose to her feet, and flung a candle at her curious and terrified sisters; another bit the rushes three times in sign of a curse. It was feared that the entire convent might become possessed, and the prioress ordered that all the offending nuns should be locked in the cellars.

It was on the morning following this unhappy episode that Dame Agnes de Mordaunt had entered the painted chamber with Sister Idonea and had described Clarice as the mother of lies.

"You have caused great grievance here," she continued. "As if swine had been running among us."

Clarice looked intently at Agnes' breasts. "A ring upon a nun is like a ring in a sow's nose."

The prioress restrained her impulse to beat the girl about the head. "You slide in your words, Clarice. You slip."

"No. I am on stony ground."

"Then pray for deliverance, daughter."

Whereupon Clarice fell upon her knees. "I pray to Mary, Holy Mother of God, that the five wounds of Her only begotten Son may appear again."

Agnes looked at her with distaste. She suspected that there was much subtle craft in the young nun's demeanour, but she could not prove it.

"They will appear in the five wounds of the city when it will be lifted into bliss."

"You speak from a dark place."

"There will be five fires and five deaths in London." Clarice, still upon her knees, then began to sing.

> "And when she came to St. Mary's aisle
> Where nuns were wont to pray,
> The vespers were sung, the shrine was gone,
> And the nuns had passed away."[2]

At the earnest entreaty of Dame Agnes the Bishop of London, Robert Braybroke, summoned Clarice to his palace in Aldermanbury. Robert was a cleric who had grown rich upon benefices, a robust and high-coloured man who had a reputation for sudden fits of violent anger. He kept the nun waiting in a small stone chamber beside the great hall where, after an hour, she was brought into his presence. He was dipping his fingers into a bowl of rose water. "Here is the little nun who begets large words. Oh, ma dame, il faut initier le peuple aux mystères de Dieu. Is that your song? Leave us." The two canons who had brought her quickly left the room. They stood close to the door, in the corridor outside, but they could not hear what was being said – only, at one point, the sound of laughter.

Robert Braybroke had his hand upon her neck when they emerged from this interview. "The wise child waits," he said to her.

"The wise child knows its own father," she replied.

"Remember, Clarice, I am your father now."

Chapter Two

The Friar's Tale

On a stormy morning, one week after Sister Clarice's interview with Robert Braybroke, Bishop of London, two figures might have been seen pacing the cloister of St. Bartholomew the Great, the priory church of Smithfield. They were engaged in earnest conversation, and moved quickly from pillar to pillar. One was dressed in the black hood and cloak of an Austin friar; the other wore a loose-fitting garment of patched leather, around which were tied an awl and handsaw as tokens of his trade. There was a third following them, a younger man who walked with his head bowed. An observer might have been puzzled by the fact that he was close behind them, but that they seemed to ignore him. His name was Hamo Fulberd.

Hamo was listening intently to them.

"We must act," the friar said.

"Why be hasty in this hot fare?" the carpenter replied. "The nun does our work for us."

"True. She inflames the city." The friar was silent for a moment.

"The incense out of the fire is sweet. But you must act, Marrow. You know what you must do."

The huge rain wrapped itself around the cloister, and there was a sudden thunder-light in the dark sky. Hamo instinctively looked towards the vaulted roof of the passage, its ribs and arches holding back the power of the stone. In the moist air it smelled of forgotten time, rancid and indignant at its deposition. To the boy it seemed that the friar and the carpenter were imprisoned by stone, enshrined by stone – that endless ages of stone lay above their heads, and that they could only find their way beneath it in subdued voices and with tired gestures. They were crouched beneath the stone, but they might have been kneeling in adoration.[3] The stone rose up, defying the rain and wind, sealing with an act of blessedness the earth and sky. What did it matter what they said? I do not wish to look upon grass or upon flowers, Hamo said to himself, I only wish to look upon stone. It is my home. I wish to become stone. If they choose to mock me, or to laugh at me, I will turn my stone face towards them.

"I have told you, Marrow, all the matter concerning the five circles of deliverance." As he spoke the friar, William Exmewe, uncovered his head; his red hair, now tonsured, had once been rich and abundant. "Five ways, and five times in each way."

"Turnagain Lane."

"In the city of God. Five senses. Five wounds."

They walked for a while in silence along the sides of the court; there was a conduit at its centre, from which all the water of the priory came, and an image of St. Chrysostom stood upon its metal cover in perpetual blessing.

"There are five letters in the name of Jesus. It is the endless knot."

The carpenter, Richard Marrow, did not reply. It was as if he were afraid, or unwilling, to speak. It was as if he had calculated how many words would lead him through this life, and was determined not to exceed that number. He was tall, with the willed slenderness of the ascetic.

The friar gestured to the light that had once more brought shade and brightness to the cloister. "But now, you see, God has breathed upon us. He is still here."

The rain had cleared as suddenly as it had descended, and Hamo felt an overwhelming desire to walk out over Smithfield. He had been brought up in the priory. He had been found abandoned in Cock Lane, only a few yards from this place, and was assumed to be the unwanted child of one of the prostitutes who plied their trade in that narrow thoroughfare. He had been left at the gate of St. Bartholomew, and discovered there by the elderly porter who looked after the horses; from that day forward he had known no life other than that of the friars. It was discovered that he was skilled with his hands, and so he was trained as an illuminator in the scriptorium. He prepared the inks and the paints; he smoothed the parchments and drew lines upon them with rule and charcoal pencil. He learned to mix black and red, white and yellow. Then he was trained in the art of drawing outlines with a brush of squirrel hair. He was taught how to plaster the walls of the church in preparation for the murals; he would cover them with lime putty, rendered damp for the better retention of colour. He had worked first on the smaller paintings on these walls, known to the friars as *Biblia pauperum* or poor man's Bible. In the chancel, for example, he had drawn the outline of Longinus piercing the body of the crucified Christ with a lance. The left hand of Longinus was pointing towards his face, as a token that he had miraculously recovered his sight. Over the years Hamo had learned the secrets of his art. The open palm denoted judgement; the upraised or pointed finger was the token of condemnation. The curved finger was the symbol of speech, while raised hands signified argument or exposition. The hands and arms spread out could be interpreted as wonder or adoration. Crossed legs were a sign of unnaturalness; that is why, in the mysteries, Herod was played in that position. The soul was always depicted as a small and naked figure, sometimes wearing a crown or a mitre. He painted all of these with red and yellow ochre, with lime white and lamp black, with green and lapis lazuli.

He was known to the others as "simple Hamo" or as "silent Hamo." He took part in the rituals of the community by rote, without conviction of any kind. He did not consider himself part of the friars' common life or fervent faith. From infancy, he had been a natural exile. When he suffered sorrow or fear, he did not consider it. This was the way of the world. Someone else might have pitied him, but he did not pity himself. He was familiar with loneliness. He was accustomed to long endurance. If he had experienced any strong feeling he would have dismissed it, since he had no one with whom he could share it. Yet over these years, he had attached himself to William Exmewe. He had begun following the young friar from a distance, staying just out of sight, but Exmewe had noticed him. He called out to Hamo one evening as he came from the refectory; the boy had been waiting for him by the corner of the building.

"What is this? Follow the leader?" Hamo looked up at him silently and intently. "What do you call yourself?" Exmewe knew his name, of course, but was determined to make him speak. He took him by the shoulders, and shook him roughly. "Do you have a tongue to use? Would it be Hamo Fulberd?" The boy nodded. "Fulberd and yet beardless, I see." St.ill the boy said nothing. "You are like wood. God forbid that you be carved from a wicked tree." But then Exmewe, perhaps recalling the circumstances of Hamo's adoption, relented. "Well, Fulberd, walk in the open way ever after. Where I may see you."

So Hamo stayed in Exmewe's company. The other friars debated among themselves the nature of his temperament and the precise mixture of his humours. Some deemed the boy to be melancholic, therefore slow and pensive, while others believed him to possess the chaste and sad piteousness of the phlegmatic. The connection between the two was impossible to fathom except that, in some obscure fashion, Hamo Fulberd had found a father.

Now that the rain had cleared, Exmewe opened the wicket gate of the priory and walked out into Smithfield. It was not market day but the open space was churned up by horses and carts and wagons of every description; pigs were rooting among the rubbish, and black kites wandered among discarded bones as if they were in mourning for London itself. The name of God was all around them – "God save you," "God's speed," "God give you grace" – muttered casually and under the breath, or cried aloud in greeting, like some susurrus of benevolence from the divine world. The smell of slaughtered animals, coming from the shambles, mingled with human scents as they passed the Broken Seld, the Bell on the Hoop, the Saresinshed, and the Cardinal's Hat.

"Filled with priests," Exmewe observed as he peered into the basement of the Hat. "They transubstantiate the wine into nothing." Above the ground-floor door of this hostelry was a sign of welcome vividly painted on a wooden panel; it displayed the image of a man entering a bed where someone else was already sleeping. "They say that March is burial month. I could fill a graveyard with these Rome-runners and chop-churches."

"They are the beads of the devil's rosary." Richard Marrow knew the litany of contempt.

"They are the kin of Cain. The children of Judas singing from the prayer book of hell."

Just then a loud argument broke out, with the cries of "Havoc!" and "Heads! Heads!" Mixed with them were the noises of the animals in a muddy yard beside the tavern, roped together and constrained by oaths and blows; Hamo could not endure the sound of horses and cattle being lashed, pummelled by fists, whipped by laughing children. It broke open for him all sense of order. He would rather have stripped himself bare and gone into the middle of Smithfield as a sacrifice. Instead he put his hands to his ears and let out a low insistent moan. All the woes of this world seemed to enter him.

Exmewe hit him upon the head. "You will mar us all. Depend upon it."

On no account did Exmewe wish to draw attention to himself. Swiftly he led them into Duck Lane, a narrow and confined thoroughfare paved with cobbles and oyster shells, with a row of open arches down its west side; there was a bench across the lower part of each arch, with variously coloured cloths and tapestries piled in profusion. Richard Marrow looked upon their rich colours and textures with disfavour. "When the fire falls," he muttered to Exmewe, "all this will burn to blue ashes."

"Be of good heart. It is the veil."

When he was a carpenter's apprentice, Marrow had been mightily impressed by the news that Christ himself had been a carpenter; he was of a naturally pious disposition and, having learned his ABC at the free school of the local abbess, picked up what scraps of learning in English he could find. He was a reflective man, not much given to speech, but he did converse on spiritual matters with William Exmewe. They had met while Marrow was repairing two side tables in the refectory of St. Bartholomew, where Exmewe had been kitchener before he was elected sub-prior, and they had soon reached agreement on the nature of Christ's example.

Now they came out of Duck Lane close by Aldersgate, where the city ditch was used as a privy. This was against the law and custom of the city, which enjoined strict rules of cleanliness upon its citizens; but in the words of the mayor, the goldsmith Drew Barrantyne, "human nature feels its way through filth and folly." The phrase had been repeated about the streets until it turned into a popular refrain. Eventually it became part of one of the "London songs" which filled the air for several days, or weeks, before disappearing. Some wooden shops and dwellings had been erected between the ditch and the wall itself, with a few planks laid down as a bridge to reach them, and Exmewe pointed out a small shed. It was painted in Naples green. "This is where you will find it," he said to Marrow. "This is where your fire will be. You will take it to the oratory. Over there. In the street of St. John." At the bottom of Aldersgate, standing just in front of the gate itself, a blind man and blind woman were holding slender white willow wands and singing in unison, "Ora! Ora! Ora! Pro nobis!"

Exmewe was staring at Marrow. "Why do you say nothing?" He had suddenly grown angry. "Do you hesitate in this high purpose?

Listen, Marrow. Our work will be as hard as hell. Do you know that? Do you?"

They passed through the gate in silence and entered the city. They were in the street called St. Martin, with its row of four-storey houses on either side. In front of them some stew was being boiled in a cauldron on a bowl of coals, and an ancient woman skimmed off its fat with a perforated spoon. A tooth-drawer, with a wreath of teeth draped over his shoulders, passed them and then looked back with an expression of delight as he loitered among the street-stalls piled high with garlic and wheat, cheese and poultry. The late rains had left the street reeking of night-old vegetables and piss. Exmewe was still filled with this mysterious and unexpected anger. It might have been the anger of God, unfathomable. "Do you hear this chatter of human-kind?" he shouted to Marrow above the press of people and of horses. "God has gone deaf!"

He stumbled over a long cart that was being drawn through the street, and the porter yelled at him, "Rouse your eyes, man! Do you not see?"

Yes, he did see. He saw the tooth-drawer walking back towards them and approaching Marrow. The carpenter was looking into the musical instrument shop.

"May I see your face, sir?"

"Why so?" Marrow asked him.

"Curiosity. I love teeth."

Marrow raised his leather hood, and the tooth-drawer sighed. "Yes. I know you. I have seen you with the Lollards in Coleman Street." The drawer looked around, seeking for witnesses, and Marrow swiftly stepped into the shadow of the shop's sign. "Loller!" The drawer pointed at him. *"False Loller!"*

At that moment someone hurled himself against the drawer. He smashed his raised arm savagely against the drawer's face. Hamo Fulberd had come to save Marrow.

The drawer fell back, concussed, and collapsed into the gitterns and fiddles, the trumpets and tabors, which were suspended from the ceiling of the shop. There was a noise of twanging instruments as Hamo kicked the head of the prostrate man. At the first sign of violence people ran eagerly across the street, ready to use violence themselves, but Marrow remained calm.

"Run, Hamo," he whispered and then called out in a loud voice. "God be here!" He pointed to the tooth-drawer. "This man is a Loller."

At once there was cry of "Stock him! Stock him!"

William Exmewe had already vanished, and in turn Hamo made his way quickly down Bladder Street. A child in a leather cap and long coat stared at him, and then ran up some outside steps to a first-floor chamber. Exmewe had often told Hamo that London was no more than a veil, a pageant cloth, which must be torn asunder to see the face of Christ shining. But at times like this the city seemed real enough. The child was calling out to someone. Hamo turned the corner of Paternoster Row, into the street of the illuminators and parchment-makers whose work was displayed all around him. He glimpsed a saint holding up his arms in ecstasy while, at the bottom of the page, an ape clambered among vines. Here was an image of the Virgin, but in the margins there were geese and dogs and foxes. There was a song sheet entitled *Mysteria tremenda*.

Exmewe had walked along St. Anne Lane and turned right into Forster Lane; after the events of the morning, he had a sudden desire for meat. His anger had quickened his appetite. He was angry because in part he despised himself. What was the phrase? You cannot have two heads under one hood. He began to crave thrushes, pies, sows' feet, anything. Yet he must take care. Always take care. He was aware that he had a tendency to melancholy, and so he refrained from fried meat and from meat which was over-salted. Of course boiled meat was better for melancholy men than roast meat, but in particular he avoided the taste of venison; the deer is a beast that lives in fear, and fear only increases the melancholy humour. If he had eaten venison, he would have fled all the sooner from Aldersgate. There was a cookshop close by, where journeymen and labourers ate their boiled mutton bones and penny ale. There would be much talk and much wind; the air would be mightily corrupted.

There were occasions when he enjoyed such close-smelling company, however, just as he enjoyed listening to the sins of the poor. It was the smell of humankind, and those who lived in the city had become accustomed to it. There were even those who welcomed human odour and would seek it out in unwholesome places – they were known as "snufflers," and would haunt privies or open jakes for their pleasure. They would follow those citizens who possessed a particular or pungent smell, until they were filled with the evil scent. Exmewe approached the door of the cookshop but the noise and confusion within, like the clattering of a mill, drove him back. Someone was singing "My love has fared inland." He could not eat with this company. Instead he stopped at a roasting-stall and bought two finches for a penny, tossing their small and fragile bones into the middle of the street as he walked westward towards Newgate.

Richard Marrow left the tooth-drawer to the mercy of the people, and managed to make his way down St. Martin into Old Change. There was much building work here, in the precincts of Paul's, and the street was filled with cries of "Yous!" and "Yis!" and "Hoo!" The builders' carts were pulled by horses or by mastiff-hounds, and the labourers played football or sang over their cups in their brief if frequent intervals of rest. It was the way of London.

When Marrow turned from their shouts and cries into Maidenhead Lane, he was in his own familiar neighbourhood. He was known here as "Long Richard," or "Long Dicoun." No one knew of his association with William Exmewe, but he was generally considered to be "touched" or "blessed" by some unworldly spirit. He showed no respect towards the rich or the high-born, for example, and never murmured "God save you" when he met them; he never bowed before them or hid his hands in his sleeve or took off his cap before speaking. He was often chided for his behaviour by his neighbours, who were concerned for the reputation of their ward, but on more than one occasion he had replied that "I would rather eat worms in the wood than bow to their folly." When asked about his tattered clothes he told the story of the peacock who in the deep of night, when he could not see himself, cried because he thought he had lost his beauty. When asked if he knew how his conduct threatened the order of the city, he asked "if the pissing of a wren can disturb the sea?" "Besides," he would remark, "I am too long to stoop low." By the more pious inhabitants of the ward he was compared to a cross that stands in the street, showing men the way.

By the evening, Hamo Fulberd had returned to St. Bartholomew. He lived in a small stone barn erected in a corner of the churchyard, by the outside wall; he slept here, upon a plank covered with straw, with the tools of his trade arranged neatly on a low table beneath the window. He drew comfort from the silent presence of these familiar objects – the hair brushes, the pencils, the earthenware bowls and the glass phials. There were no woollen blankets here, no tapestries or cushions; all was as plain as the barn itself, except that the floor was of earth and turf like the rest of the churchyard in which it stood. He sat down upon his stool, and began to work upon a parchment which he had been given by his teacher, Father Matthew, as a reward for his assiduousness. He was drawing an image of the Three Living and Three Dead. The living ones held scrolls, on which their oaths were written. "By God's bones that was good ale" and "By the feet of Christ I will beat you at the dice" were complemented with "By God's heart I will go to town." Hamo was erasing part of a badly drawn figure, rubbing it with the skin of a stockfish, when Exmewe quietly entered the barn. "This is a brittle world, Hamo." He stood behind the boy's shoulder, peering down at his work. "A cold world."

"This is a cold night."

"There is a city of janglers, and a city of God. That man belonged to the janglers."

"The tooth man?"

"His dwelling is now in hell."

"Are you telling me that he is dead?"

Exmewe put his hands upon Hamo's shoulders. "There is no shorter way." Hamo would never have guessed, or suspected, that Exmewe was lying to him. The tooth-drawer lived, and was even then repeating the story of his attack in a tavern called the Running Pie-Man. "His body has been recovered and now lies in the Barber Surgeons' Hall for the greater glory of his profession. We must keep you close and secret until he is buried."

Hamo rocked upon his stool. "Why? Why do I not belong to the play of the good people?"

"What good people? The world is thick with thieves." Exmewe felt the strangest sensation of pity. "Do not lose heart. Your best friend is still alive."

"Who?"

"You."

Hamo cried, and then laughed aloud, at this. "So I am as alone as I was born."

"You are not alone. You are part of the kingdom of the blessed."

Hamo had listened when Exmewe had expounded to Marrow the secret religion. He had listened incredulously when the friar had told the carpenter that Christ had not voluntarily gone to the sacrifice of the Cross, but had been a victim of a "coivin" or conspiracy between the two other members of the Trinity. He had heard, too, their debates about the nature of destiny and providence. "So what comes, comes by destiny," Marrow had said.

Hamo remembered this now, as he sat upon his stool with the stockfish in his hand, and questioned Exmewe. "So all is foretold by providence?" It was a comparatively new debate, instigated by the theologians of Oxford. In recent years many people had been driven to despair by the idea that they were foredoomed, and that nothing in the world could avert the fate that was awaiting them. There were some who flagellated themselves as a preparation for the punishment to come. It had become so serious a problem among the clergy, for example, that a papal encyclical had been issued against the sin of wanhope. The notion of providence, and of the timelessness of God, induced feelings of helplessness and lassitude. And yet for others the same doctrine was a cause of celebration; they did not feel responsible for their actions, and as a result could sin without remorse. The choice of heaven and hell was beyond them, entirely out of their control, and therefore they could act – or refrain from acting – with impunity.

"Did I destroy the tooth-drawer by providence or by destiny?"

"All will be well."

"Will it?"

"Do not walk or ride outside Bartholomew without my express commandment."

Exmewe left him then, and Hamo Fulberd continued work upon the parchment. Then quite suddenly he put his head upon it and began to weep, calling upon the unspeakable mercy of God.

Chapter Three

The Merchant's Tale

The hour before dawn had come quietly into St. John's Street. A pig wandered down Pissing Alley, having escaped the attentions of the night warden, and from one of the many small tenements along the street came the sound of a baby crying. The haberdasher, Radulf Strago, was about to leave the bed while his wife was still sleeping. He had suffered a bad dream, in which he had said to his mother, "I will give you two yards of linen cloth in which to wrap your body when you are hanged." Even at the time he knew that she had died peacefully, some three years before, from a surfeit of strawberries. In his dream there had begun to fall great flakes of snow, as if they had been locks of wool. He had been trying to knock them away with the flip-flap used to swat flies, but the wool then turned into pieces of frieze cloth and broad cloth. He had awoken in a sweat but, as a practical man whose thoughts were already forming around the business of the day, he dismissed these visions as fantasies. The cramp or flux in his stomach was still there; he had trusted himself to shit it out, but it remained like a hard knot within his body.

He blessed himself and rose from his bed; with a groan he crept over to a small wooden table where he combed his hair before washing his face and hands in a basin of water. He was still naked but he slipped on a linen shift before kneeling on the floor for his pater noster and credo. Then he sat down upon the side of the bed and, muttering a litany to the Mother of God, he drew on a pair of short woollen socks and some woollen hose striped in blue and mustard yellow. There was no need for a doublet on this spring morning, and so he put on a simple jacket of blue serge cloth; he whispered the invocation "Memento, Domine," so as not to disturb his wife, as he donned his green tunic and scarlet hood. I have prayed faithfully, he said under his breath, so the Lord send me good profit. He slipped on his pointed red shoes, fashioned out of the finest leather, and laced them carefully before walking down the wooden stairs to the solar below. His apprentice was sleeping on a pallet, and he roused him with a "Torolly-lolly, Janekin. It is the spring time of the world."

Radulf Strago, at the age of fifty-seven, might have been considered to be in his declining time; but he had married a much younger woman two years before, and had reason to consider himself blessed. It is true that he had been sore and sick in recent weeks; he had cause to vomit every day, and his stools were as loose as running water. He sometimes feared that he had a cancer or imposthume, but he tried to dismiss these symptoms as part of his sanguinary complexion. A change in the aspect of the stars would change everything. His business continued to flourish, in any case, situated as it was between the priory and the city; St. John's Street itself led directly to the gate of the priory of St. John of Jerusalem, and many visitors passed Strago's door. All the travellers to Smithfield came this way, too, in search of hats and shoelaces, combs and linen thread.

The shop itself was on the ground floor facing the street and, without waiting for Janekin, he descended; he unlocked the wooden shutters and unfolded the counter. He opened the door, too, and breathed in the air of dawn. The rays of the sun touched the painted cloths and the children's purses, the whistles and wooden boxes, the beads and parchment skins, solemn and still in the early morning. Then the bells began to ring, and the street itself seemed to know that it must awaken.

At the top of the stairs Janekin coughed and spat; he muttered some oath, unintelligible, to which Radulf replied, "God give you good day!"

The evening before Janekin had been engaged in a battle of words with the young citizens who supported Henry, duke of Lancaster, in his struggle with King Richard. Janekin was of the king's party, and wore a pewter badge of the white hart in his tall hat of felt. John of Gaunt, father of Henry, had died seven weeks before. Now King Richard had revoked Henry's inheritance, keeping the Lancastrian legacy for his own use, and had consigned Henry to perpetual banishment. Whereupon some Lancastrian supporters had rioted through the streets, overturning barrels and breaking down signs.

Janekin had been watching them at the corner of Ave Maria Lane, and had called out "Torphut! Torphut!" as a signal of his contempt. Two of them heard this and ran in chase of Janekin, who turned upon his heels and fled down the lane. There was a fish-stall at the corner of a small yard and he sent it flying across their path. As they slipped upon herring and eel, he laughed out loud, with an exhilarating sensation of panic and excitement, before taking shelter in the porch of St. Agnes the Cripple. An old woman there offered him a candle. He took it, and walked reverently into the nave of the church. He blessed himself, lit the candle and left it by the shrine of St. Agnes with the prayer that he might escape his pursuers.

St. Agnes must indeed have looked down upon London and touched Janekin with her blessing, since he made his way to St. John's Street without any injury.

He had been Radulf's apprentice for the last three years. Before entering the merchant's service he had sworn in the Hall of the

Haberdashers and Drapers that he would not copulate or commit any fornication, and that he would not play at dice or hazard; on these matters, however, he had not proved entirely faithful to his oath. He had also agreed that "ye shall be obedient unto the wardens and unto all the clothing of this fellowship," a stipulation which he had also disobeyed; he favoured the short hair and short tunics of the fashionable youth, and his slender legs were shown to best advantage in scarlet hose. Radulf was not a harsh master, and dismissed these failings as the way of the world. His wife, Anne Strago, had also pleaded on the apprentice's behalf. "Can a young man," she asked her husband, "be happy in such sad and wise stuff? Can he wear a slashed doublet in West Chepe? The dogs would bark at him."

Anne had been present at the ceremony in the guild's hall. When her husband had been asked, according to custom, whether his apprentice was of good growth and stature, and whether he had any disfigurement of the body, she looked at Janekin with curiosity. He was not disfigured at all; he was slender and graceful, already taller than her husband. She had been married to Radulf for two years, in a union properly conceived for purposes of trade. Her father had been a haberdasher, also, with a substantial shop in Old Jewry; she was an only child and, on his death, she had inherited the business entire. It was now only lent to Radulf Strago for the duration of his life; when his soul changed house, she would be a wealthy widow indeed. In the meantime she was disgusted by her duties concerning the merchant's cod – his coillons, his bollocks, his yard, his testicles, call it what she would in her disgust – and she prayed God for an ending. She devoutly wished her husband to die.

Janekin was Radulf's only apprentice. The guild had asked him to employ at least one other, but the merchant insisted that he had been made feeble by life and had not the strength to raise two. Anne Strago supported this plea, adding only that two boys in one house would never accord. "There are three things full hard to be known which way they will go," she had said. "The first is of a bird sitting on a bough. The second is of a vessel in the sea. The third is the way of a young man." With remarks such as these she had already acquired a reputation for wisdom among her neighbours.

So Janekin lived in a household where there was little restraining hand. Contrary to oath he played at hazard with other apprentices in the ward, and engaged in a violent game known to them as "breaking doors with our heads." He had also participated in the frequent struggles between the competing groups of tradesmen and merchants. The cobblers and cordwainers, for example, fought each other over the right to mend shoes; the grocers and fishmongers pitched against each other in running street fights. After one such fight Janekin returned with a broken head. Anne bathed it for him, and anointed the wound with an ointment made out of sparrow grease. "What sharp shower of arrows reached you, fool?" she asked him.

"From the butchers of the Chepe. They made a great roistering."

"And you did not? What woman would love such a wretch as you?"

"They say, mistress, that pity runs swiftest in a gentle heart."

"But I have no gentle heart. I have no heart at all."

"Then fortune is my foe."

"Why so?"

"I had looked to you for – for grace."

"Grace, wretch? Or favour?"

"Greedy are the godless. I want all."

"Who taught you courtesy?"

"A lighthouse hermit."

She laughed at this, and soon an understanding was reached between them. They could do nothing in the presence of the little haberdasher but, when he was gone for a day or even for an hour, they played the devil's game.

After their first lovemaking Anne Strago had sighed and complained that Radulf did not keep her in her proper estate. "Other women," she said, "go gayer than I."

"Fine gear will come your way."

"From you? You have no more of money than a friar has of hair."

"When the will is strong, there is a way."

The fate of Radulf Strago was then determined.

Janekin had buckled his shoes and now, on this spring dawn, he came down the stairs with an ivory box in his hand. "What is this," he asked, "left with the woollen caps in the solar?"

"What do you think? A comb case." Radulf Strago walked over to his apprentice, and opened it upon his palm. "Here are your ivories. Your scissors. Your ear-pickers and all your other knacks."

There was suddenly a loud explosion, which sent Radulf and Janekin flying across the open counter. It had come from the other side of the street, where a hermit's oratory stood. The hermit himself had died some three months before, and the adjacent parishes were arguing over the appointment of his successor; but the oratory had remained a well-known place of prayer on behalf of those who had departed into purgatory. The loud explosion sent people shrieking into the street. The walls of the oratory had been blown out, and its thatched roof demolished. Radulf could not rise to his feet, and he lay among the hats and purses as wisps of straw floated through the air.

Janekin had roused himself, and was brushing the dust off his taffeta jacket when he thought he saw a tall figure running towards the city. He was too shaken to raise the hue and cry. Instead he helped to support Radulf as he struggled upright, murmuring, "Christ and His tree save us!" All those around them were shrieking "Fire!" Some were wrapped in cloaks, some had quickly pulled on hose and jacket, while others were already dressed for the day's work. They clustered around the smouldering oratory, where a wooden image of the Virgin lay in fragments among the blackened stones. The air smelled of sulphur, as if the smoke of hell itself had ascended into the outer world. Radulf walked unsteadily towards the ruin, and noticed traces of dark powder on the earth floor. "They have used Greek fire," he said to no one in particular.

But who would wish to destroy a place of prayer, a corner of London where the souls of those in purgatorial fire were perpetually remembered? It was for the living as well as for the dead. The chantry priest of St. Dionysius the Martyr, a small church in a nearby side street, had claimed that anyone who prayed in the oratory all night would be rewarded with ten years' release from purgatory. Who would violate such a place with fire and gunpowder?

Two brothers hospitallers had come running from the gate of St. John, and begun howling that the nun of Clerkenwell had prophesied this. The merchant glanced at them with contempt, and in that instant he glimpsed something daubed upon a wall beside the oratory. It was some crude device, depicted in white lead paste. On peering closer at it, he saw circles linked one with another. His head ached, and he felt himself falling forward.

He was woken by the strong scent of vinegar in his nostrils. He opened his eyes, and found himself gazing at his wife. "Have you closed the shop?" he asked her.

"Janekin has bolted it and locked it. All is as safe as could be."

"Did you hear the din? The oratory has gone." She nodded. "Today is Friday. Friday is a hard day. An unfortunate day. An Egyptian day. It was on a Friday that I bought that false silver."

"Hush. Rest."

"Monday's thunder brings the death of women. Friday's thunder portends the slaughter of a great man. Who will we lose after this? May it be the king himself? The foxes of division are among us." He had been undressed by his wife. He lay beneath a white cover garnished with golden lambs, moons and stars. "I must go to siege," he said. "Help me."

He had told his wife some weeks before that he had felt a "wambling" in his stomach, but nothing had cured it. He had also experienced an airiness in his head and heels, as if he were walking on moss. He ascribed these symptoms to newly corrupted blood, and had been cupped on several occasions. But the letting only made him more weary. Then he had begun to vomit. His wife encouraged him to try every remedy although she knew that nothing would save him.

She had gone to the apothecary in Dutch Lane, some way from her parish, and had asked him what poison was needed to kill rats. She had also told him that there was a weasel coming into her yard to eat the hens; this, too, must be destroyed. She had taken away some grains of arsenic in a linen bag, with careful instructions how to use them, and from that evening she had begun to mingle them with the pottage which Radulf always consumed for his supper. She had not told Janekin, fearing that he might blab her secret.

"Help me," Radulf said again as he rose impatiently from his bed.

"Here. Take this cloak. And tread upon the cushions. Your naked feet should not touch the tiles."

The house of office was in a yard behind the shop, next to the kitchen and the stables. He walked slowly downstairs, his hand upon Anne's arm, but he was still very feeble. He stopped on the next landing underneath a woollen tapestry depicting Judith and Holofernes; he felt the ague in his stomach, and sat down upon a large wooden chest. "Friday is the day of the Expulsion and the Deluge, the Betrayal and the Crucifixion. Take me into the yard."

She assisted him down the last flight and watched him as he walked slowly across to the privy. "May Friday be your own doom day, dear husband. May it be your expulsion and your betrayal." And then she remembered the scriptures. Let old things pass away.

Radulf Strago sat down carefully on the hole of the siege.[4] He could feel his stomach turning in its agony. It was a fire. There was a wooden pipe in the corner, leading to a stone-lined latrine pit beneath the soil, and for a moment it seemed to move as if it were a living thing. He was bathed in a great sweat. "The sun," he said, "is none the worse for shining on a dunghill. So may it shine on me." There was a trickle of water in the lead cistern just outside the door, but it seemed in Radulf's ears like a storm. Blessed is the corpse that the rain rains on. But if I besmear the seat, no one else will come at it. He put out his hand to grasp at the arse-wisps, the pieces of hay and the cut squares of cloth which were piled beside the privy.

Anne Strago found him crouched upon the clay floor with a piece of cotton in his hand; there was a stream still flowing from his buttocks.[5] She did not want to touch the body: those days were over. So she ran out into the street, crying, "A death! A death!" Then she came back into the house, and embraced Janekin. "The apprentice no longer has a master," she told him. "He has a mistress."

At the subsequent inquest the coroner declared that Radulf Strago had suffered a fit after the oratory had been visited by fire, and had died a death none other than his rightful death; his verdict satisfied the five guardians of the ward, who paid for a trental of Masses to intercede for Radulf's soul. And what could be more natural and appropriate than that, after a period of mourning, Anne Strago should marry Janekin? She told her neighbours that excessive grief only harmed the soul of the departed, which was considered a wise saying. It was then generally agreed that the business would prosper, as indeed it did. As Anne Strago told Janekin, "Friday is a good day." There was an ancient belief, however, that murder could never be concealed in London and that it would always find its season to appear.

Chapter Four

The Clerk's Tale

Five days after the death of Radulf Strago the friar, William Exmewe, could have been seen entering a bookseller's shop in Paternoster Row; friars were a common sight in this street, since the bookshops sold psalters and hours as well as canons and doctrinals. This particular bookseller devoted himself to prick-song books with their kyries and sequences and, although much of his stock had been cleared in the week of the Passion, he hoped that the Seven Dolours of Our Lady would renew interest in the allelujahs. April was the month, too, when folk longed to go on pilgrimages. He managed a good trade, in all circumstances, and also worked as a scrivener adding new feast days to the holy books.

He was not on the premises, however, when William Exmewe came through the door with his black cloak billowing behind him. Emnot Hallyng, a clerk, entered a few moments later; he wore his hat under his hood and it knocked against the lintel, causing him to step back in surprise. There was a manciple already present; Robert Rafu was testing the strength of the chains, which locked and protected the books, by pulling at them sharply. Then there entered another citizen who, by his dress, was a franklin of rich estate; Garret Barton owned land across the river in Southwark, and was the freeholder of many inns in that neighbourhood for pilgrims and other travellers.

A voice was calling out, "Come down! Come down!" The four men greeted one another with the whispered phrase, "God is here," before walking down a stone stairway into the undercroft of the bookshop.

They came into a room of octagonal shape, with a stone bench running round its walls; there was a high stone seat in the east of the wall, and a wooden desk in the middle of the chamber. Other men and women were gathered here but the low murmur of voices stopped when William Exmewe crossed over to the eastern seat. His audience settled upon the low stone bench.

"It was a good beginning, Richard Marrow," he said without any formal exordium.

The carpenter, standing among the others, bowed his head. "It took only a candle and some black powder."

"Well said, Marrow, well said. Do you not know the verse, We will search out Jerusalem with candles?"

The franklin, Garret Barton, now spoke out. "The oratory was but a pie-crust, made to be broken. Like all the promises of the false friars. All their indulgences and prayers and trentals are deceptions of the devil, invented by the father of lies himself."

Robert Rafu felt moved to speak. "Prayers cannot help the dead any more than a man's breath can cause a great ship to sail."

William Exmewe took up this theme. "The purse-proud prelates and curates pass all their life in dark night. Their sight has been filled with darkness and with smoke, and therefore they are full of tears. What is a bishop without wealth? Episcopus Nullatensis. Bishop of Nowhere. What do they do now, but tremble before the mad nun of Clerkenwell?" They laughed at this. They had all heard how Sister Clarice had been taken before the consistory court, on the grounds that she had uttered false prophecies, but had been immediately released at the insistence of the citizens who had surrounded the court with imprecation and clamour. "These prelates are dumb fools in the realm of hell, dumb hounds that do not bark in time of need."

A woman cried out, "They pray to Our Lady of Falsingham. They do reverence to Thomas of Cankerbury!"

"Their images may do neither good nor evil to men's souls," Exmewe said, "but they might warm a man's cold body if they were set upon a fire. The wax wasted upon their candles would be fit to light poor men and creatures at their work."

These were the true men, otherwise known as the faithful, the foreknown or the predestined ones. There were few of them but they were known by many names – in Paris as the *apostoli* or the *innocentes*, in Cologne as the men of intelligence, and in Rheims as the *humiliati*. They believed that their sect had existed since the time of Christ, and that their first leader had been Christ's brother; they were assured that they were the true followers of the Saviour and that they comprised the invisible church or communion of the saved known as *congregacio solum salvandorum*. They rejected all the ceremonies and beliefs of the established church, and condemned them as the trappings of the god of this world who is called Lucifer. The pope was a limb of the fiend, as rotten in his sin as a beast in his dung; the prelates and bishops were also perpetual matter for burning in hell. Churches were the castles of Cain.

They were called the *innocentes* or the foreknown ones because, as Christ's true followers, they were absolved from all sin. Each one of them partook of the glory of the Saviour, and their actions were prompted wholly by the spirit of God. They could lie, commit adultery or kill, without remorse. If any one of them robbed a beggar, or caused a death by hanging, he or she had nothing to fear; the soul whose bodily life had been taken would return to its source. The predestined ones could commit sodomy, or lie with any man or woman; they must freely satisfy the promptings of their nature or else they would lose their freedom of spirit. They could deservedly kill any child conceived by their actions, and throw it into the water like any worm, without confession; the child, too, was going back to its source.

They met in secret, in small conventicles, because of all heretics they were considered to be the most dangerous. Only six months earlier, an order had gone out from the bishop's court forbidding "congregations, conventicles, assemblies, alliances, confederacies and conspiracies" against Holy Church.

Their names were known only to one another, and they would often pass in the street without any greeting. The predestined men were so convinced of their sanctity that they eagerly sought for the day of doom. Exmewe had explained to them that the great Antichrist would be an apostate Franciscan friar; he was now twenty and would appear at Jerusalem in the year following. The anointed one, the second Christ at the day of judgement, would be a foreknown one like themselves; he was the Son of Man foretold in the Apocalypse. He had already drunk Christ's blood and, at his coming, he would free God of his suffering for the creation of the world; he would be known as Christ imperator et deus.

In the undercroft of the bookseller's shop, a few months before, Exmewe had discoursed to them of the several signs. "There are many diverse tokens which shall come before that day," he had told them, "by which we shall fully know that the day is near and not far. Among which signs or tokens Christ proclaims in the Gospel when he says that 'There shall be signs in the sun, moon, and stars.' You should understand that Christ speaks not only of wonders that can be seen in these visible planets which are set in our sight, but also of ghostly tokens which are more subtle to understand for the coming of that doom."

So in succeeding weeks he spoke of the circles interlinked and the five wounds of London. Just as the blood of a murdered child will cry out unless it is covered, so the blood of Christ is only visible when the painted cloth of the world is removed from it. "We must fix Him upon the tree once more, so that His image shall stretch across creation. Christ suffered five wounds in His mortal death; we must inflict five mortal strokes on five sundry places in the carnal church which is the church of this world. Wherefore five? It is the image of all that exists. The five joys. The five wits. We have the threefold universe, the trine compass of earth, air and sea, but we must add to them time and space which are the angels of God. Therefore, five. It has been revealed to me in words that are a chosen song before God, a lamp to our life, honey to a bitter soul. When the circles of fire are painted upon London, it will be a sure sign that death is within the gate. That the judgement is not long."

He had persuaded them, therefore, that five London churches or sacred places must be visited by fire and death. Only in this manner could the day of doom be delivered.

The clerk, Emnot Hallyng, had left the conventicle and was striding down Bladder Street towards his tenement in Bevis Marks. It was close to curfew; the last street-traders were packing up their chests and boxes, while in the dying light the fruiterers and waferers pressed their merchandise upon all those hurrying home. He passed an inn known as the Wrestlers, and heard the words "crown" and "peace"; those deep in drink were arguing about King Richard's decision to sail to Ireland, even as he was being threatened by the enmity of Henry Bolingbroke who had been banished to France. But Emnot was not concerned with such matters; he regarded the events of this world with a boredom amounting to distaste. What was the king to him? Less than a straw.

He had taken up a wafer for a farthing and, as he bit into its crisp baked surface, he asked himself a question. What is the quantity of this night? He was teaching himself geometry or art-metricke. This day the sun was 21 degrees and six minutes of Taurus, a good day for the sinews and the heart. It was well known that the world was created at the vernal equinox, and that God first made mankind in the month of April; so this season was filled with magical properties. But was it a good night for experiment? Emnot practised alchemy in the hours of curfew, making sure that all the windows of his lodging were covered with black cloth so that the burning coals could not be seen. It was he who had manufactured the gunpowder, and had brought it to Richard Marrow in the green shed outside the walls.

"This is good powder," he had said to him. "You take two ounces of your sal petre and half an ounce of your brimstone, and temper them together in a mortar with your red vinegar. Do you smell the brimstone? Then you add your sal ammoniac and your nitre blended with small coals. That accounts for its blackish cast. You dry it in your earth pan over a soft fire and, when it is well dried, you grind it until it becomes this small powder. It is so small that it can be put through a sieve! There is no coal that serves better than the coals of the lime-tree."

These were also the coals which he used in his pursuit of alchemical gold. He was not an avaricious man. He was always eager, and curious, but not greedy. He had no conception of worldly things and, like the salamander of legend, lived only in the fire of his imagination. He had calculated his nativity as that time when the sun was in Gemini and a little from his declination in Cancer; this was the period of Jupiter's exaltation, thereby confirming to Emnot that his life would be one of study and of learning. The worth of the gold did not concern him, therefore; it was the pursuit itself that pleased him. As one of the predestined men, he believed himself to be singularly blessed in all his operations and did not doubt his ability to create gold out of inferior substances. It was a question both of meditation and of calculation, of locking all the forces of the world into one pattern. When the sun grows old and in his hot declination enters Capricorn and shines pale, then begins the work. When the spheres were in alignment with his own bodily humours, when the elements of the base matter were calcined and revived in proportion to the eight and twenty mansions which belong with the moon, then the radiant hour would enter his alembic.

Emnot loved number and pattern. He had tried to devise a geometry for the movement of pigeons in the yard below his tenement; he calculated the chances of seeing the same stranger more than once in a certain street; he looked into the night sky, and tried to divine the distance between each of the nine spheres. That is why he was so powerfully convinced by William Exmewe's image of the circles which were part of some larger circle; it corroborated all that he thought and believed. Emnot Hallyng was always eager, always active; he licked the egg and cheese off his fingers before running up the stairs.

Something was crouched in a corner, waiting for him there.

"Whoa! Who are you? Why are you here in the darkness?"

"It am I. Gabriel."

Gabriel Hilton, a jeweller by trade, was Emnot's cousin. They had attended school together, at St. Anthony's in Threadneedle Street, after which Gabriel had gone into his father's business and Emnot had been enrolled at Oxford. Emnot's sponsor was the late Bishop of Ely, who had surmised by various signs that he was one of the predestined and had trained him accordingly. Emnot became known in the family as "the clerk of Oxenforde," and was often gently ridiculed for his pale face and spare frame; it was widely remarked that he was even leaner than his horse. Yet he was clever and quick-witted. It had been he who taught Gabriel Hilton the properties of the stones which he sold. He told him, for example, that the diamond must always be worn on the left side; its strength was always growing to the north, which is the left side of the world. If an emerald was kept with little pieces of rock, and watered with the dew of May, then it would grow. An amethyst gave hardiness and manhood. A sapphire kept the limbs of the body whole. Agate protected its wearer from evil dreams, enchantments and illusions of wicked spirits. If venom or poison were brought into the presence of the ruby, it became moist and began to sweat. He taught Gabriel, too, that all of these stones could lose their virtues through the sin and incontinence of those who wore them.

"What wind has guided you here, cousin? I have not seen you in a long time." Emnot took his cousin by the shoulder. "Quick. Come in. Take off your overslope. Sit." Then he noticed Gabriel's face. "Have you seen harm?"

"Yis. There is harm approaching me. Of that I am certain."

"Sit."

"Emnot, you know the sliding science very well?" His hand was moving quickly, as if he were shaking invisible dice. "You know of dreamers and geomancers?"

"I am a clerk, Gabriel, not an enchanter. Do sit."

"Yet you told me that in the stars is written the death of every man, clearer than any glass."

"It is so." He hesitated. "Are you in sickness?"

"Not one that any leech could cure." Gabriel sat down upon a little wooden stool, but then immediately rose and walked over to the horn window. "I am in wanhope."

"Never say so, Gabriel. Even to speak those words is a great sin."

"But mine is a great trouble." He was looking down into the street below. "I am marked down."

Then he began his story. He had been resting in his lodging in Camomile Street, when he heard noises in the room above his own. He noted the footsteps of several people, as well as voices engaged in conversation; the words were so muttered and confused, however, that he could not make them out. They made a low and indistinct sound, which reminded him of the noise of the city when heard from the fields. He had been lying quietly upon his mattress, but suddenly he sneezed very loudly. The conversation above him stopped, and for a moment there was absolute silence. Then there was the noise of footsteps, and the door of the upstairs chamber was flung open. Gabriel could hear two of them coming down the stairs very quickly and, to his horror, there was a ferocious banging upon his door. It continued until Gabriel could bear it no longer; he crept over to the door, and put his ear against it. It was then he heard the sound of heavy breathing, loud and intense. Slowly he unlocked the door, raised the latch, and looked outside. There was no one there.

Emnot could not help breaking in. "So these were bloodless and boneless ones behind the door?"

Gabriel enquired among his neighbours, but no one had heard or seen anything that evening; the room was itself untenanted, given over to worms and spiders. Gabriel would have dismissed the matter from his mind since, as he said to Emnot, "men may die of imagination." But then two days later he had been walking down Camomile Street towards his shop in Forster Lane, when he was possessed by the strangest sensation of being followed. He looked around, but could see nobody except the traders and the casual populace of the area. He thought that he had heard someone calling out, "Head him! Head him!," but amid the general clamour it might have been the baker's cry of "Bread!" He also recalled that, at this moment, a horse reared up and threw its rider into the kennel of water and rubbish in the middle of the road.

On his way to work the following morning, in the same part of the street, he believed that he was once more being pursued; someone then put a hand upon his shoulder but, when he turned in alarm, there was no one. The same fear had come upon him, in that street, many times since. "It is more horrible than all monsters," he told Emnot.

"When does it press about you?"

"At dawn. And then again about curfew. Sometimes, too, I hear the steps above me in the room."

"Can you cast in your thought what they may be?"

"No. I cannot."

"They say that the souls of those who betray friends or guests go to hell, while their bodies continue to live."

"But there are no bodies. They are without shape or form."

"It is marvellous and strange to me. They seem to be of this earth but they cannot be seen upon it."

"Yet they are more menacing than cruel mouths."

Emnot rose from his chair and joined Gabriel by the window in the waning light. "Let me consider. If their anger arouses in you these floods of tremblings, then they possess an influence like that of intolerable heat or cold. Now it is said that where a great fire has for a long time endured, there still dwells some vapour of warmness. Could this be your case?"

"How so?"

"They may be creatures of a time beyond human memory." Emnot was troubled by his cousin's story in another sense, since these invisible meetings were like a ghostly image of the predestined men who met in secret places. All his fears of pursuit and capture were aroused by Gabriel's haunted life. "Like the mist which is made of disintegrating clouds, they may be a memory of passed things."

"If that is so, Emnot, then they have come to my infinite harm."

"Or these people may be upon a different path. What if they were ahead of us?"

"And are yet unborn? Why would they come into Camomile Street?"

"Yes. True. So they must be a sad token of what is gone." Emnot was distracted by a memory of William Exmewe's vision of the circles interlinked, circles that partook of each other's nature so that it was not clear where one began and another ended. He thought of the round drops of light rain, or mist, or dew, running into one another. If you looked into the circles deep enough, all would be cured.

"Whatever path they tread, I am foully vexed with them."

"They are but dead, Gabriel."

"One touched me, Emnot."

Emnot went over to a small cupboard, took out an enamelled jug, and poured two cups of wine. There were some crumbs of bread floating on the surface, and he picked them out with his finger. "How great be these darknesses. And therefore David says, Abissus abissum invocat. Deepness calls unto deepness."

Gabriel looked at him with pity. "You are still a man of learning, I see. A very perfect gentle clerk."

"And as a clerk I will give you my avisement."

"Go to the nun?"

"By no means see that witch. Remove from your lodgings, and shun Camomile Street."

Gabriel Hilton did indeed take his cousin's advice. He rented three rooms in Duck Lane, and never ventured again down Camomile Street; it became what he called "an avoided place." [6] Yet he did not follow all of Emnot's counsel. He had heard that Sister Clarice was to visit the female prisoners of the Mint, beside the Tower of London. He waited there by the postern gate on the appointed day and, as she approached, he held out his hands to her in the familiar gesture of supplication. "Release me," he said. "Release me, dear sister, from a world of woe."

Clarice saw his handsome face, and his dark eyes rendered darker by tribulation. "What is your trouble?" There was no one with her but another nun, Sister Bridget, and she gestured her to stand apart.

Gabriel Hilton then told her of the spirits haunting him. She bit her underlip, and shook her head in apparent dismay. "There are other such stories in the wind. There is a great perturbation of spirits in London. They see some evil day approaching." Then she kissed her finger and touched his cheek with it. He stepped backwards in surprise, but she smiled at him. "Are you afraid of me, or of my sex? You see from my dress that I am devoted to God. Why fear me then?"

He suspected that the nun was mocking him. "I am afraid not of you, nor of any woman born."

She put her finger upon his forehead. "Your cousin will be in great joy and comfort."

"Emnot?"

"He is being led to the light. Other men are at his back, hastening him onward into bliss."

"Emnot is solitary. He is a full learned clerk."

"Listen to what I say. He must continue his course without fear. Exmewe is his fast friend. Tell him that he must not weaken or waver. Will you tell him this?"

"Of course. If you wish it."

"I wish it." She left him there, and entered the little gate of the prison.

With many other citizens Gabriel watched her as she mounted a stone block in the yard, put out her arms as if she were Christ crucified, and spoke to the narrow gratings which concealed the female prisoners. The wind from the river was so strong that he heard only snatches of what she said. "I am in irons. I am in fetters. This body is my prison house. My eyes are my grilles." Then she spoke of a day when all doors would be opened and all locks would be broken.

There was no sound from the prison itself, but suddenly a pale face appeared at one of the gratings. A mouth opened, screaming out, "False witch of hell! Ripe for the burning! When rotten fruit falls to the ground, the dogs disdain it!"

Sister Clarice turned and descended from the stone block. She called Sister Bridget to her, and together they went out of the prison of the Mint. She passed Gabriel Hilton, but she did not acknowledge him. He noticed that she whispered something to her companion, and that she laughed out loud. Surely, to be so merry, Clarice must be blessed by God? Even as he considered this, he determined not to mention her advice to his cousin. As his father had taught him, it were best not to mingle heaven and earth.

Chapter Five

The Canon's Yeoman's Tale

In the week following the explosion in St. John's Street, the under-sheriff had made public proclamation by the cross in Cheapside that this ruination by fire had been "rotten, stinking, and abominable to the human race." If the offender was found he would be taken with trumpets and pipes to the stocks by the market, there to stand for a day and a night. If he were still in life, he would be taken from there and hanged beside the elms in Smithfield. He would be utterly excommunicate, and his body thrown into a lime-pit outside the walls.

There was much speculation about the identity of the miscreant, with city opinion inclining to the belief that the Lollards were responsible. These were a loosely knit group of Christian men and women who approached their faith with an egalitarian fervour. They doubted the efficacy of certain church practices, and were in any case inviolably opposed to the wealth and social power of the Church in the world. Confession could only be effective if the priest was full of grace, but no such priest had ever been found. Bread could not be made holier by being muttered over by priests. It was a sin to venerate images of the saints. Pilgrims to Canterbury were in danger of damnation, since St. Thomas had been consigned to hell for endowing the church with possessions. There was no purgatory other than this life, and so all masses for the dead and all chantry priests were without value. The Lollards asserted that it was contrary to Holy Scripture that priests should have any temporal possessions, and that friars were bound to obtain their living by the labour of their hands rather than by begging in the streets. They protested against chanting and church bells, saints' days and precious vestments, oaths and festivals, fastings and pilgrimages.[7]

Some days after the proclamation by the under-sheriff, the members of the Guild of Mary the Virgin met for a solemn dinner in the Hall of the Mercers along Ironmonger Lane. The guild encompassed the worthies of London, the richer merchants, the abbots and priors of city foundations, the more notable landowners and clerics; there was among them, too, a certain canon named William Swinderby. He was accompanied by his yeoman, Drago, who always followed him at a respectful distance. Swinderby lived in the clergy house of St. Paul's Cathedral, and had acquired fame as a preacher at Paul's Cross; his sermons against the Lollards in recent days had excited many London crowds.[8] He had attacked John Wycliffe, dead for fifteen years, as "the arch-parent of this heretical depravity." He had then dismissed the Lollards themselves as "beardless blabbering boys who, yes, believe me, deserve to be well birched"; at that aside, Drago looked at him strangely.

Drago gave his dagger to the porter of the Mercers' Hall before attending to his master. Swinderby handed his cloak and gloves to him at the door of the hall, and stood before the screen until the usher took him to his table. It was often wondered how such a powerful voice came from such an attenuated body; Swinderby was short and a little stooped, with a face so pale that he looked to some as if he were being led towards his death. The sweat often stood out on his forehead, and his clothes smelt of nutmeg and ink.

There was the usual music of pipes and tabors, echoing beneath the great hammerbeam roof, as the guests greeted their neighbours at the tables. On the left side of Swinderby sat the London knight, Geoffrey de Calis; the squire, Oliver Boteler, sat upon his other side.

"Well, sir," de Calis asked Swinderby, "what is the new news?"

"King Richard has grown honest." A servant brought over a basin of water, and Swinderby washed his fingers before crossing his mouth. The bread, and trencher, had already been laid before him.

"Honesty will not save him now." Geoffrey de Calis looked around for service with the gusto of one longing for meat. "His followers will be hunted as wolves are."

"Oh, that is not the case." Swinderby grimaced, as if in sudden pain. "He may yet win all." There was a silver salt-cellar upon the table, in the shape of a chariot with wheels so that it could be passed down the table. Swinderby pulled it towards him as he spoke. "The followers of Henry Bolingbroke are as errant as the moon. And as moneyless."

To the sound of a bell the marshal led the procession of servants bringing in the food. In order came the panterer, the esquires and the valetti, bearing dishes according to their rank. They placed them reverently upon the tables, while on the meat-board were piled baked pheasant, goose, wild fowl, pullets and pork. At the high table sat the Archbishop, Roger Walden, and the mayor of London; beside them were the lords and bishops while all the others were arranged by estate and by degree. It was generally assumed that the diners would form pairs; the sheriff, for example, sat beside the prior of Bermondsey. They all arose as the archbishop said grace, and then began that general din of eating and conversation which was known to the speakers of Latin as *taratantarum*.

Drago stood silently behind Swinderby; he had been in the canon's service for six years, and had been instructed in all the arts of courtesy. He was trained to be careful where he spat, and to put his hand in front of his mouth before doing so. If a superior spoke to him, he took off his hat; he did not glance down upon the ground but looked steadfastly into his face without moving his hands or feet. He was taught not to scratch his head, and to ensure that his nails were always clean. He learned how to sponge Swinderby's clothes, to make his bed and to lace his shoes. He was taught certain other lessons, also.

On the tables dishes of peacocks with pepper sauce lay beside partridges roasted with ginger; pigs' ears baked in wine were scooped up with fish served in a green sauce made out of various herbs; a bowl of lobster with vinegar was put next to some small game birds covered with feathers so that they still seemed alive. All the food of the world appeared to be lying here.

The squire, Oliver Boteler, was in good humour. "Do you know," he asked, "what the Proctor of the Arches told me this morning? You know that he is lately married. Well, I asked him why he had chosen so little a wife. She comes up to my hip-bone, you see. To which he replied, Ex duobus malis minus est eliendum. That is, to say in English, among evil things the less is to be chosen. Was that not well answered?" There was a flagon in front of him, carved in the shape of a knight on horseback, and he poured some wine into his cup. According to custom, they stopped talking while he drank. "Yet how," he said, wiping his lips with his sleeve, "does he pierce her?"

At the end of the meat course a subtlety was brought forth; it was carved from sugar and paste and was in the shape of a man, wrapped in weeds, holding a sickle in his hand. It was not to be eaten but was known as a "warmer" to signal the next course of almond cream, baked quinces, sage fritters and dates in comfit.

By the time that the salads were placed upon the table, the conversation had returned to the topic of the king. "These are hard times," the knight said. "Stony times." He picked among the parsley, fennel and sage, as if choosing the herbs closest to his natural humour.

"No estate abides." The squire had gathered up a handful of garlic and spring onion. "It is the wheel. And I am bound upon it."

They knew the cause of his complaint well enough. In order to pay for his expedition to Ireland the king had been levying huge fines upon his opponents among the lords and commons; he had instituted a system of payments for legal "pardons," but he had become cruel as well as greedy. As the verse sung about the streets put it:

> The axe was sharp, the stocks were hard,
> In the twenty-second year of King Richard.

"The people are stormy." Swinderby was still inclined to support the king. "I know London well. I know the citizens. They are as indiscreet and as changing as a weather vane. They delight ever in rumble that is new. Now they say that Henry Bolingbroke is casting some plot against the king. Then it is all denied as a deceit. Like the moon they wax and wane. They are full of chattering. One moment it is good King Richard, God keep his neck-bone from the iron. And then it is Richard the ruthless, the inconstant one."

"Yis." The squire sighed. "What may ever last?" At which conventional sentiment, the three men burst out laughing.

"I have heard talk that Henry Bolingbroke may incline to Benedict. So Boniface writes to the king, 'Age igitur,' which is as much to say, 'Do something.' " Geoffrey de Calis was alluding to the Great Schism of recent years, in which two popes had been elected by rival groups of cardinals.[9] Richard II fostered the claims of Pope Boniface IX in Rome, while it was rumoured that Henry Bolingbroke would cast his allegiance with Benedict XIII of Avignon.

"I hear," Swinderby was saying, "that Benedict wears the hair."

"He is nothing but a hedge priest. A waterless cloud." Oliver Boteler was a firm supporter of orthodoxy in religious matters. "Benedict's bulls are fit only to cover mustard pots."

"But Boniface chases our gold." Geoffrey de Calis was less orthodox. "They say that he is a blind mole rooting about in earthly muck. The priests – saving your good self, William – bear the king's gold out of our land and bring again dead lead."

Swinderby graciously ignored the knight's allusions to priests. "The mad nun has been singing a high song on the matter."

"Oh?" The knight filled his mouth with mint. "Wherefore?"

"You must ask Dame Agnes. But I hear that Clarice fell into a fit at the time of vespers and saw in vision a beast with two heads. She prophesied that the Church would fall asunder, and that the crown of Richard would be forfeit."

Oliver Boteler was repeating "tush" under his breath. "That nun is the devil's left hand. Can she not be taken from Clerkenwell and walled?"

Swinderby smiled at this image of perpetual duress. "For one who thinks her a harlot, another finds her holy."

"She is a jangler. Her wit is all away."

"I cannot say whether it is this or that. But she moves the citizens marvellously."

Tarts of apple and of saffron were placed upon the table, together with nuts and spices coated in sugar. The mawmenee was passed around in great jugs, a sweet wine for a sweet end. Then the archbishop rose from his central seat. He saluted them in order, "in high reverence and obedience" as he put it, and spoke of his incapacity. "Excuse me for my plain speaking," he told them. "I never learned the arts of rhetoric, and all that I say must be bare and plain." This was a conventional disavowal and did not at all reflect his ability, in the manner of the oratorical models, to match his voice and facial expression to his words. "The reason for which we have assembled here is a full heavy thing and a high matter, because of the wrong and the wickedness that have been done. We are troubled also because of the great damage that in the time coming may fall out in the same cause. Consider now the evil men of Lollers or Lollards, lewd and open fools fallen into blindness –" there was a general murmur of approval among the assembled Londoners, despite the known fact that the Lollard sect thrived in certain parts of the city. "These poor preachers of Lollardy do act plainly against Christ's gospel. I can smell them in the wind. They are hypocrites and heretics who have brought fire down upon the precious places of salvation. Their lewd lust must be utterly quenched. These are black things that strike terror into us. It is well known among you that full two years ago the reverend bishops of both provinces petitioned the parliament house for a statute of burning –" again the London worthies signalled their assent. "The damnable blinding by antichrists of Christian people must cease in the flames. These devil's jugglers who put out men's ghostly eyes, and who lay Greek fire around our altars, should be put to the death. Now I turn to another high matter." Archbishop Walden then surprised the company by revealing that "the nun of Clerkenwell" was being questioned by a group of learned clerks to determine whether her visitations were blessed or cursed; he prayed Almighty God to bring them wisdom. "I say no more but leave you to your dinner."

That meal was then quickly completed, with cheese and white bread being cut and put upon the trenchers. The citizens rose in unison, bowed to the archbishop, and left in procession. The other worthies then departed according to their estate. The pieces of bread, cheese and discarded meat were put into voiders, to be distributed to the beggars who were sitting cross-legged on the floor of the stone chamber beside the hall. William Swinderby passed them with a grimace. "Do you have pepper in your nose?" one of them shouted after him.

Drago followed his master into the London air. He was a tall youth, with hair the colour of wheat; he had mild blue eyes, as if his head were filled with the sky. He was talking quietly to Swinderby as he followed one pace behind. "You have as much pity for poor men as pedlars have for cats, that would kill them for their skins if they could catch them."

"Mea culpa." The cleric's pale face was suffused with sweat.

"You are purse proud. Piss proud."

"Mea culpa."

"You are an ape in a man's hood."

"Mea maxima culpa."

"I will enshrine you in a hog's turd."

"Benedicite fili mi Domine." He turned his head back, and looking imploringly at his yeoman. "Confiteor tibi."

"You should be fettered and put in the pit."

"Ab omni malo, libera me."

They were walking down Cheapside towards the cathedral. A passer-by would only assume that the canon was murmuring his devotions. "A flagello, libera me." It was clear, from the settled expression upon Drago's face, that this was some customary ritual; in truth he had been taught his words by the canon himself. They passed through the Little Gate of St. Paul's churchyard, in the north-east corner, and entered the precincts of the cathedral; they followed the familiar sandy path to the houses built there for the thirty greater canons. As soon as they entered Swinderby's dwelling the canon took off his cloak and lay down upon the floor of the principal chamber with his arms and legs spread wide.

Drago locked and bolted the door. "Show me your buttocks, like a she-ape in the full of the moon." He knelt down and pulled off the priest's shirt and hose. "Phew! Your breeches are stained with your arse."

"Agnus Dei, qui tollis peccata mundi, miserere nobis."

"You are a lost man." Drago walked over to a wooden chest, from which he took out a whip of lead. The cleric looked up at him again imploringly, and then closed his eyes. "You are a sack filled with shit." He raised the whip.

"Peccavi."

He let it fall. "You are a parcel of dirt covered under clothes."

"Clamavi."

A few minutes later Drago left his master's chamber, whistling, and went out into the fields for a game of archery.

On the following Friday the canon preached at Paul's Cross on the need for a statute *de heretico comburendo*, so that the Lollards might be burned at Smithfield. Among the crowd assembled before the Cross were William Exmewe and Emnot Hallyng. They avoided each other's eyes.

Chapter Six

The Franklin's Tale

Garret Barton, the franklin and predestined man, was walking through the Great Gate to the south of St. Paul's Cathedral. He could not help but consider how many pilgrims had gone to their damnation along this cobbled path. The air itself seemed rank with their shrill cries, like the putrid smell of other churchyard matter. Garret was one of the most ardent of the foreknown ones who, at Exmewe's instigation, had written on a parchment "The Eighteen Conclusions." He had rolled it carefully and placed it in the pocket of his coat. A wrestling match was being conducted in the usual place, an open space just behind the tomb of the parents of St. Thomas Becket, to the cries of "Yis!" and "Nay!" from the spectators. Outside the charnel-house, a scrivener had set up his stall; on a board above him had been painted a hand holding a pen. He stared solemnly at the franklin, as if divining his purpose in coming to this place.

The clock in the belfry stood at two as Garret Barton entered the cathedral by the west door. It smelled of the stables. All the sounds of the tradesmen and the hucksters mingled in the great vaulted space, and resembled the strange buzzing and humming of thousands of bees; it was a still roar and a loud whisper, much like a sea of voices and of footsteps. Barton could just make out the slow chanting of the pilgrims who clustered around the gleaming shrine of St. Erconwald. This world was nothing but a cherry fair! The barristers stood by their respective pillars, awaiting clients, their scarlet hoods scarcely visible among the press of porters, stall-keepers and priests. Hay had been strewn across the cold and shadowy stone floor of the nave. It would have been a dark place, even in the middle of the day, were it not for the candles and torches blazing upon the images and the painted walls. A broad band of sunlight crossed the nave, but it seemed pale against the glistening pillars.

The franklin approached the shrine and noticed with distaste the little limbs, modelled out of clay or lead, which hung there as objects of intercession; a clay penis was swaying beside a crippled leg, in the cool wind of human breath, as the people murmured their prayers to the golden figure of the saint whose alb and mitre were encrusted with bright jewels. He could see the monks peering at the pilgrims from the wooden watching chamber, where they guarded the holy treasures; one of them had fallen asleep. There was a faint smell of urine in the air, together with the smell of old stone and the familiar odour of humankind. A man was fumbling with his leather hose in a corner of the transept. And this was Garret's thought: What is praying but piss against a wall? He walked back down the aisle among the dogs and pedlars. Three candles for a penny. Two Spanish onions for a penny. Five biscuits for two pennies.

Yes, there was singing at the high altar. This plainchant was supposed to be pleasing because it copied the music of the spheres; its pattern was precise art-metricke, or geometry. It explored the length and the breadth, the depth and the height, of sound. These voices encircled each other like the heavenly spheres; they passed smoothly over each other as if they were already part of the empyrean, their marvellous moving and wonderful turning combined to create harmony. Then the voice of a boy rose up in the psalm, "Quam dilecta tabernacula tua," and it seemed to Garret Barton to be the voice of one raised up against the many. It was the sounding of the soul outside the Church Universal. It was his voice, lucid and melodious, until once more it was caught up in the divine machinery of noise. The choir had answered with "Domine virtutum!"

He leaned his forehead against the stone screen which stretched below the rood displaying the crucified figure of the Saviour. It was said that the rosemary tree could never grow taller than the height of Christ. He looked up at the painted image, scarred and suffering. Could it be true, as the astrologers claimed, that the infant body of Christ was influenced by the planets and the constellations? That his death was prefigured in the stars? That would be strange indeed, if creation could have power over its creator. Yet it was no more strange that, as William Exmewe had taught the predestined ones, God must sometimes obey the Devil. It was time.

Garret Barton walked out of the north door into the cloister known as Pardon Church Haugh, the walls of which were covered by the Dance of Death.[10] The franklin noticed the pope cavorting beside a skeleton. Ah, you, is it you that leads the dance of sorrow? He came out of the cloister and stopped before the *Si quis?* door, so named because of the notices pinned there by clerks looking for benefices. He took out the parchment of the Eighteen Conclusions, while in his other pocket he reached for the stone and the nails he had concealed there. With a few swift strokes he fixed the parchment to the door.[11]

"What do you do here?" The scrivener was standing behind him; he had followed him through the cathedral, and into the cloister.

"What do I do? I lead you to heaven's gate." He still had the stone in his hand and, with a savage movement, he struck the scrivener down.

Then he hastened back through the cloister and across the Dance of Death. He had just entered the north transept and was passing the fresco of the Miracles of the Virgin, when he heard his name. He looked first at the figures upon the wall, glowing in the decorated light, and then he licked the blood from his right fist. He was in fear until he saw Robert Rafu, the manciple, beside a pillar. "Quick, Barton. God is here. Come with me." Rafu knew the shortest ways, and led Barton towards the newly built south transept where some furriers had already set up their shops. "Did you nail the Conclusions?"

"Someone was watching me."

"Watching?"

"He seemed to threaten me. I had the stone in my hand, so I had no need of my dagger."

"You killed him?"

"God killed him."

"And you were not seen?"

"Only by the angels. Their wings covered me."

They left the south transept, crossed the churchyard, and went out through the south gate into the warren of tumbledown houses and tenements which always seems to spring up in the shadow of great churches.

"Have you ever considered," Garret Barton was saying, "how each fresco has its own light? Virtues shine more clearly in them. Like a tapestry." He scarcely knew what he was saying. All was a dream. They had stopped at the corner of Paul's Chain and Knightrider Street, beside the Cardinal's Hat.

A group of apprentices pushed past them, shouting out "Bonjour!" and "Dieu vous save!" and "Bevis, à tout!" In the inn there was a harper, sitting cross-legged upon a table, waiting to play. The franklin and the manciple walked through the room, and then re-emerged into the street by another door. The Hat was too disordered for their quiet talk. So they made their way down Farthing Alley, where the Bethlem men begged.

"It was a scrivener," Garret Barton said, "who asked me what I did."

"You have favoured him. He has gone back."

"Where no pens or receipts will trouble him."

"You did a good deed, Garret. He is dissolved into time. Here is the place I sought."

It looked like a house, but it was a tavern. Some men were playing checkers on a bench outside; Rafu and Barton stepped over the threshold into a room filled with laughter and raised voices. "Put the case," someone was saying at Rafu's right hand. "Put the case that the cloths were not good. The dye would not hold. Am I to be blamed for it?" Just behind Barton a man and woman were arguing. "It is all very well for you, dame patience. I grant you, patience is a great virtue. But not every man is perfect. I am not perfect." A cat leapt down from a table on to the floor. A young man was staring down into a cup of ale, talking slowly and hesitantly to his companion. "The poor man is hard pressed on all sides. If he does not ask for his meat, he dies of hunger. If he asks for it, he dies of shame. I would rather die a better death. More, please. Fill it up."

Rafu and Barton found a small table with two round stools and, when the tapster came over to clean away all the spilled beer and wine, they asked him what was best. "Ask your purse, sirs." He was a surly man, used to dealing with customers who might be violent as well as drunken. "My best ale is fourpence a gallon. A gallon of Gascon wine is fourpence also. The Rhenish is eightpence. If you wish for sweet wine, then you must go to another place." And how good was the Rhenish? "It will defy the dust."

They sat in silence over their drinks and could distinctly hear the conversation between a pedlar and an old woman. "The parrot is luxurious and very fond of wine," she was saying. "The drake is wanton and the cormorant is gluttonous."

"What of the raven?"

"Oh, sir, the raven is wise. While the stork, you see, is jealous."

"And a drunken old woman," Barton murmured, "is as wallowing as a sow and as foolish as a she-ape."

"They say of a drunken man," Rafu whispered, "that he has seen the devil."

"What of it? Lucifer himself cannot touch us."

"So we can never be drunken? Never piss-pots or cup-shot?"

At another table one man was asking for the reckoning, even as the cry went up from his companions to let go and pass round the cup. One of them fell from his stool and, as he was pulled up by the tapster, began to urinate in his breeches. "When I said to put down your shot," the tapster told him, "I meant your pennies and not your piss."

There was general laughter, and Garret Barton leaned towards the manciple. "There is no heaven or hell for these, except earth itself."

"Butler, fill the bowl!"

"God created them without souls."

"Cast your counts first, friends. Sixpence each one."

"They will return to earth and air, fire and water, without ever knowing that they have lived."

"One pot more!"

A huckster selling laces peered into the tavern. The tapster shook his head at him, and put out his hand in warning, but he entered. "Have you heard, good masters? A murder in the cathedral! And a proclamation made by the Lollers! All is in havoc." He asked for a jug of pudding wine, which was speedily purchased. Garret Burton and Robert Rafu did not speak, and kept their faces averted from the huckster as he told his tale. "It was Jacob the scrivener – you know him, all goggle-eyed and tongue-tied – who was struck down and died upon the spot. Goodwife Kello found him, and fainted away."

"Do we know who did it?"

"No. Not a word in the wind. Yet a Lollard must be suspect. Above him were some words written which damned the clerics and the friars."

"Truth enough there." It was the old woman who had discoursed upon the qualities of birds. "Jacob has departed to God, sure enough. It will come to each of us." She crossed herself. "Then we will know who are the holy men."

The drunken man now roused himself. "Is there not any man here who will make good cheer? Tomorrow is still untouched."

After a full husting[12] the aldermen of each ward called together the worthier and more prosperous citizens. They met at various locations – a pump, a well, a corner of a street – but their purpose was the same. They were to visit each hostelry and investigate the aliens or travellers who were staying on the premises. It was considered likely that the poorer sort might fall upon any strangers, as angry bees might cluster around an intruder, and it was necessary to be seen to act. "You must make surety for every person you harbour," Alderman Scogan told Dame Magga of St. Lawrence Lane.

"God forbid I should swear for those I do not know."

"You must. You are held responsible for all their deeds and trespasses."

"Oh Lord, that is too great a burden for a widow woman. Whatever next? Will you wish me to follow them in the highways and byways?"

"Just answer me this, Magga. Do you have any strangers?"

"They are all strangers to me, as you know, Ralph Scogan. Have I not kept this house for twenty year without causing the least harm? Why, the mice are better fed here than most households. It is a sad day when a widow woman is judged to keep Lollards under her roof!"

"Nothing of the kind, Magga. We only wish you to open your eyes. Look to any suspected person."

"Infected persons? I have none such. Can you keep a good tongue in your head? Soon you will have me locked up in my chamber with a bowl of vinegar before my door. I shall be painted with a red cross for all the world to see. Oh, has it come to this?" She held out her shawl of blue serge. "This is not a winding sheet, is it? Or am I mistaken?"

"You are in the right, Magga. But no one –"

"You disturb me like thieves." She gazed scornfully at the small group of citizens who were accompanying the alderman. "Am I to be mocked in my own street where I have paid scot and lot? Inform me, Ralph Scogan, if I have not paid it." She was a thin and bony woman, upon her head a parcel of false hair, which she believed the world to mistake for genuine hair. There was real hair upon her upper lip, however, which she rubbed each morning with a pumice stone. "Every goodwife now will mouth me behind my back, I am sure of it."

"Calm yourself, Magga. You have done nothing."

"So I am to be put in the ducking stool for doing nothing, am I? This is the king's justice, is it? Well, it is a hard day for London." She was about to close the door, when she opened it again. "And as for the rest of you – you are good only to fry pilchers in hell. Good day!" She slammed the door shut.

Alderman Scogan looked up at the sky, and whistled. "Well," he said to no one in particular. "The wheel will roll on."

The parchment of the Eighteen Conclusions was solemnly burned by William Swinderby, standing at the right hand of the under-sheriff by Paul's Cross; Drago watched him with interest, as he raised it high in the air before plunging it into a brazier of fire.

Chapter Seven

The Nun's Priest's Tale

"What is truth and what is seeming?" Dame Agnes de Mordaunt had just put this question to John Duckling, the nun's priest, who was removing a piece of excrement from beneath one of his fingernails. "The mayor believes her to be as true as a stone in the wall, but of course she serves his purpose by stirring the people against heretics. The king has gone to Ireland, and the mayor feels himself to be alone. So Clarice blears his eyes." On this Day of the Ascension of Our Lord, the candles of the convent church were wreathed in flowers; according to custom, too, John Duckling was wearing a garland of flowers upon his head. "She weeps too readily."

"That is her complexion," he said.

The nun's priest was studying the image of a pilgrimage in the margin of the psalter which the prioress had opened; a knight and a squire were striding gaily forward amid a cloud of words. A nun was riding through the phrase, "Ascendit Deus in jubilatione," with a second nun following close behind.

"I am not so sure of that." Agnes was very severe. "Beneath all that mummery, she is a gay mare."

"Of course some hold her to be mad."

"Oh no." Dame Agnes turned from the window, and stared at him. "She uses covered language, but Clarice is not mad."

"Then God send her better words." John Duckling had witnessed an interview which the bishop's chaplain had conducted with Sister Clarice two evenings before.

"I am not like a hawk," Clarice had said to the chaplain. "I will not be lured with something under the thumb."

"I am not offering you gifts, sister. I am offering you a sure way to repentance."

"Of what should I repent? Of hearing the word of God? You sit at the dais, but I sit between His feet. He touches my head. He touches my ears. He touches my eyes. He touches my mouth." With her finger she outlined her lips.

John Duckling had looked away.

"But more venom than sugar comes out of you, Clarice." The chaplain whispered to her, as if their talk were dangerous. "Why do you speak of burning and slaughter in the city?"

"Because I see fire and powder. Because I see companions disguised with false faces, both foreigners and those free of the city. Because I see many perils arising."

"Well done! Well done! You will put London in a fury."

"Well, sir priest, it is better to be forewarned than unarmed. There are a hundred churches within the walls. Not one of those hundred will be safe. Do you believe me, John Duckling?" She turned to the nun's priest, took up her wimple and showed her forehead to him. It was a sign denoting faithfulness; but he had shaken his head.

Now he hesitated before looking up from the psalter and gazing at Agnes de Mordaunt. "She is not yet proven a liar or a suspect person. Hold yourself in patience, ma dame. Link after link the coat is made at length. So piece after piece things will come to light."

"Watch her. Follow her. Listen to her. Stay as close as a hound to his bone."

"I must be sure not to bite her."

"Oh, she will bite back. Take care, John Duckling. Let her be her own roper, and hang herself."

Sister Clarice had been given a chamber in the guest-house of the convent, on the instruction of the Bishop of London, Robert Braybroke, and was constantly attended by a monk as both guard and protector. He had been given a chamber next to her own, but they had been permitted to pray together at the sacred hours. This holy man, Brank Mongorray, had previously acted as a confessor and prayer-reader in the parish of St. Sepulchre and was considered to be skilled in all matters "above this world." It was not clear, however, whether he had been placed beside Clarice as a spy or as a companion; he may have assented privately to both roles. The prioress feared that in any case Clarice would bewitch him.

Brank Mongorray opened the window of the nun's chamber to enjoy the air of May. He was on the first floor, above a lead cistern of water which the birds used for their refreshment. John Duckling was crouched silently against it, so that he might hear any words that were spoken.

"Did you hear the thrush this morning, Brank?" It was the nun's clear voice, known now by so many. "They say that if a man is sick of the jaundice and sees a yellow thrush, the man shall be cured and the bird shall die. Is that not too cruel?"

"A man has an immortal soul. A bird does not."

"Who can be sure of that? Dieu est nostre chef, il nous garde et guye."

Duckling had never heard her speak Anglo-Norman before; for

some reason this seemed to him to be evidence of her duplicity. There was more conversation but the monk and nun had moved away from the window; Duckling could make out only occasional words until he heard her cry, "When will come the day of the Seven Sleepers?" Then she called out, "Deus! cum Merlin dist sovent veritez en ses propheciez!" These were marvellous strange words from a young nun: Merlin was no more than a devil worshipped by the little folk who lived in the moors and marshes. He could hear Brank Mongorray talking quietly to her. Could they be in league against the world of holiness?

Sister Clarice then began to chant, in a high voice, "Lords wax blind, and kinsmen be unkind, death out of mind when truth no man may find." Duckling repeated the words over to himself, so that he might better recall them. "Wit is turned to treachery, and love unto lechery, the holy day unto gluttony and gentry into villainy."

He had once known a young man who always stood on the corner of Friday Street and Cheapside and who raved only in rhymes such as these; eventually he had been taken up and tied down with chains in Bethlem. He had said that he was the King of Beeme or Bohemia, and the local people called him the King of Beans. He had been released from Bethlem, wearing the badge of that place, but had thrown himself into the Thames in a fit of desperation.

A candle was lit in the nun's chamber, just as it grew dusky. Duckling slipped into the shadows. He had heard Clarice say, "Let it be ready made at the cordwainer's with the crooked back, next to the water gate at the Cow Cross."

Just as the other nuns were gathering for vespers, Duckling heard footsteps upon the turning stair of the guest-house. It was Clarice. She was wrapped in a dark cloak, and glided past him across the lawn towards the side gate; he took care not to be seen, but followed her as she opened the gate and hastened down the lane towards the Fleet. Then she took the path along the river and walked in the direction of the city. It was not the place for any nun to walk alone. This bank of the Fleet was notorious for loiterers and wanderers, and was also a trysting place for effeminates called scrats or will-jicks.

Clarice walked past wooden huts and small outcrops of stone, past refuse and the sodden remains of small boats, until she reached the bridge at Cow Cross. On the other side of the river rose the slope of Saffron Hill; it had become the haunt of tinkers who had spread their camp as far as Hockley in the Hole. The glow of their fires and torches was reflected in the quietly moving water of the Fleet, while the sounds of hammering and beating could still be heard. There was no curfew beyond the walls.

Duckling stayed as close to Clarice as he dared, but she had stopped. She had reached the stone cell of the bridge hermit. He thought that she was simply giving alms but, approaching the little hermitage, he could hear the nun and the anchorite talking quietly together.

"And the height of Moses?"

"Twelve foot and eight inches," Clarice replied.

"Christ?"

"Six foot and three inches."

"Our Lady?"

"Five foot and eight inches."

"St. Thomas of Canterbury?"

"Seven foot save an inch."

The hermit then helped her down some ruined steps to the bank of the river, and into a small wherry like those which crossed between Lambeth and Westminster. Duckling could hear the splash of oars, and saw the boat move slowly down the Fleet towards the dark city and the Thames. The Fleet flowed softly here, but its quietness was deceptive. It was filled with unclean things, from the dead dogs of Smithfield to the refuse of the tallow chandlers. In some places it was deep and perilous, and in others more like a mire or marsh than a river. It was known to be dangerous to children and to drunkards, who were often found floating in the filthy water or caught among the reeds.

John Duckling began to walk across the bridge, when he heard something sighing or whispering in the water. It was just below his feet, waiting to raise its hands towards him, and he turned back in horror. As he rushed past the hermit's cell he heard a thin voice calling to him.

"Right dear brother, great worship be thy sacred order unto you. Do you have any offerings for the sake of Christ?" The cell stank of the age-old sweat that had settled into its stones.

"One nun came this way. Sister Clarice. Do you know of her?"

"No nun has come here, sir priest. There is no nun who may leave her house alone. What novice are you? Do you have hair under your hood?"

"I saw her take boat here and depart."

"Do way! Do way! I know nothing of this!" The bridge hermit, a man no more than thirty, was wearing an unclean shirt which touched his knees; now he banged his head savagely against the wall behind him. "Do way! Do way!"

The nun's priest retraced his steps along the Fleet towards the House of Mary; he opened the side gate and walked across the lawn to the guest-house and the cloister beyond. A candle was still gleaming within the nun's chamber and, as he came closer, he could distinctly hear the low voice of Brank Mongorray coming from the open window. And then – but this could not be – the reply of Sister Clarice. It was her own clear, light voice. John Duckling had just watched her floating down the Fleet in the direction of the Thames. How could she still be here? Had he seen a hobgoblin of the night? Such figures were known to haunt convents and other places of God; but why had it taken the form of a nun? He heard her suddenly singing, "Oh one that is so fair and bright." And at once the strangest memory descended upon him.

*

Three years before he had been the confessor to the Alder Street compter, a local prison of ancient foundation where the more serious malefactors were confined before they were hanged. He had been ordered to undertake this dangerous work as a penance by the Bishop of London, after he had been found consorting with a married woman of his parish. The prison itself comprised two connecting vaulted chambers constructed at a depth of seven feet, with an aperture in the roof as an entrance; on each side ran a stone bench for the whole length of the room, and in a platform on the earthen floor against the western wall were inserted six huge rings of iron. It was here that John Duckling, fearful of the gaol fever, had first conversed with Richard Haddon, a fishmonger who had suffocated three children. Haddon had admitted his crime at the sheriff's court and, since he could not read and therefore not plead benefit of clergy, he was sentenced to hanging at the site of the murders on Dark Tower wharf.

On the day before his death he had told John Duckling *in secreta confessione* that he had seen his own mother stifle her newborn child and take its body in a basket down to the Thames. His mother, ever after that time, had beaten and whipped him; he believed that the devil had entered him when he first opened his mouth to scream. He confessed to Duckling that he had only once found contentment in all his life – when his mother sang him to tearful sleep with the song that begins, "Oh one that is so fair and bright."

More curious still was the manner of Haddon's departing from this life. When he was lifted out of the stone prison and tied to the hurdle which would drag him from Alder Street to Dark Tower wharf, he opened his mouth and began to sing. As he was jolted along the stone cobbles he sang out, "Oh one that is so fair and bright," in a strong and melodious voice.

Duckling could still hear the nun singing as he crept from the guest-house and walked quickly through the cloister. It was only after he entered his lodging that he wondered if the monk, Brank Mongorray, had assumed her voice:

"Oh one that is so fair and bright
   velud maris stella
Brighter than the day is light
   parens et puella
I cry to thee, I sue to thee,
Lady, pray thy son for me
      tam pia
That I may soon come to thee
      Maria."

Chapter Eight

The Knight's Tale

On that same spring evening, even as John Duckling was walking through the cloister of the Clerkenwell convent, certain Londoners might have been seen entering a round stone tower of Roman construction; it stood a few yards north of Castle Baynard near the banks of the river by Blackfriars. It had one great portal, around which were inscribed certain words in Latin which might be translated thus – "I am not open to them that knock as they pass by, but to those who stand and knock." Each of these evening visitors was greeted at the entry by a liveried servant, and led down a winding stair to a vaulted chamber beneath the ground. Some of those present at the dinner of the Guild of Mary the Virgin, the previous month in the Hall of the Mercers, were also in attendance here; among them, for example, were the knight, Sir Geoffrey de Calis, and the canon, William Swinderby. But they were not dressed in the robes of their degree. Their cloaks and hoods were of some striped cloth; their colours were blue and white crossing diagonally, which to a trained eye were the tokens of time crossed with patience.

A sergeant-at-law, Miles Vavasour, had joined them, together with one of the two under-sheriffs of London. This was a high meeting but curiously enough it was the knight, Sir Geoffrey de Calis, rather than the under-sheriff who called them to order.

He summoned them with a Latin invocation. "Hoc est terra quaestionis . . ." This is the ground of our seeking. This is the ground, the beauty and beginning of all good order. It was not a prayer of the Church, but they knew it well and joined in all of its responses.

After these preliminaries the knight turned to one of them.

"Well achieved, William Exmewe," he said.

The friar, Exmewe, stepped forward, among the men of high degree, and bowed towards Geoffrey de Calis. "The game is begun," he said in a low voice. "The oratory was well burned with Greek fire. The death in the cloister of St. Paul's came by chance, as I believe, but it served our purpose well enough."

"Who are these people you lead?"

"Broken-down people. The helpless and hopeless ones of this world. There is Richard Marrow, a carpenter who would creep to the cross if he could. Emnot Hallyng, whose head is higher than his hat. Garret Barton, a malignant man who fights the world. There is one of Paul's manciples."

"Oh?" Geoffrey de Calis raised his head. "Which one is that?"

"Robert Rafu."

"I know him to be cowardly disposed. He eats too little."

"Hamo Fulberd, a marvellously ill-favoured youth. He is marked down for an especial doom."

"And they know nothing of our purposes?"

"Nothing whatever. They have not the least suspicion of me. They believe me to be, like them, a foreknown one."

Miles Vavasour raised his voice from the back. "The common report is that your people are Lollards."

"No matter." Geoffrey de Calis put his hand on Exmewe's shoulder. "If Lollers are blamed, so much the better. The Lollards have not hearts or livers great enough to burn down churches, but let them be burdened with the guilt. They will arouse the people. The king will be considered weak and foolish in the face of these violations. If he cannot protect Holy Mother Church, he is the shadowy one who cannot bear the sun. The anointed one will fall. Not even Christ and his holy blood can save him."

They laughed at the allusion to Christ's holy blood, for they were neither deceived by nor afraid of the tricks and japes of the Church.

These men comprised a group known as Dominus[13] which had been secretly assembled eighteen months earlier, with the sole purpose of dethroning Richard II. In this company were well-known clerics as well as several of the king's councillors. There were also dignitaries of London, including an under-sheriff and two eminent aldermen. Geoffrey de Calis himself had been appointed by King Richard as Constable of Wallingford and the Chilterns, a sinecure which he had successfully "farmed" for an annual payment. Yet now, as a result of the king's depredations, their lands and their wealth were not safe; Richard demanded new taxes, and confiscated property on mere pretext. So they were willing to risk all in order to destroy him. It was they who had agreed to finance Henry Bolingbroke's invasion. It was they who, a year before, had persuaded William Exmewe to establish a group of rebellious ones who would be willing to challenge the pope and the bishops within the city of London; they had decided that outrage and confusion among the citizens would speed their course and the destruction of the king. William Exmewe had by chance found Richard Marrow, in the refectory of St. Bartholomew, and had conversed with him on matters spiritual; Marrow had in turn informed Exmewe about the group of foreknown men to which he was joined. Exmewe eventually accompanied Marrow to the meetings of these men, and soon gained mastery over them with his rhetoric and his piety.

*

"And how is this gear to proceed?" Miles Vavasour took pleasure in asking questions.

"I have spread the report among the predestined men," Exmewe replied, "that there must be five wonders to hasten the day of deliverance. You know the old device of the five circles interlinked?" It was the sign used by Joseph of Arimathea, and a token of the early church. "It has wonderfully impressed itself upon them."

"So there are three remaining?" Miles Vavasour, as a sergeant-at-law, prided himself upon his quick wit. "The oratory and Paul's have been first and second."

"There then follow St. Sepulchre, St. Michael le Querne and St. Giles. At all points of the city."

They murmured approval. Their voices had the confidence of power, and they were on easy terms with one another. They were jovial, almost careless, in their demeanour; they were frank, and confiding and free. The unstated belief among them would have been that, just as there was nothing before birth, so there was nothing after death. It were wise, therefore, to enjoy this world while you may. Matters of religion were to be used to quell the people and to promote good order. This was a belief that the prelates among them also accepted.

Sir Geoffrey de Calis called them to order once again. "There will be more fires," he said, "and more destruction. Henry will return to England and summon a great host. If Henry is to defeat Richard, he must be looked upon as the saviour of the Church. The first law of reverence is need. There then follows fear. In the meantime we must be still as any stone. No one must know of our devisings. Not what we do but what we do not do."

As they left the chamber, some of them stooped to kiss Sir Geoffrey's ring; it was on the third finger of his left hand, which communicated directly by the nerve to his beating heart.

When they had all departed into the night he mounted the stairs of the tower into the muniment room on its second floor. There was a cubiculum here in which someone was kneeling, whispering the holy words of the Hidden Gospel. Sister Clarice was saying, "Vertas. Gadatryme. Trumpass. Dadyltrymsart." Then she turned to Sir Geoffrey. "All will be well, good knight. And all manner of things shall be well."

Chapter Nine

The Reeve's Tale

The prioress, Agnes de Mordaunt, stood by the principal gate of the convent and sighed. She turned to her reeve, Oswald Koo, with an expression of fury only partially softened by the dimple upon her chin. "On no account give them leave to use our barns. Look at them! Nasty, vile tregetours! They have already pissed on the straw we were about to lay in the church." She was staring at the workmen who were even then building Noah's ark upon the green. It was the second day of the mysteries held each year in Clerkenwell, during the week of Corpus Christi, under the guidance and supervision of the guild of parish clerks. A raised platform had been erected near the ark itself, and the painted cloth hung upon it represented the front of Noah's house. It was depicted as if it were a merchant's house along Cheapside except for a see-saw, or merry-totter, which had been placed in front of the cloth.

There was much activity behind the stage, as the cast prepared themselves for their roles. Noah and Noah's wife had performed as Adam and Eve on the previous morning, and had exchanged their white leather costumes for the more familiar gear of smocks and gowns. "Let go, Dick. Let go!" Noah's wife was played by the clerk of St. Michael in Aldgate; he was laughing as a pair of false breasts was tied to his chest by the keeper of the costumes. "This is so tight I cannot breathe."

"For a little woman, you cause a great commotion. Put on your hair with your own hands." The wig of Noah's wife resembled a great yellow mop, but the clerk of St. Michael raised it reverently above his head.

In the cart of costumes there were several masks, with stars and spangles glued to them, ribbons, hats, jackets and paper streamers as well as various false beards and wooden swords. The parish clerk of St. Olave, who was playing Noah, was leaning against it; he was drinking pudding ale out of a leather bottle.

"If you rut-gut in my face," Noah's wife warned him, "you will feel my fist."

"It is a necessary, good wife. When my stomach is empty, I have no strength."

The faces of Ham and Japhet were being painted with grease and saffron, while God practised upon his stilts on the bank leading down to the Fleet. Already a crowd had gathered beside the green. Some of them were exchanging jokes with the carpenters who climbed across the ark and were even now raising its mast.

Something indelicate was shouted by one of the players, and the prioress put her hands to her ears. "Oh this sinful life. Aufer a nobis iniquitates nostras." The reeve blessed himself, and asked if he might return to the cart-house. "Yes. Leave this valley of vanity." Yet Dame Agnes lingered, and watched as the audience assembled; the wooden stalls were filled with distinguished visitors – among them the knight, Geoffrey de Calis, and an under-sheriff – while the crowd settled down upon the green. And then at nine o'clock, on this last morning of May, she might have been heard whispering to herself, "Whatever is this approaching?"

A man in a tight red costume, and wearing a pointed red cap, had drawn up beside the well; his horse was caparisoned in red, and its saddle sewn with bells. "Oye! Oy!" he cried out, waiting until the noise of the audience had subsided. He was the clerk of St. Benet Fink, better known to Londoners as the pageant master who for many years had organised the Clerkenwell plays. He was known to be a merry man; he was too merry, perhaps, since his evident and inexhaustible happiness left others feeling inadequate and uneasy. "Oye! Oy!" All were still.

> "Sovereign citizens, hither am I sent
> A message for to say.
> I pray you all that be present
> That you will hear with good intent
> The message of our play."

It was a bright morning and the sun gleamed upon the gilded mask of God, who now walked on his stilts before the crowd; he was dressed in a white robe, embroidered with golden suns, and his arms were raised in greeting. He looked straight ahead, above the eyes of the crowd, to the rows of wooden benches where the dignitaries of the city were seated.

> "It is my will it should be so.
> It is, it was, it shall be thus,
> I am and have been ever."

The clerk of Mary Abchurch, who played this part, was known for his harsh and unyielding temper. He had once accused a child of sacrilege, for playing football in the nave, and had suspended all services within the church for a week; he had brought the boy before the bishop's court, asking for his excommunication, but the charge was wisely dismissed. In the role of the Creator, however, he seemed to command authority over the hundreds of citizens assembled. He was, after all, playing the angry deity of the Old Testament. His mask augmented and amplified his voice.

"I, God, that all the world have wrought,
Heaven and earth, and all of nought,
I see my people, in deed and thought,
Have pain upon their own heads brought."

The high chant of God had summoned up a stillness in the
audience which was close to fear; but this mood was suddenly broken
by the voice of a child crying, "Make room! Make room, masters!
Here comes a player!" A boy, riding upon a donkey, advanced into
the open area before the ark and the stage.

"All hail, all hail, both blithe and glad,
For here come I, a merry lad,
I am named Japhet, Noah's son,
My father bad me not speak too long."

The boy playing Japhet was in fact the courier and messenger at
the clerks' hall in Garlickhythe. He was named "Bullet" and often
competed with his colleagues from other guilds – "Slingaway" of the
Mercers, "Gobithasty" of the Grocers and "Truebody" of the
Fishmongers – in races around the streets of London. "Bullet" was
known for his impudence and his quick wit, which he used with such
effect in the role of Japhet that it seemed that he was acting out the
type of the young city boy. The donkey was now talking to him.

"To smite me now it is shame.
You know well, Japhet, pardy,
You never had an ass like me."

To which Japhet replied, "Go kiss my arse, ass." It was only the first
of many obscenities passing between the boy and the donkey,
culminating in a mock attempt by the boy to penetrate the beast's
rear end. Dame Agnes gathered up some of the nuns watching the
performance, and with many threats drove them within the convent
gates.

All this time God remained before the crowd, his gilded mask reflecting the sun of early summer. Eventually the boy rode off, to great cheers and cries of "Yas, Bullet!" Then, on cue, Noah appeared upon the raised platform. The parish clerk of St. Olave, Philip Drinkmilk, had studied all the arts of disguising before ever taking on the role of Noah. His father was still a scene-painter for the city's pageants, and he had accompanied him to the great mummings and interludes that celebrated the cycle of the city's year. It happened that a group of travelling players had been hired for the entry into London of King Richard's young bride, Anne of Bohemia, in the early days of 1382; Philip Drinkmilk's father had then been employed to fashion for them the masks of the various passions. They had been lodged at the city's expense at the Castle inn in Fish Street, and with his father Philip had visited them in what they termed their "robing room." He particularly remembered his overwhelming fear when a bear approached him, moaning, and his sudden relief when a man's face popped out from the skin. "Welcome," the face said. "If the rats do not slay you here, the lice will do it."

He became acquainted with this man, a young actor whose only name was Herbert and who, to the great joy of the company, would burn his farts in Fish Street. Herbert showed Drinkmilk the thirteen signs of the hand, tokening the various feelings, and the eight signs of the face. He also explained to him the mummery of the colours; yellow was the colour of jealousy, white of virtue, red of anger, blue of fidelity, and green of disloyalty. A good actor would wear several of these, and so create a performance of the utmost interest and subtlety. Philip Drinkmilk, under his tutelage, had become a natural mimic; he learned the dialogue of *Grimalkin, Our Cat*, and mastered the gestures and the expressions within a very short time. In the little vestry of St. Olave, he would perform elaborate bows and intricate dance steps; sometimes he would twirl around in the middle of the room, and sing snatches of the latest songs.

In the role of Noah, however, he adopted the attitude of weariness; his palms were flat, parallel to the ground, and his body was bent sideways. His face had become the mirror of his soul, with his eyes raised upward and his mouth half-open. He was wearing a blue and scarlet gown; he touched the blue as a memorial of his faithfulness, and the scarlet as a token of his fear, while the two colours conjoined were an emblem of suffering. When God turned from the crowd and stood before him, he lay down upon the stage.

In the same rhythmic chant, which seemed to the audience to come from some source beyond speech or song, God commanded Noah to build an ark and to shelter there two of every beast or bird upon the earth. The fact that the ark could already be seen upon the green was of no consequence; past, present and future were intermingled in the small area of Clerkenwell. The audience assembled knew precisely what would occur in front of them, but they were always surprised and entertained by it. They laughed now as Noah addressed God in fear and trembling. It was clear that he was shaking not out of respect for the presence of divinity but out of fear for the wrath of his wife.

There was Noah's wife see-sawing on the merry-totter, with one of her female "gossips" rising and falling on the other end. It was a comic moment devised by the pageant master, and their lower smocks now billowed up to reveal their dirty undergarments; both of them were holding flasks, and were miming the words of a violent quarrel. Noah's wife slid from the see-saw and began scratching the face of her gossip, to general laughter. When she saw Noah coming towards her with slow step, she hitched up her smock as if preparing herself for combat.

Oswald Koo, the reeve, had retreated to the cart-house before the mystery had begun; one of the carters had complained about the quality of the nails, and Koo wished to weigh and measure them for himself. There were also the instructions of Dame Agnes to be followed. He had cleared away the damaged straw and, just as Noah and his wife began to fight, he had walked carefully and quietly around the back of the stage. He did not wish to disturb the players, but he was convinced that the workmen had stolen some of his wood for the construction of their ark. He was searching for the mark of the convent, a hind outlined in red ink, on the edge of the planks. He had found nothing and, keeping out of sight of both players and audience, he crossed the end of the green and walked a little way down Turnmill Street. At which point he glimpsed something in Black Man Alley; it was leaning against the wall, but now it rose to its full height and turned to face him. It was more horrible than any dragon. It had the feet of a lizard, the wings of a bird, and the face of a young girl; it put its claws up to its face and, with a shriek, fled from him down the alley. The noise of the crowd on Clerkenwell Green could distinctly be heard, as it passed the fishpond and the bowling alley. What monster was this? It had not yet occurred to Oswald Koo that it might be some player in costume, perhaps in the part of one of Lucifer's demons. Instead he had instantly recognised an image of damnation and judgement. He believed that the face he had glimpsed was that of Sister Clarice.

Eight months earlier he had followed her into the fields; he had been watching for her there, and waiting for her. When he saw Clarice leaving the mill, bearing two sacks, he asked if he might assist her. He gazed earnestly at her as he spoke and, refusing his help, she lowered her eyes.

"Well, sister, how do you?"

"Pretty good, God be thanked."

"You like this life well enough?"

"I have known no other, Master Koo."

"True enough. Ever since you were a child –" He stopped, fearing to speak. The years of silence then broke around him; he could keep quiet no longer. "I knew your mother, Clarice."

"No one knew her." She crossed herself, and stared down at the muddy earth of the field. As a child she had been told by Agnes de Mordaunt that she had been found, abandoned, upon the steps of the chapter-house.

"That is not true," he said as gently as he dared. "She was once among us."

"What is it that you mean? Among us?"

"She was of the order."

"How do you know this, Oswald Koo?"

"I was under-bailiff to the convent then. I was a young man. With the heat of a young man. Her name was Alison." He hesitated. "She was the chantress. She died in the travails of birth." He walked away from her, and then returned out of breath. "Do you by any chance remember the tunnels?"

The story of the tunnels had reached her, even as a child, and she had often wondered why the other nuns treated her as if she were some unregarded piece of the convent itself. She did indeed recall some place of stone that seemed to her to be secret. It was full of wailing and of anger. She associated stone with tears and iniquity.

"I was a young man, as I said. Your mother and I – well, it was error. Accident." He had copulated with Alison by the Fleet river. He could still recall with horror that moment when his thin leather yard-case, or prick sheath, had split and his seed had tumbled into the queynte of the young nun.

"I was the fruit of her womb?" Clarice remained very calm.

"I was your seed."

"But you did not claim me. Or recognise me."

"How could I? I was a servant here."

"You did not love me then." She still betrayed no feeling at all.

"Love you, Clarice? I did not know you. But I watched you grow up within the walls. The nuns were often harsh with you."

"I know it. I was the token of sinfulness."

"I suffered with you when you were beaten with candles. Yet I was uplifted when I heard you sing 'O altitudo' at vespers. I was proud of you then. No one knew that I was your father. Your birth was blamed on a monk hospitaller. So I never ceased praising you to Dame Agnes. I still pray each night for your soul to God and to the congregation of saints."

"You may save your prayers for yourself. I have no need of them." With a sigh Clarice put down the sacks of wheat. "Will you carry them to the cook-house?" was all she said.

She walked away across the field until she was out of his sight. Then she lay down upon the grass, and beat her fists against the earth. She was whispering, "Dear mother, let me in. Let me in." It was the next day that she experienced the first of her visions.

When Oswald Koo saw the serpent with the child's face, he feared it as some phantasm of the evil he had committed. He determined to follow its path even if, as he believed, it had no true outward form.

The reeve passed the fishpond, in which he saw his own guilty image hastening across the surface, and walked over the empty bowling green. The noise of the audience, a few yards to the north, was growing louder. He turned a corner – and stopped short. Sister Clarice and her monk, Brank Mongorray, were in earnest conversation. The monk stepped back in order to remonstrate with her, and the nun raised her hands as if in prayer. The only words he heard were "Ireland" and "bounty," but he could not construe their sense. He had not talked to his daughter since his revelation in the field, and she had averted her eyes whenever they passed each other. It sometimes seemed to him that her voices and her prophesying were means of not talking to him. She gazed at him now and he heard her say, as if in a dream, "Noli me tangere." He stepped out of sight, and retraced his steps to Turnmill Street.

When he returned to the green, two of Noah's sons, Ham and Shem, were holding out painted images of the animals that were supposed to be entering the ark. There were two unicorns, two monkeys and two wolves as well as other creatures which seemed to have no name. Then Noah and Japhet entered with pairs of real beasts – two cows, two sheep, two oxen, two donkeys, two horses, which passed through a gap in the wooden front of the ark. The reeve observed them carefully, in case they were part of the convent's stock. The ark was then rocked to and fro by several carpenters while painted cloths, depicting great seas and waves, were raised and shaken behind it. Eventually a great ribbon glued with painted feathers was held up, in token of the rainbow, and God once more walked out upon his stilts.

He was about to speak when a sudden movement within the crowd was followed by whistling and jeering. Some members of the audience ran out, screaming "Idols!" and "The devil's images!" One of them rushed up to God and, to the crowd's horror, knocked him off his stilts. Another took the gilded mask from God's face and crushed it beneath his foot, crying out "Whoreson false face!" It seemed to the reeve that, at this point, the crowd became one living creature with a single purpose. It hurled itself against the assailants of the mystery. There were cries of "Loller!" and "Antichrist!" as the offenders were set upon and beaten. One man was hit with a hammer between the shoulders, and then struck in the face with the butt of a sword; another was stabbed with a long dagger known as a "misericord," and died instantly.

The rage ended as soon as it had begun, but only two Lollards were left alive; their bones were broken, and their bodies bloody, but they still breathed. They were speedily committed to prison, where they soon died of their wounds. It was the only occasion, in this fearful year, when the Lollards were seen.

Chapter Ten

The Physician's Tale

The prioress had fallen into a fever, or an ague, or a rheum, or she knew not what. She was sore sick, as she told everyone around her. She felt sorry and heavy. She sent her water in a flask to the physician of the convent so that he might, in her words, "understand his conceit upon it" and discover whether "I shall mend or mar." By the same porter, who bore the urine, he sent back the message that she would prosper in this world if only she would eat shrimps. Shrimps recovered sickly and consumed persons because they were the most nimble, witty and skipping creatures; they also possessed the best juice for cures, although she should be sure to unscale them in order to vent their windiness from which lust and venery arise. The allusion to venery was taken by her as a personal insult.

On the recommendation of the nun's priest, then, she consulted Thomas Gunter, a famous leech whose shop was in Bucklersbury. She sent him a letter listing her symptoms, among which were heaviness of stomach and mistiness of sight. He wrote back in a very elaborate hand. "Do you have marigolds? Only to look on marigolds, dear sister in God, is to strengthen the eyesight. Yet they must be picked when the moon is in the sign of the Virgin." He added that "the juice of the marigold is very useful for the inflammation of the breasts," but the prioress let her eye pass over that sentence. He was much discomfited by her heaviness of stomach, but suggested that she mix the grease of a boar and the grease of a rat, the grease of a horse and the grease of a badger, souse the concoction in vinegar, add sage, and then put it upon her belly. "I can write no more to you at this time, ma dame, but the Holy Ghost have you in his keeping. Written at London the Monday after Corpus Christi." He added, in a postscript, that he did in fact possess a pot of the said stomach ointment if the dear sisters were unable to procure the necessary greases.

The wind changed in the night. It now came from the north, and was deemed to purge all evil vapours. Thus Dame Agnes had read in *Cantica canticorum*, "Rise up, north wind, and perfect my garden." But the new air did not refresh her. She sent a message to Master Gunter asking whether he would be so courteous and so gentle as to visit the convent "where you will find a suffering body." He arrived on horseback three hours later.

Thomas Gunter was a small man, who seemed physically overwhelmed by the furred hood and robe of his profession. He moved quickly – as if he were on wheels, Dame Agnes said later – and his bright eyes quickly took in all the details of her gestures and appearance. The prioress was sitting in a high-backed chair when he was escorted by Idonea into her chamber. He kissed her ring, and glanced at the plate beside her. "Shrimps? What are shrimps doing here, ma dame?" He had a quick and lively voice, like that of a bird in a cage. "A fish with this flesh hurts sick people excessively. It nourishes bitter humours."

"I was advised –"

"Do you not know that a tame beast is better for sick people than a wild one? You need a carp from your pond, dear lady, not a shrimp from the sea-shore." The prioress's monkey was fingering Gunter's leather satchel, in which he kept all the tools of his craft. "Have patience, dear Adam," he whispered to it. "All shall be revealed. Tell me somewhat about your humours, my lady."

"Melancolius." The prioress gave a little burp, and covered her mouth. "A portion phlegmaticus."

"Then I shall not cup you."

"I wish you would purge me, Master Gunter. I feel some noisome matter sitting within me. I cannot sleep."

"I have pills which can provoke sleep. Tell your nuns to go to the dove-house. The dung of doves is a soporific when it is applied to the soles of the feet."

"Do you have that ointment which you wrote me of?"

"I have considered further, and I am not sure that its natural virtue fits your case. Give me room and space to wonder." He opened the satchel. "The prison of your melancholy lies in your spleen." He brought out an earthenware jar. "This medicine is good, since it purges the humour of those night places. Do you drink much milk?"

"I have that weakness."

"It is good. Excellent. Milk is very good for melancholy. Abstain from hazelnuts. They discomfort the brain. But eat green ginger. It quickens the memory, and may yet make you gay."

"My memory is not of gay things, Master Gunter. I have my burdens."

"Nevertheless, good prioress, I heartily recommend it to you. Indulge in eggs also. Poached eggs are best at night. New roasted eggs are good in the morning, with a little salt and sugar. This is not a hard diet, you see. It is full easy. And remember this, my lady. If you be unobedient or unpatient to my commandings, you may fall into a full great peril. May I?" He put his hand upon the tips of her fingers. "Rose oil is needed to heat you here." He took from his satchel a little glass vase. "Before you lie down to sleep, you must lay this stuff upon your stomach with as even a stroke as you can."

"What is it?"

"It is a mixture of my devising. There is horse dung here, that is called lutum sapien. Together with the powder of burnt hen's feathers and the fur of a hare. It is dry to the fourth degree." He held up the vase for her inspection. "As it comes from diverse bodies, so it works in diverse complexions."

The prioress sighed. "Do your cunning on me. All is mixed beneath the moon."

"Then beware of pissing in draughts."

"I never thought of pissing in draughts."

A short while after this exchange, Thomas Gunter rode out of the convent. He was indeed glad to be gone, since his healing would be affected if he were in the company of menstruating women. He had not seen the young nun, about whom so many scandalous reports had circulated, but he feared the taint of her blood. He had wanted to question the prioress about her, but her melancholy and evident exhaustion had persuaded him to remain silent on what must have been an unhappy subject. He turned his horse towards Smithfield, and within a few minutes had arrived in his neighbourhood; he crossed the Walbrook at St. Stephen's Bridge, and turned down Bucklersbury. He lived among other druggists and herbalists, and in the shop next to his own he noticed a display of the dried flower known as "Hallelujah"; it was so named because it blossomed in the period between Easter and Whitsuntide, when the one hundred and seventeenth psalm was sung, but Thomas Gunter was more interested in its curative properties. It was known as a sure antidote to cramps and seizures, and the physician made frequent use of it. The druggist was watching him from his doorway as he dismounted. "God be with you and his cross comfort you, Thomas."

"You are pious this morning."

"I have been proclaiming. Hallelujah!" Robert Skeat, the druggist, was well known for his somewhat ironic attitude towards the Church's devotions. "I trust to be saved."

"In God's time, I hope. What do you have for me at present?"

"I can give you spurge laurel for the flux. And the ground ivy to stop bleeding." Skeat was smiling as he spoke, almost as if he did not credit his own words. "Here is corncockle, Thomas –"

"Agrostemma."

"If you say so, leech. For those who will not shit, I believe. And here is mayweed."

"Which smells like shit. I gave some to Goodwife Kello only last evening."

"All her matter comes out of one hole. Lord, is she a chattermouth."

"There is no cure for that, alas." Thomas Gunter was about to enter his house – his hall and solar were built above his shop – when a tall man dressed in a grey cloak approached him. "Is it you, Lambert? Why muffle yourself on the edge of summer? Excessive heat will provoke the piles."

"It is not so warm in the pits, sir." Lambert was one of the gaolers in the Poultry Street compter; he had a wide hat, which he took off as he entered Gunter's shop. "You know why I have come."

"Is it fresh?"

"It died yesterday night. A Loller. It was taken at the Clerkenwell rumble. It has yellow hair."

"The more hot a man is, the more hair he will have."

"I will have five shillings."

"So much? For a body that none will wish to bury?"

"Five shillings. Yellow hair."

It was well known to Gunter, and to others, that a corpse with yellow hair was of enormous efficacy. The body must have been killed, however, and not died from some disease. The flesh was then cut to pieces and placed in a powder of myrrh and aloes; it was imbibed for twenty-four hours in the spirit of wine and turpentine, and then hung in a shadowy place where it would dry and would not stink. The flesh then became an excellent adjunct to Thomas Gunter's surgery, since it congealed flowing blood and helped to close wounds. It also helped to assuage the stinging of serpents and the biting of mad dogs. "When can you bring it to me?"

"After curfew."

*

The body was indeed that of a Lollard who had been taken as a result of the riot during the Clerkenwell mystery; he had died in the gaol in Poultry Street, from a wound delivered to him by the parish clerk of St. Benet Fink with the aid of a wooden staff tipped with iron. He had not died in mercy, since no priest was willing to shrive him. No one would care what happened to the body of a heretic; Lambert need only say that, for fear of infection, he had tipped him into the lime-pit outside the walls.

That evening, two men could be seen carrying a sack across the Walbrook. It was not heavy work, and Lambert refused Gunter's offer of wine. He looked angrily at his companion, Nicholay, who on principle accepted a drink of any description. They stood uneasily in the leech's shop, their burden thrust on a bench in the corner, among bottles and phials, boxes and flasks, parchments and skulls of small beasts. They had little to say to one another.

"That wart is ripe for cutting." Gunter was looking at Nicholay's neck.

"Now, Master Gunter?" Nicholay seemed suddenly anxious.

"No. Not now. It is not the month for the neck. Taurus is the sign for neck and throat. A surgeon, Nicholay, may not cut any member of a man's body until the moon is in its proper sign. Take your head." Nicholay did not know how to accede to this request. "Aries, which is a fiery sign, moderately dry, governs the head with all its contents."

"If any." Lambert was eager to be gone.

"So when the moon is in Aries I am ready to operate upon your head and your face, or to open one of your head veins. A surgeon must also be an astronomer, you see. Similarly, consider your cod. Your testicles." Nicholay was now staring at him very earnestly. "They lie in Scorpio."

"You are wrong, master leech. They always lie in his wife. We must go now, Nicholay." Lambert cleared his throat, and glanced towards the corpse. "But not without our silver."

Gunter climbed the stairs to his hall, and returned with five shillings wrapped in a cloth. "May I ask you to carry him below?" The two gaolers were then directed down the stone stairs of an undercroft; in the vaulted space, there were hanging knives and saws and various small instruments. They put the sack upon a slab of marbled stone which was raised upon two thick columns of limestone.

After the men had departed, Gunter cut open the sack with a pair of shears and inspected the body. The smell of the prison was still upon it, so he washed it with a linen cloth soaked in turpentine. The body was slight and thin; it was worn, as Gunter observed out loud, with praying and sighing. Before he could begin his secret ministry, there were two other rituals which he wished to perform. He took a flaming candle from its sconce in the wall, and examined very carefully the eyes of the corpse; no image of the murderer could be seen, but during those moments the parish clerk of St. Benet Fink had the curious sensation of being watched. Then the leech smeared oil upon the thumbnail of the corpse, and scrutinised it closely for images immediately preceding the death. Once more there was nothing visible.

With a sigh he took down one of his knives, a newly sharpened instrument known by surgeons as "Follow me," and cut into the breast of the body. Then he parted the ribs. One of Gunter's passions lay in tracing the paths of the body's spirits. He knew that the natural spirit resided in the liver, the vital spirit in the heart, the animal spirit in the brain; yet he wished to have some physical evidence of their operations. He concentrated first upon the liver. The livers of whales and dolphins smell like violets, little Lollard. How will yours smell?

On the following Sunday Gunter rode out at dawn into the countryside. After six days of work and study, he wished to refresh and recreate himself. He passed the crossroads of Gracechurch Street and Fenchurch Street on his way to Aldgate, where the poet Geoffrey Chaucer had once lived, and then he galloped out through the opened gate to the eastern fields past the Minories. It was a ride to reach them, however, since the road beyond Aldgate itself was marked and pitted by the scars of the horses, carts and wagons which passed this way in endless procession. There were wooden houses on both sides of the road, offering cheap lodgings for travellers, as well as ramshackle inns and dirty cookshops; there were myriad signs of hands, and plates, and flagons, to attract the vast army of wayfarers. The fields closest to the city had also become dumping grounds for all manner of refuse together with piles of stone and heaps of ashes, deep pits and marshy places. Yet beyond them lay the open fields. He rode for a few furlongs, until all that could be seen were the wooden shacks used by those who watched the crops at night for thieves and pilferers. The air was clearer here. He had read of all the gardens in the love visions, but nothing delighted him so much as the prospect of open country. It was quiet now, with only the sound of his horse trotting upon the road.

He heard someone moaning. There was a pony tied to a gatepost by the side of the road, and Gunter reined in his horse. There was a field beside him shielded with trees, but he could make out a figure walking across some patch of grass; Gunter dismounted and walked over to the edge of the field, standing behind a tree so that he could not be seen. There was a young man in the field, with his hands pressed against his face, walking backwards and forwards. When he let his hands drop to his sides, Gunter could see that he was crying.

The physician was successful at his craft because he possessed a sensitive and sympathetic nature; he could tell, from a gesture or an expression, the nature of the illness he was called upon to treat. Now, on the edge of the field, he was consumed by a sadness so intense that it seemed to drive out every other emotion and perception. How must it be to live friendless and alone in this world? With no one sad for your sorrow? He watched the boy for a moment or so longer, but he could not bear his suffering. He no longer wished to ride onwards – there was no more to see. Instead he mounted his horse and returned in the direction of the city. When he came up to the wall he began to sing, "Draw me, draw me near, draw me near the jolly juggler."

The young man whom Thomas Gunter had seen, and pitied, was Hamo Fulberd. He had chosen the field as the place fittest for him. It was known as Haukyn's Field; there was a brook running upon its southern side, with a copse of trees upon its north. When he was later asked to describe it, Hamo said that "it was just a plain bare field only." He had come here before the events of the spring, but now for the first time he had disobeyed Exmewe's command and left the precincts of St. Bartholomew's. The field had called him, as if to share his misery. He had taken the pony and had ridden here during the night. He had come because he could no longer bear the sight of his familiar world; it seemed to encircle him or, worse, to enter his soul. What if this world were all that is, and was, and ever would be? What if, from the beginning to the end of the thing men called time, the same people merged continually with one another?

Ever since Exmewe had told him that he had killed the tooth-drawer, he had considered himself lost. He had heard no more about the man, and he assumed that any pursuit of the murderer had passed. But, for some reason, that rendered him all the more fearful of judgement. He looked into the night sky, at those stars of the circle which is called Galaxia or Watling Street, but found no comfort there. He had asked Father Matthew, the head of the scriptorium, if there were forgiveness for all. The friar had replied that "no one knows if he is worthy of the love of God." This also did not comfort him, any more than Exmewe's belief that he was a predestined one and therefore blessed. Nothing was right or wrong. We are all in the night.

He saw nothing ahead of him but darkness, as if he were trapped in a vaulted space of cold stone. He had an image of God, laughing, as he doled out dooms and destinies. Or was there some over-whelming grief always waiting to seize upon a poor spirit such as his? Would there always be people as sorrowful as he? Or did that grief seize upon one place? Was that why he was drawn to Haukyn's Field? Did all the forces of the world, which wise men said was round, work together? So in his adopted place, in this small field, he pondered these questions. He looked down upon the ground, since he did not wish to be distracted from his ever increasing thoughts. His head was bowed, as if those thoughts had already grown too heavy. Sometimes he would mumble to himself; he believed that his words were not worthy enough to be spoken out loud.[14]

He was bewildered by himself. He did not care particularly whether he failed or prospered, but this was worse than all – he could not grasp what was happening to him. He stayed in Haukyn's Field until the moon appeared above him, and then he rode back slowly to St. Bartholomew. When he arrived there, William Exmewe was waiting for him. "You disobeyed me," he said. "You wandered abroad." He struck him across the face.

Hamo did not flinch. Instead he brushed back his hair, and stood more upright. "I must go somewhere. I am mewed up here like a bird."

"I am protecting you, Hamo, as a nurse protects her innocents. I will soon have work for you. So be steady." Exmewe said nothing else, and left the barn.

Chapter Eleven

The Monk's Tale

"Well, there is no new guise that has not been old."

"True enough. This wide world turns upon a wheel. Ancient things return." They were conversing in the library of Bermondsey Abbey, surrounded by many old parchments and chained volumes; the dust of the ages seemed to have settled upon them. The sergeant-at-law, Miles Vavasour, and the monk, Jolland, were sitting at a long table with a copy of *Expositio Apocalypseos* by Primasius before them; they were discussing a sentence by Primasius in which he lamented the greed and hard-heartedness of certain second-century bishops. A casual observer might have wondered why a lawyer of high degree had taken off his white silk hood in order to speak familiarly with an ordinary monk; but Miles Vavasour already knew the Cluniac by repute. Jolland was a learned man who had laboured for many years upon a commentary to Bede's *Historia Ecclesiastica Brittaniarum et maxime gentis Anglorum*, and was considered to be the greatest of all scholars on the early history of England and its Church. But Vavasour had come to test the monk's faith. He respected him for his learning, and wished to see how far Jolland's knowledge stretched towards the things of his God. Vavasour, like the other members of Dominus, had no faith or belief in matters that the common people reverenced. Yet the sergeant was an intelligent man, spurred on by curiosity; he was a lawyer, too, and had an infinite zest for debate and dialectic. He was an impulsive and argumentative man, also, who loved dissension. He had a large nose and wide mouth, as if his features were trying to betray his true character. He had come to Bermondsey in order to discover more about certain miracles connected with the history of Glastonbury Abbey, but the conversation had taken another turn. As the monk had said, the events of the world must keep on breaking through.

Jolland had lately heard of a surprising incident in neighbouring Southwark. Joan de Irlaunde, one month old, had been left sleeping in her cradle on the floor of a shop which her parents had rented for the sale of the shoes which they cut and stitched; in the hour before vespers this couple had decided to take a stroll along the high street leading towards the bridge, but they made the mistake of leaving the door to their shop partly open. A pig had entered from the street and, despite the fact that the baby was tightly swaddled, had as Jolland put it "mortally bit the right side of the head." On returning, the horrified mother had snatched up her child, but had only managed to keep her alive until midnight. The monk knew no more, but the incident rekindled his fascination with the presence of destiny in human affairs. Was the pig prefigured to eat the child? And did the bodies of animals bear the marks of the stars? "It could be said that, even if Venus was compounded with Jupiter, it was still unable to repress the malice of Mars against the pig. As the heavens began to turn, the child was subject to the bad aspects of Saturn that ordained she would be destroyed. Or so it is argued."

"This is all matter for children." The sergeant seemed annoyed that so learned a man should speak of such things. "You are like those enchanters who see the future world in a basin full of water, or in a bright sword, or in the shoulder-bone of an ass."

"I am not so serious as I may seem, sir judge. I only put the case. But there are those who believe that all is prejudged and predestined, even to the number of the souls in bliss."

Vavasour suddenly put his hands together as if in prayer, and imitated the pious declaration of the predestined men whom Exmewe guided. "Above the world I am. In this world I am not."

"How do you know that chant?"

The sergeant laughed in order to conceal his confusion. "It is nothing. I have heard it somewhere in the courts. But tell me this, Jolland. How do we find the distinction between providence and destiny?"

"Providence is the governance of all mutable nature as it exists in the mind of God. Destiny is that plan as it is worked out on changeable things in time. We are going on a pilgrimage to Canterbury. I would know that Canterbury was our end, but I would not of necessity know the myriad accidents of fortune upon the way."

"But that is not God's way, is it? Does not God know the path thoroughly? Has it not been said that God causes a man to sin and to become a sinner? For the man who sins is but conforming his will to the will of God. If that man feels hatred for his sin, he need only remember that God is the antecedent cause. Is that not so?"

"It has been concluded by some, I grant you, but it is a false reasoning. If all were preordained, what would be the use of choosing any one course above another?"

"You know that Henry Bolingbroke has landed in England with sixty followers?"

"What is that to me?"

"He means to kill Richard and take the crown. Will that be necessity? Has God foredoomed it?"

"He has and He has not."

"And while we await His judgement, the nation wades in blood. Is that it? I merely ask the question."

The monk recognised the sergeant's impatience, and took it as the sign of a heavy heart; he realised that his uneasiness, too, was a form of bad conscience. He was happy to augment it, if only to curb Vavasour's pride. "I have by me a very learned work, Hieronymus his *De situ et nominibus*, which justly expounds the matter. Let me unclasp it." He unlocked the chain holding a book, lying upon the shelf above his head, and then with another key opened the clasp around it. Here was a rich volume indeed, illuminated with great coloured capitals through which birds and monkeys ran. Jolland felt the vellum paper with his forefinger. "Every page takes the skin of a sheep. So here we have many flocks before us." He turned the pages very carefully, in case one of them might crack or tear. "Hieronymus argues some-where that all comes of necessity, and that our destiny is shaped before our shirt. Now let me read this to you. Ah. Here it is." He translated from the Latin, as he recited the words. "For some men say, if God has seen all before – since God may in no manner be deceived – then must it fall out that way, even if men had sworn that it would not happen. No other thought, nor deed, can ever be but such as providence decrees. Otherwise we would be claiming that God does not have clear knowledge, but to lay such an error upon Him would be false and foul and wicked cursedness. There is more to this effect."

Vavasour shifted uneasily in his seat. "There is a stone laid upon a tomb in the nave of Paul's. It has an inscription carved upon it. 'Now I know more than the wisest of you.' Is that not just?"

"You may be sure of it." The monk was still intent upon the book. "Here is the argument of the learned father. It is not necessary that things happen because they have been ordained but, rather, that things that do happen have indeed been ordained. It is a subtlety worthy of a great clerk, is it not?" The sergeant, who was accustomed to the legal sophisms of Westminster Hall, gave the remark his professional approval. If the world were words, then the more erudite the better. "Hieronymus has another exposition. If a man were to sit by that trestle table, it would be your opinion that he had indeed sat down?"

"It would."

"Two types or forms of necessity are here in operation. One, for him, is the necessity of sitting. Two, for you, is the necessity of truthful vision."

"No no, Jolland. Ignotum per ignocius. You cannot explain the unknown by the more unknown. What is this necessity of sitting? And how are we to peer into divine things by means of a trestle table? Your God cannot be known."

"My God?"

"The God who shapes all our destinies. He is invisible."

"The nun tells a different story. She talks to Him."

"Oh, the nun. The witch. She is the whore of the people." Once more the monk recognised the extent of Vavasour's thwarted passion. The anger was alive within him. "She decks herself with her false faith and deludes the fools whom she is leading over the abyss."

"Yet the good doctor Thomas tells us that the soul has a faculty of its own for apprehending the true and that it may reach towards God with will and understanding. Could that not be her case?"

"The good doctor is mistaken, Jolland. God is beyond our will. Beyond reason itself. Reason pertains to matters belonging with this world, not to the things of God. Let me put an example. Self-murder is right if it is commanded by God."

"Oh no. To be damned perpetually by God Himself?"

"Who is to prevent it? Can you prevent a pig eating a child?" Vavasour quickly rose from the table, and walked to an oriel window which overlooked the mill-house and bake-house of the abbey. "Why do you suffer yourself to sit here so long, sir monk? It is a miserable mouse that hides in one hole."

The monk took no offence; he had been trained in humility. "I find peace among my parchments, Sir Miles. You are in the world of men and of affairs, and cannot in your cell fantastic imagine any other life. But there is a book lying in my chest which tells me of angels and patriarchs walking over the face of the earth. Why, you and I –"

There was the sound of loud argument in the courtyard below, and Jolland joined Vavasour by the window. Some four or five beggars had somehow passed through the gate, and were now crowding around the bake-house calling for bread. "They are so poor," Jolland said, "that they will put anything in their mouths. Their meat is commonly grasshoppers." The monks of the bake-house were throwing them horse-bread and gruel-bread, at the same time beseeching them to leave in peace. "They have had purgatory enough in this earth. They will rise into heaven."

"They are so poor, monk, that they scarcely care what will happen to them. Heaven or hell. It is all the same if your place of rest is some stinking stable on the highway."

" 'Forth, pilgrim, forth! Forth, beast, out of thy stall!' " It was clear from the sergeant's expression that he did not recognise the monk's text. "I sit solitary in my thoughts, Sir Miles. You spoke of a mouse in a hole. I am more like a hound. When a hound gnaws a bone he has no companion. These old books are my bones." There was now silence in the yard outside, broken only by the clatter of the watermill against the current of the stream which ran towards the Thames. "We were speaking of eternity. Did you ever hear anything concerning the dancers of St. Lawrence Pountney?"

"I recall some far-off thing –"

"The churchyard has now been hemmed about. Where the houses stand in that part of Candlewick, there was once a good fair space. It was Midsummer Eve, some two hundred years ago, when certain young people of that parish began their revels in the churchyard there. In those days, as in ours, dancing and jumping were forbidden in the ground of the church; yet they were busy with pigs on the back, tugs of war and other such flim-flams. The priest came out among them and commanded them to bring their unholy assembly to an end. 'Have peace!' he called to them. 'Have peace!' They were as hot as toast, but he determined to cool them. He reminded them that they had strayed into a churchyard with their noise and banners. 'Hold your tongues,' he said, 'and let our neighbours under the soil continue their rest.' But these buffoons, these gay horses, held hands and danced around him. They mocked him as the Jews once did Christ. The poor priest then took a crucifix from his bosom and, holding it before them, solemnly cursed them to the effect that they would dance all summer, and all winter too, handfasted until the end."

"It was a strange curse."

"Yet it was *efficiens*. The youths could not stop their dancing. They could neither eat nor drink, but they could kick and leap. They cried out for rest, but their legs and feet still moved in faster and faster measures. So their nights and days passed. They wailed like the wind, but they could in no wise help themselves. A father of a dancer made to pull her away from the ring, but his arm was wrenched from his body. The year passed, but the priest's malediction did not pass. They were still in continual motion. The dancers gradually sank up to their waists in the ground. The clay was clinging to them. The earth of the churchyard was soon over their heads, yet still the people could hear them dancing. Some say that the dead had joined them in their revelry."

"Terrible indeed."

"Others say that they are dancing still." The monk paused in order to turn a page of *De situ et nominibus*, and examined an illumination of some ancient walled city. He noticed in particular a procession of its citizens issuing from one of its gates, holding aloft gitterns and cymbals as if they were on their way to some sacred shrine. "That is what I hear wherever I go, Sir Miles. The dancing under the ground."

"Is this held to be true, or commonly reported as a fable?"

"Who can say?" The monk turned the page again, and saw the outline of a beast tale. Reynard the Fox had been tied by Couard the Hare, and was now being dragged to judgement before Ysangrin the Wolf by Chanticleer the Cock and Pinte the Hen. The wolf held up a spherical object, like an astrolabe, in which a spiral pattern seemed to circle endlessly. "If the past is a memory, it partakes of a dream. If it is a dream, then it is an illusion."

Sir Miles Vavasour left the abbey of Bermondsey soon after, turning his horse north-west towards London Bridge. He was jostled by crowds as he went across the bridge, and their smell seemed to linger above the river; his horse had difficulty in moving between the carts and wagons, but when it reached the road on the other side it broke free. Quite by instinct Vavasour galloped along the bank to Old Swan Stairs, and then continued northward up Old Swan Lane towards the church of St. Lawrence Pountney. He had barely recalled the legend of the doomed dancers; it was for him one of those dim far-off things which he associated with his childhood, like those stories which began "In old days there was a man . . ." He came out at the corner of Candlewick Street, which Jolland had described as part of the old churchyard. In its place now was a row of houses, a stable owned by a hackney-man, a saddler's shop, and a tavern called the Dog on the Trot. He could hear music in the air, and the sound of someone singing "This world is but a whirligig." The noises were coming from the tavern. Vavasour rode up and bent over his horse to look through a little mullioned window; he saw a circle of revellers, holding hands and dancing in a ring.

Chapter Twelve

The Manciple's Tale

"There shall be youth without any age. There shall be fairness without any spot of filth." It was Lammas Eve, the last day of July. "There shall be health without any sickness. There shall be rest without any weariness. There shall be fullness without any wanting. There shall be worship without any villainy." William Exmewe was addressing the predestined men, in the style which he had subtly fashioned for them.

He praised Garret Barton for his pinning of the Eighteen Conclusions on the *Si quis?* door; the killing of the scrivener was an unlooked for benefit, since the words would be easier read by the light of his death. "The floodgates are up," he told them, "and all goes forth. When the pattern of the five wounds is complete, then shall we see the day of challenge and of wretchedness, the day of darkness and of mist, the day of high cloud and whirlwind, the day of trumpets and noise. He shall come in majesty; that is in great brightness, full comfortable to His friends and His darlings. But where shall we fix our sight next? In St. Sepulchre the doom is to be delivered."

St. Sepulchre was the popular name of the Church of the Holy Sepulchre Without Newgate; it was the largest parish church in all London, even though it stood close to the prison of Newgate. Newgate was so noisome itself that, it was said, the rats ran from it; it had acquired a strange power over its neighbourhood, and its stench lingered in the alleys and doorways as a continual token of the gaol fever. It made the bones ache. The cries of the prisoners could sometimes be heard, and the whole area had become known as "the assize." It was no wonder that the church beside Newgate should bear the name of the sepulchre – but from this tomb no one could be resurrected.

"This is our text," Exmewe was saying, "all is well that ends well. The first two wounds have been opened with the help of Almighty God. Now, with the help of the same, go to the third. The oratory was wonderfully burned by hand; this one must be engined." He showed them a manuscript, entitled *The Book of Fire for Burning Enemies*, in which was explained the means of fashioning a *balle de fer* which would cause a great explosion. A hollow lead sphere was filled with gunpowder, and then wrapped around with leather; this ball was then placed in a box or chamber which contained the charge and was kept in place by a wedge. It were necessary only to remove the wedge and, lo, Greek fire would spread within the church. There was little danger. "Yet you know," Exmewe continued, "that we are eternal in the knowledge of God. We are *materia prima* created in the beginning of the world. We are freed from all harm. Robert Rafu, God is here! His will is that you have the chief governance of this matter."

The manciple sighed, and looked at the others as if for mercy. "This comes sooner than I looked for."

William Exmewe saw the fear on Robert Rafu's face, and exulted. He had chosen well.

After the predestined men had departed, he walked back with Rafu to the common stable where their horses were tied and watched. "Be comfortable, Robert. God will be with you." He observed the manciple carefully. "Are you comfortable?"

"Is the moon made of calves' skin?"

"This is a hard matter."

"As hard as adamant."

"But it can be softened somewhat."

"Signifying?"

"What is done can be undone. If the shoe does not fit, it can be slipped off." Exmewe had baited the trap, and now stepped back.

"Whoever can relieve me of this burden is my good friend." Rafu stopped in the street. "If my fate is ordained then I will suffer it, but I can serve the faith in many other ways." He spoke more eagerly now. He was wearing the hood of his habit over his head, but now he shook it off. "If I were to be destroyed in this matter, there would be a huge din and much searching after causes. The manciple of Paul's is a high office —"

"I know it."

"Any moot or inquest would be a long one." He stepped aside as two men crossed between them with a ladder. "Will you show me your will in this matter?"

"There is a boy of mine. One Hamo. One of God's simple creatures, without thought. He may be persuaded to carry the mechanism to St. Sepulchre and to unlock the fire. Would your mind be easier then?"

"Oh yes."

"Then you must speak with him. We will meet this evening, before the sun declines."

Exmewe had known that the manciple would wish to avoid the task that he had set him. Despite his brave faith as a predestined man, Robert Rafu was of a fearful disposition and easily discouraged. He was a heretic, but no martyr. Exmewe had already decided that Hamo must be sacrificed. The boy knew too much. Exmewe's fears had in recent days been mightily increased, ever since he had learned that Hamo had visited the nun of Clerkenwell. Exmewe knew this because he had been informed by the bailiff of the House of Mary, an acquaintance who had been seasoned with gifts of cloth and pottery from the abbey's store. Exmewe did not know what had passed between boy and nun; but he suspected much. They were both children of darkness, born out of wedlock, and there was no doubt a bond of secret sympathy between them. If Hamo had mentioned the death of the tooth-drawer, would she have told him that the man still lived? Or had Hamo sought for simple absolution? Had he betrayed the predestined men? Had he overheard secret matters concerning Dominus? The sweat came out of Exmewe's body, hot and pungent before turning cold; it poured from him, as if he wished to be dissolved.

In fact the boy and the nun had said little to one another. The mystery of their lives was too great for many words between them. The nun knew of Hamo's origins, and had asked for his blessing. This had astounded him but, before he could stammer out a reply, she put her finger to his lips. "Not from your mouth," she had said. "From your loneliness."

"How do you know of me?" he asked at last.

"Your sorrow is the angel that I see. You do not know why you came into the world."

"And do you?"

"I was summoned, Hamo Fulberd."

They had sat in silence for a while. "There is a place called Haukyn's Field," he said. "A great bare field only –"

"Where you walk the ground and weep? It is the place of your conception." She bent over and touched his knee. "It is said by some, Hamo, that God has given life out of forgetting or neglectfulness. That He is bored by his Creation. Others say that He multiplied humankind so that He might outwit the demon, like a gamester who piles up lead tokens in a game of hazard. The more souls, the harder the labour to ensnare them."

"I am like to be ensnared. There is one called William Exmewe –"

"Hush. I know of him." Once more there was silence between

them. "We say in English, Hamo, that we feel a man's mind when we understand his intent or meaning. When the same is very dark and hard to be perceived, we do commonly say 'I cannot feel his mind.' That is not my case. I can feel your mind."

"How do you, when I cannot find my own mind?"

"Feel."

"When I cannot feel my own mind? All is in darkness." And, with these words, he left her.

Now Exmewe was planning his fate. If Hamo were successful in the firing of St. Sepulchre he would be a wanted felon; if he were taken in the attempt, Exmewe would cast blame upon the nun. If Hamo were to die, well, what cannot be mended must be ended. Need knows no law. And so he invited the manciple to have conference with Hamo that evening, at dusk, by the bank of the Fleet.

Robert Rafu rode along the Thames to the meeting place. The wives of the citizens were fetching and taking up water, or washing their clothes, as they had done for time out of mind. Children stripped and plunged into the river, their harsh shrieks leaving Rafu uneasy. There were two or three groups of foreign merchants talking earnestly to one another. But Rafu did not need to approach them to understand their expressions and their gestures. In the last several days Henry Bolingbroke had ridden across the north and had acquired a great army; the keeper of England during Richard's absence in Ireland, York, had surrendered to him in the parish church of Berkeley. A week ago King Richard had finally landed in Wales, but his support was weak. Would battle now be joined? The merchants were concerned for their ships, already sailing towards the Port of London. One of them spat upon the ground, but it seemed to Rafu that the man was spitting at him. He hastened north towards Clerkenwell.

When he arrived by the saffron fields on the west bank of the Fleet, he saw William Exmewe holding the arm of a young man and remonstrating with him. Exmewe noticed Rafu and waved. The young man had his back turned and was staring down into the running water.

"Here is Rafu," Exmewe said. "One of the good men."

Rafu dismounted, and they started to talk intently.

Exmewe put his hand upon Hamo's neck. "I have told Robert Rafu that you are as fit for this purpose as any man I know. That is the truth, is it not?"

"William Exmewe tells me, Hamo, that you are a faithful man."

Hamo looked from one to the other, and said nothing.

Exmewe was angered by his silence. "What else is there for you upon this earth? You are already marked." The boy was silent. "The tooth-drawer rots in his grave. If I were to surrender you, your life would be forfeit."

Then Hamo smiled. It was a smile of recognition. Suddenly he saw the shape of his destiny. He saw the whole web of his fate shimmering before him. What had seemed hard now became simple; what had been confused was clear. The nun had told him that she had been summoned. And this, too, was his purpose. He must accept his hard fortune: that was all. He had been born for trouble in this world, and must embrace it. There was no more to say.

"See," the maniciple said. "You are already of good cheer. God give you grace, and all will be well."

"This boy is as still as a lamb which recognises its master," Exmewe said. "It is time, and more than time, to requite me for all my past kindness to you. I pray God, Hamo, that you bring this matter to a good end."

Hamo walked away from them and once more looked at the course of the Fleet, as it flowed down to the Thames before it reached the open sea. "Well," he said. "He must needs swim that is borne up to the chin."

The maniciple rode back to St. Paul's in high spirits. He had been relieved of a difficult and dangerous task. There had been the prospect of death or maiming. If he had been taken up, there would have been the certainty of Murus, the wall or perpetual imprisonment. As a predestined one he knew that he was part of God's breath and being, but this knowledge was tempered by the painful experience of the flesh in which he presently served. Robert Rafu was a practical man, or a "useful man" as he was called by the canons, but his successful conduct of the cathedral's affairs was based upon indifference and dislike. He despised the beliefs of the Church. He knew that its pardons, and other of its trumperies, could be bought and sold in Lombard Street as you would buy and sell a cow at Smithfield. You could pay for time in purgatory as men bought twopenny pies in Soper Lane. As for the sacrament of the Mass, well, the little mouse will eat the wafer and profit nothing from it. The so-called sacred wine waxed sour and stank, just as the holy water which had lain too long in the font.

He had ridden close to the north gate of the cathedral, when he saw the glare of torches raised in the air; several clerks and canons had gathered in the churchyard, and were examining something lying upon the ground. Their voices were raised; whether in excitement, or fear, the manciple could not tell. He dismounted and walked over to them with his usual soft tread. A pit, or hollow, had opened in the ground a few yards from the north porch. The master of the novices came up to him and murmured, "A child fell. The earth suddenly gave way and behold —" Rafu stepped closer to the pit and could see the outlines of a shallow walled grave. Lodged within it was a coffin of ancient shape, some eight feet in length. The upper part had decayed, and a great skeleton could be seen. At first sight, it seemed to be the skeleton of a giant that roamed the earth before the Flood. Yet on its right side lay a small chalice, covered with a patten, and a piece of silk or linen wound around its stem. On its left side were the remains of what was clearly a bishop's crozier. But what giant bishop was this? Rafu peered into the dust around the thigh-bone of the body; there was a ring, glinting in the torchlight. He lay down upon the ground, and reached into the pit. When he had retrieved the ring, he saw at once that the emerald stone at its centre had been embellished with a curious device; it was that of five circles within a circle.

Chapter Thirteen

The Summoner's Tale

The physician, Thomas Gunter, observed the Mother of Christ presented pleasantly by the Kings of Cockaigne. A gallant young man, piping and singing, was standing on a cloud called Spring. A verse, painted in red letters upon a long strip of parchment, was hanging from this cloud:

> "With these figures showed in your presence
> By diverse likenesses you to do plesaunce."

On a gaudily painted stage, carried by six porters, were two citizens playing Providence and King Richard II; they were embracing and kissing as they processed down Cornhill. The stage was followed by a pageant wagon, drawn by two horses with gay gilt saddles and shining bridles. Gunter, his eyes alert and bright, saw everything clearly. The wagon contained a great coloured model of the cosmos, with naked boys positioned upon the glittering circle of each sphere. Close behind them was a young man riding upon a platform with his arms and legs tied; he was wearing a white leather costume, borrowed from Adam of the mysteries, upon which numbers had been painted. Beside him stood one dressed as an astrologer, in long furred cloak and hood, who sang out to the crowd, "What solemn subtlety is this? It is the subtlety of figures." Gunter could scarcely hear him, however, above the din of the minstrels who walked between the wagons and the stages with harps and fiddles, bagpipes and gitterns, strings and trumpets, bladders and tabors, hurdy-gurdies and pipes. It was the feast of the midsummer watch, on the Vigil of the Assumption, when the might and glory of the city were celebrated.

Gunter grimaced as the guns upon the walls and bulwarks were "shot for joy," in the phrase of the mayor, while the merchants of the several crafts walked in procession past the Great Cross of Cheapside. The men of the wards then progressed in their ancient array; the citizens of Bridge and Walbrook carried lances all red, for example, while those of Farringdon and Aldersgate had black lances powdered with white stars. There followed behind them a group of citizens riding in disguise, as if for a mummery. Some were dressed as knights, in coats and gowns of red, with visors upon their faces; one was arrayed as the emperor and after him, at some distance, came one like the Italian pope accompanied by twenty-four cardinals. In the rear were seven others masked with black visors, unamiable, as if they were in the service of some foreign prince; they were hissed by the crowd of spectators, who were eager to enter the spirit of the proceedings.

He walked over to the corner of Friday Street and Cheapside, where he could better see the traditional procession of the poor men, each one wearing a straw cap with a badge of lead pinned to it; they were assembled to personify the Book of the Midsummer Watch's claim of "None but rich men charged, and poor men helped." Gunter knew them well and knew, also, that they took their place in the vast hierarchy of need and service; they were not citizens free of the city, but they were not loiterers or lost men. Nor were they beggars known as "louse men," from the proverbial expression, "he is not worth a louse." These were in the third degree of want, and were known as "masterless men." They would change their employment according to the season – woodcutters in winter and shoemakers in the autumn – and whenever they had earned as much as they required they simply stopped working. It was their unwritten rule. Or, as Gunter used to say, it was the law of London. Their garments came at second hand, with faded colours and frayed hems. They were at the lowest level of the commonalty before the stage of abject need and misery, and they made up a considerable number of the city's population. That is why they were given their own procession.

As the physician watched them passing by, raucously singing a hymn to the Virgin, he felt for an instant that he was being watched. He turned instinctively, but all those clustered around him seemed intent upon the moving pageant. Two tall men were now walking past on stilts. They were impersonating the giants, Gog and Magog, who were the twin guardians of the city; they were masked as lions, and wore artificial wings. Thomas Gunter decided to walk down Friday Street, where each door was garlanded with green birch and long fennel, white lilies and orpin or "live-long," in honour both of London and of the Virgin. He still felt uneasy, as if someone else's natural humour were shadowing his own. He walked faster and looked back once or twice, as the sound of minstrelsy began to fade.

"For Christ's love!" Gunter was startled by this voice coming from nowhere. "For Christ's love give meat or money to a poor man!" A beggar, with bag and staff, had stepped from an alcove by the corner of Watling Street; it was a "passing point" known to the citizens as a "pissing point." "I am in heaviness, master. I have lost all that I had." The light of the sun surrounded him. Gunter observed the shape of his prominent nose and the breadth of his wide forehead. He might have been a great scholar, but by chance or destiny he had become one who sits in the dust and stares at the world.

The physician took out a penny. "God comfort you," was all he said.

"Sir, I thank you of your goodness towards me." It was clearly a ritual acknowledgement, long practised. "I pray God I may one day make you amends."

Gunter was used to all the odours of the human body, and he was not offended by the smell of this man which suggested night things. He seemed in good health except for curious ring-like markings upon his forehead. "Do you have the scabbado beneath your hair?" The beggar nodded. "When you go into the fields, gather the weed commonly known as liverwort. It grows in wet places. Make a paste of it with your own spittle, and then press it down upon your head."

The beggar laughed at this. "It is a hard world, my master, when a man must grow grass instead of hair."

"Not so hard that it may not help you. God keep you." The beggar's laughter had recalled to his mind the song he had learned as a child. He repeated it under his breath as he turned the corner.

> "Nos vagabunduli
> Laeti, jucunduli,
> Tara, tarantare, teino."

There was also a saying, beggars are God's minstrels. The song was still in his head as he walked along Watling Street, but once more he was filled with fear of being followed. Quickly he turned down Lamb Alley and into Sink Court; he heard footsteps behind him, and he waited impatiently for the one whom he feared. There came out a man in middle life, wearing an old-fashioned surcoat of leather and a leather cap. It was Bogo the summoner, whom he had lately treated for an inflammation of the thigh. In his sudden relief Gunter called out to him. "How is this, Bogo? You know my door. Why haunt me in the street?"

"I saw you standing in the way of the pageant, Master Gunter, and I could not refrain from breaking my mind to you as soon as may be. These days be evil, as St. Paul says." Bogo was not well liked. He was the summoner of the newly made ward of Farringdon Without, which included Smithfield and that part of Clerkenwell encompassing Turnmill Brook and Common Lane, but his reputation was more generally known. He was employed to call citizens to the church courts and to the local assize, although it was suggested that warrants might be destroyed upon the payment of a certain sum. He was known as "the devil's rattle-bag," and was shunned. Bogo came so close to the physician now that Gunter could smell his breath; it had the savour of some interior sickness, some cancer. "You have heard that the king fled Carmarthen in the guise of a monk?"

"That is old news, Bogo."

"A few nobles are with him. I am told it was a piteous sight."

"Now Richard and Henry parley. We must await the time. But why disturb me with this now, Bogo?"

"It is joined with another matter." He looked into the physician's face. "Somebody, Master Gunter, has darked the city."

"You talk too mistily."

"Did you know of the giant bishop found at Paul's two weeks past?"

"Of course."

"There was a ring found with him, a ring of emerald." Gunter said nothing. "Upon that ring was the curious device of circles."

"It is an ancient sign of sacredness. What of it?"

"It is a good sign but it is now in the service of an evil cause. It has been turned to great harm in recent days."

"How so, master summoner?"

"By the oratory fired in St. John's Street, a circle was found painted upon the wall. I know it. I have seen it. Where the scrivener lay dead, by the *Si quis?* door, another circle was to be found. I tell you, Master Gunter, it is a pumice stone to smooth London."

"Bogo, you are a child. You can imagine the thing that was never thought nor wrought."

"When I took up one Frowike, on the charge of heresy, I saw in his chamber the book that did prognosticate all this. There are five in one and one in five. The wounds of our Blessed Saviour numbered five, as did the strings upon David's harp which make up the music of the spheres."

"This is strange speech, Bogo."

"I know strange things."

The physician believed the summoner to be a crafty and subtle man, but not a creature of vain fantasies or imaginings. He suspected, too, that Bogo trod various secret paths and byways to keep pace with news of the city; he knew night walkers and strangers. "Have you seen these circles in other places, Bogo?"

"I have seen the signs everywhere. They are about our death. They chant placebo and dirige."

"So who are these who are writing down their purpose upon the walls? Heretics such as Frowike?"

"There are bands and affinities in this city who stay concealed, Master Gunter, and who in the broad day pass among us as honest citizens. They use quaint craft. The world is brittle."

"Not so brittle, I am sure, that you cannot see through it."

"Then remember, for the passion of God, what I have said. Are you still acquainted with Miles Vavasour?" The physician had cured the sergeant-at-law of a fistula, three years before, and they ate supper with each other on the anniversary of the operation at the sergeant's lodgings in Scropes Inn. "Make all this known to him. He is a worthy man who will know what to ask and what to tell. Look. Do you see the torches?" There were footsteps coming down the alley. "The pageant is ending. God be with you."

The summoner slipped away. Instinctively he avoided crowds and torchlight; he might be buffeted or threatened. In fact one of those now entering Sink Court among the group of revellers was a known deceiver and beguiler of the people, John Daw, who had been arrested by Bogo only a few months before. Daw's offence was to pretend to be mute and deprived of his tongue in order to beg for alms. He used to carry in his hands an iron hook and pincer together with a piece of leather which looked, in shape, like a little part of the tongue; it was edged in silver and had writing around it which spelled out, "This is the tongue of John Daw." He had made a noise like that of roaring, continually opening and closing his mouth in a manner which cunningly concealed his tongue. The summoner, suspecting him, had followed him to a tenement in Billiter Lane where the same Daw was seen by him to talk easily and fluently to a woman of the house. He appealed him to the beadle, and Daw was taken up; he was sentenced to the pillory, but after this ordeal he had elected to remain in the city. No one knew how he earned the money he possessed, but he always drank in the same low tavern. The summoner had seen him in the light of one of the torches, but had walked quickly away.

Bogo now came out into Old Change, where several bonfires had been lit. They were known as the fires of amity, a custom of Midsummer's Eve, but they were also designed to purge the infections of the air during the long days of summer. Cresset lamps were placed before each door, lending a strange brilliance to the clustering flowers and branches around the threshold. Tables, with meat and drink, had been set up in the street; already one of them had been knocked over by a party of drunken dancers. That is why Bogo disliked the festival of Midsummer's Eve; the general spirit of licence threatened his safety.[15] A group of women was dancing around one of the fires, singing the song of the prancing pony; some were wearing masks as a token of their liberty, while others wore false beards fashioned out of dyed wool.

And then he was noticed. One of the women screamed out, "There goes Bogo the summoner!" He was not in his own parish, but he was known by sight to many Londoners. "There's Bogo!" He was grabbed by both hands and dragged into the dance; he was held tightly underneath each arm, and found himself being whirled around the fire at what seemed to him to be an ever increasing speed. And then the women came closer to the flames; they swayed by the edge of the fire and Bogo was aware that the leather of his shoes, and the cloth of his hose, were being singed. He cried out in alarm and the women fell back, laughing, as he scrambled to his feet. Two of them pursued him, kicked him to the ground, and beat him with their fists. Then one of them, instinctively imitating the common practice of street fights, bit off the lobe of his ear. He howled and the women, sensing his pain, yelled in triumph. It was the savage yell, hard, prolonged, exultant, which often sounded through London. It was the cry of the city itself. They left him lying in Old Change, the blood running from his wound into the earth and stone.

Chapter Fourteen

The Miller's Tale

Coke Bateman, the miller for the convent of Clerkenwell, was kneeling in the north transept of St. Sepulchre. He had just delivered twelve sacks of flour to the parish priest of that church; the priest had agreed to act as arbiter in the miller's dispute with the bailiff over that stretch of the Fleet that ran between them. The bailiff had in turn presented him with a mastiff, since the priest had complained of roarers and masked men who seemed strangely drawn to the Newgate prison.

The mill beside the Fleet was less than a mile beyond the city gates, and Coke Bateman often drove his cart within the walls. For him it was a city of springs and streams. He had grown so accustomed to the sound of water rushing beneath his mill that it seemed to him to be the sound of the world. He slept with the rush of waters, and awoke with their rhythms in his head. He knew the harsh and hasty sound of the Fleet, therefore, and compared it carefully and deliberately with the other rivers within the city. He recognised the soft sound of the Falcon soughing through reeds, the disturbed and excitable Westbourne with its hidden springs sending out competing currents, the slow and heavy Tyburn winding through marshes, the light Walbrook gliding over stones and pebbles, and the Fleet itself with its strong and sweeping central current running like a sigh through the city. And then of course there was the Thames, majestic, many-voiced, at one moment a mass of dark turbulence and at the next a gleaming sheet of light.

Was that the river in this Jesse window above the north transept, stained in the colour of verdigris, upon whose bank St. Erconwald was standing with arms uplifted? The priest had urged Coke Bateman to see this newly installed treasure, the work of Janquin Glazier who lived in Cripplegate. "Do you recall," he had asked the miller, "the blazing star of three years ago which kept its course rising west in the north?"

"A great glowing thing. Yes. I recall it very well. It appeared less and less until it was as little as a hazel stick."

"That star is in the window!"

There it was, glowing in the glass where Richard II knelt before the figure of John the Baptist. Among them curled the branches of the Jesse tree itself; in the central stem, issuing from the body of the sleeping Jesse, were placed in ascending order David and Solomon, the Virgin and the crucified Christ, with Christ in glory above them. At the Mass for the window's consecration two young brothers, joined by the hip-bone, sang "Mater salutaris" very sweetly.

Coke Bateman was particularly interested in the figure of the king; he was draped in a robe of red and white, with a large golden crown upon his head. The miller had seen the king once at close hand, when Richard had dined at Clerkenwell with the abbot of the Monks Hospitallers at St. John's. The king had ridden there beneath a great canopy of gold in order to celebrate the rebuilding of the great hall of the priory, after it had been fired by Wat Tyler and his ragged army. The miller had noticed then how the king had behaved as if he were in the pages of a psalter. He had been wearing the gown known as the houpelande which went down to the knee; it was of scarlet and was studded with fleurs-de-lis in pearls. The king's ermine cap was embroidered with golden letters, and he wore pointed shoes of white leather tied to silk knee-stockings with chains of silver. Even when he was greeted, and given the kiss of fellowship, he remained impassive. His own silence seemed to enjoin silence upon others, so that the proceedings continued within an expectant hush. It was as if time itself had been suspended. To Coke Bateman, Richard seemed neither old nor young, but somehow the age of the world. In this stained window he seemed to be no different; in five hundred years, in a time beyond the imagining of any then in life, he would still be kneeling there in quietness and piety.

It was difficult for Coke Bateman to contemplate the king's present troubles. How could this image of sacred order be subject to distress and change? The miller, like everyone else, was acquainted with the news of Richard's plight. Only five days earlier Richard had surrendered himself into the custody of Henry Bolingbroke. Henry's words to him had already been repeated in the streets and taverns of the city. "My lord, I have come sooner than you expected, and I shall tell you why. It is said that you have governed your people too harshly, and that they are discontented. If it is pleasing to the Lord, I shall help you to govern them better." The king's reply was also well known. "If it pleases you, fair cousin, then it pleases us well." Certain reports added another detail. Richard had turned to the earl of Gloucester and had said, "Now I can see the end of my days coming."

The king was not altogether popular in London. The stage on which his effigy had been paraded during the pageant of Midsummer Eve, for example, had been hooted at. Two years earlier he had demanded the wool and leather duties for life, and in recent months had imprisoned a sheriff for failures in his office. It was rumoured, too, that he intended to impose new taxes on the merchants in order to finance campaigns in Ireland and in Scotland. He was in Ireland when the present rebellion of Henry took shape in the north of England. The king had also become increasingly autocratic. A rumour spread among the citizens that he had erected a throne in Westminster Hall "where he sat from after meat to evensong speaking to no man but overlooking all men, and if he looked at any man, what estate or degree that ever he were of, he must kneel."

Yet Coke Bateman had defended the king on many occasions. His nature was prone to awe and wonder in the contemplation of majesty. It was the same awe which filled him when he looked into the night sky and its revolving spheres. He knelt down in front of the Jesse window, and began to pray. "Beata viscera Mariae Virginis." Blessed is the womb of the Virgin Mary. "Quae portaverunt aeterni Patris Filium." But he was disturbed by errant thoughts. "Which bore the Son of the Eternal Father." How could the Virgin's womb have carried God Himself? How could divinity be contained? How could it hide in human flesh?

The miller's daughter, Joan, had recently produced a child out of wedlock and he had asked Sister Clarice to advise Joan upon her course. The young nun had now become the most important source of authority within the convent, much to the dismay of Dame Agnes de Mordaunt, and Clarice was even visited by deputations of citizens asking for her counsel on civic matters. The prioress had sent a petition to the Bishop of London, Robert Braybroke, begging – or, rather, demanding – that Sister Clarice be sent to another religious house where there might be "plus petits dissensions"; but he was still considering the matter. He seemed strongly inclined towards the nun. In order to teach her humility, however, Dame Agnes had insisted that Clarice continue certain menial household tasks. She washed the floors of the frater and the dorter with a mop and wooden bucket; she scrubbed the bowls and ladles after meals, letting them dry in the sun. The miller had found her shelling peas at a trestle table in the kitchen of the convent; she was wearing a white woollen gown, thick and soft, with a white linen coif and veil. "God send you," he said.

"Is that not how we address beggars, Coke Bateman, when we are not minded to give them alms?"

"Very well, Sister Clarice. I wish you great abundance of ghostly comfort and joy in God. Does that please you more?"

"It is sufficient. Sit down beside me and talk. I have not seen you in a long time."

So for a while they conversed upon the little affairs of the mill and the convent. Then Clarice tapped his hand with the shell of a pea. "You have come to confer with me concerning your daughter's case. Is that not so?" The miller was not surprised by her remark, since he suspected that the nuns had been discussing his daughter's obvious condition.

"I have been considering upon it," Clarice said without waiting for his answer, "and I have been thinking of this. When the Virgin was swollen with child, did anyone know or guess its father?"

"It must have been commonly known to be Joseph, sister."

"Yet in the Clerkenwell play Joseph denies any such matter." The miller was not clear what Clarice was supposing. "If Mary claimed that God had entered her, who would have believed her? So she was mocked. God loves abasement, you see. And we poor women are frail of kind."

"What are you telling me?"

"Sit closer, and I shall whisper. I have seen the Questions of Mary. The Genna Marias has been revealed to me in golden letters as I slept. She was taken to the temple as a sacred priestess, a maryam, and there she did copulate with the high priest Abiathar. Do you know the Latin *meretrix*?" It was, as the miller discovered later, the term for a harlot or courtesan. But he had already heard and understood enough to be profoundly shaken by Sister Clarice's words; to him it seemed to be a great storm of uncleanness.

"Bring Joan to me," she said. "She will become my loved sister in Christ. I will drop sweetness in her soul."

He muttered something about his daughter's coming confinement, and then left the nun still shelling peas in the kitchen. He guessed that she had spoken plain heresy, but he decided to say nothing. The nun was travelling down strange paths and, from that time forward, he vowed to avoid her company. He did not wish to be in any way tainted by her blasphemies.

As he knelt before the Jesse window in St. Sepulchre, he heard a movement in an aisle behind him. A young man was crouched in front of a side altar dedicated to the saints Cosmos and Damian, and seemed slowly to be moving towards it; he was holding something beneath his cloak. Coke Bateman thought that he was creeping to the cross but then, suddenly, the young man rose to his feet and walked quickly towards the west door. There was a sudden loud explosion; the banners and cloths about the side altar began to burn, and a fierce blaze started in front of the tabernacle. A wax image of the Lamb of God had melted in an instant.

Two days earlier William Exmewe had brought Hamo Fulberd to this church. St. Sepulchre was only a short walk from the priory of St. Bartholomew the Great in Smithfield, and they had crossed the market without talking. The noise of the animals filled Hamo with alarm, however, and he put his hands to his ears. When they came up to the steps of St. Sepulchre, Exmewe whispered to him, "I will show you the stage of your action. Come withinside." Hamo climbed the steps slowly, looking down at the worn stone.

They entered by the west door and Exmewe led him towards the altar of Cosmos and Damian. "This is where you set the fire," he said. "I will draw your mark for you. Here."

There were polished floor tiles surrounding the altar, and Exmewe took out a sharp knife used for cutting the lead badges purchased by the pilgrims to St. Bartholomew; he knelt down and neatly cut the shape of a circle into one of the tiles, so subtly that it might have matched its pattern of diamonds and lozenges. "Are you watching this, Hamo? We are not playing blind man's touch."

Hamo was looking apprehensively at the Lamb of God upon the altar.

"The wedge goes here." Exmewe cut another circle. "A small spark can kindle a great fire."

After the explosion two or three people ran into the church, shouting and calling out for help. One woman cried, "Havoc! Havoc!" Hamo Fulberd was already making his way down the steps and yelling, "Alarm! Alarm! Each man preserve his own life!" It was the ritual shout of danger, uttered by him as if he were an innocent witness of the event.

The miller had been too surprised by the explosion to say or do anything; instinctively he looked up at the Jesse window and, to his relief, it was intact. As soon as he saw Hamo rushing out of the church, however, he rose from his knees and screamed, "Him! Him! It is him!" He was the first finder, after all, and it was his obligation to raise the hue and cry.

He ran out in pursuit, and saw Hamo turning the corner of Sepulchre Alley; he called out "Smite fast!" as a signal to anyone close by, and then ran after Hamo as he passed Pie Corner into the open ground of Smithfield. Two citizens joined him in pursuit and in their sudden excitement were calling out "Slay! Slay!" and "Give good knocks!" Hamo had reached the stalls where the swine were shown for sale, and turned round for an instant; Coke could not see the expression upon his face. Hamo then swerved to avoid a cart and knocked over a wafer-seller; he hesitated, but then ran even more quickly past the bulls and the oxen towards the gate of St. Bartholomew. Coke Bateman now knew his course: he was about to enter the church and there claim sanctuary. The wafer-seller and a farrier now joined them in this fierce chase; the farrier took off his leather apron and whirled it above his head. Their cries mingled with the noise of the sheep and cattle, so that it seemed as if the whole market were in violent uproar.

Hamo could hear them as he passed through the gate, ran down the cobbled path and pushed open the great door of the church itself; he raced down the aisle and then, fighting for breath, slumped against the high altar. He put his head against the cold stone, and wept. He could smell the stone around him; it smelled of forgotten things, primeval stone quarried from the bedrock of ancient seas. The world was of stone.

The constable and beadle of Farringdon Without had been summoned, and informed of the great and cruel offence against the peace in the church of St. Sepulchre. They in turn had called upon the alderman, Christian Garkeek, who was at the time busily engaged in the Custom House where he was controller of the wool custom. They told him that the malefactor was now claiming sanctuary. They also informed him that the prior of St. Bartholomew knew the accused man: he was one Hamo Fulberd, an illuminator in the service of the priory.

"Is he a clerk?" Garkeek had asked them.

"By no means. He is half-witted."

"Then he can be hanged." Garkeek looked out at the dock, where several ships were now being unloaded. "Yet my lord bishop may prefer a burning."

There were now many citizens watching the church; they were ready to take Hamo if he should come out, or to seize him if he should try secretly to escape. The rules of sanctuary were known to them all. While he remained in the church, no man might hinder anyone bringing food or drink to him. He could remain within the safety of the church for forty days, after which he could formally be expelled by the archdeacon. If Hamo wished, however, he could choose to abjure the realm within this period.

As soon as Hamo had claimed sanctuary the prior summoned William Exmewe and the oldest monk to the chapter-house.

"There is a storm of trouble come upon us," Exmewe said to the prior even as he entered the chamber. "How did the boy fall among abominable heretics?"

"He must needs walk in the wood that may not walk in town."

"Meaning, father?"

"There was a wildness in him. He was born for grief."

"Now," the elderly monk murmured, as if he were in danger of being overheard, "he has become a wolf's head that everyone may cut down."

"Do you know what he said when he claimed sanctuary from me?" The prior bit the inside of his mouth.

"What?" Exmewe was quick to ask the question. He could feel the sweat gathering within him.

" 'God has ordained that I should suffer. So this is my house.' " The prior crossed himself. "Poor boy. Listen. Can you hear them?" He opened a small door at the back of the chapter-house; outside, in the churchyard, there was a tumult of singing and shouting. "Some wicked aspect of Saturn has given us this." The prior believed in the efficacy of the stars and planets. "I have dark imaginings. Could there be others in the abbey who are casting some plot?"

"Oh no." Exmewe was again quick to speak. "I can smell a Lollard in the wind. There are no others here. Hamo was alone in this."

"Then how did he contrive the Greek fire?"

"He is skilled in all workmanship, father. I have seen him build quaint devices."

"Is it so? Well, he has created infinite harms. Why have I lived so long to see the abbey desecrated? My grass time is done. My white top writes my old years." The prior sighed and walked about the room. "We will shrive him and then urge him to leave of his free will."

"If he leaves here," the old monk said, "he will be engined and pained. Perhaps he will die in the pain."

Exmewe smiled, and then wiped his mouth with his hand. "Certainly he will be in woe and not in bliss."

The prior was growing impatient. "If he has committed sacrilege then he has no place here."

"He may cry innocence, father."

"He must go. Otherwise our souls are in jeopardy. How can we harbour a burner of churches? It is a thing impossible."

"Leave him a little," Exmewe urged. "Let him sleep upon the altar tonight. The sun may bring back his wits."

"I doubt that. But give him barley-bread and water from the brook. Let him drink with the ducks. We will challenge him at daybreak."

William Exmewe was perturbed and angry. He had never expected Hamo to flee for sanctuary and return to St. Bartholomew in so open a fashion; the boy was like a mad dog running to his kennel. If the prior heard his confession, he might tell all.

So, later that night, in the silent time between vespers and compline, Exmewe walked quietly down the stone stairway which connected the dorter to the church; there could in any case be no devotions while Hamo remained beside the altar. He went up to the boy, who was already watching him with wide eyes.

"How now, Hamo. How have you fared?"

"Badly. I am spilled." He seemed to be fighting for breath still, as if he had just escaped pursuit.

"Checkmate?"

"So it seems."

"Have patience, Hamo. The sorrows of this world are short. They pass like shadows on the wall."

"It is easy to say. Hard to endure."

"Go on. Make your moan. But consider this. You have not served me well. Could you not accomplish your purpose without all this noise and clattering?" Hamo said nothing. "Have you filed your tongue? You are dumb as any stone." The boy began weeping silently. Exmewe wiped his eyes, as clear and as trusting as those of a child, with the sleeve of his gown. "You have caught a thorn, and I cannot prise it loose."

"You have taken away the key of my world," the boy whispered to him.

"Am I to blame? Did I mar all? I might as well hold April from rain as keep you steadfast. Your wit is overcome, Hamo. I give you up for now and evermore." The boy looked at him in shock. He had been Exmewe's shadow and had not expected this last dismissal. That was perhaps why he had fled to St. Bartholomew – to be protected by Exmewe. But now his protector had cast him out. "Fortune has thrown the dice for you, Hamo."

"Is fortune the cause, then?"

"The far cause is Almighty God, that is the cause of all things. But fortune is your foe." Exmewe smiled. "How do you like the foul prison of this life?"

"I would that I were out of this world."

"Then I may help you a little." Swiftly he took a long dagger out of his belt, and put it through Hamo Fulberd's heart. "Hoo," he whispered to the boy. "No more. It is done." He drew out the dagger and replaced it in his belt.

When he was sure that Hamo lay dead, Exmewe walked softly to the porch and unbarred the main door.[16] He opened it very slightly, so that those on watch outside would eventually notice the faintest glimmer of churchlight. Any one of them might have entered and murdered Hamo upon the altar.

Chapter Fifteen

The Wife of Bath's Tale

As soon as he learned about the explosion in St. Sepulchre, Thomas Gunter rode out to the church; he had been intrigued by the summoner's murmurings about the conspiracies of secret men, and wished to examine the remains of the latest fire. When he saw the tumult he dismounted, and gave his horse in keeping to a porter. A large crowd had gathered on the steps. According to custom, the body of Hamo Fulberd had been removed from sanctuary and returned to the place where he had committed sacrilege. Here he could be viewed as an object of God's vengeance. He had been stripped of his clothes, and various devils' heads and zodiacal signs had been daubed upon his naked corpse. He had been placed in the aisle, in a square cart made of wicker, with a cross placed upside down upon his chest. The coroner had already declared that Hamo Fulberd was lying dead, but no one had seen the wrathful agent of his killing; this was considered to be an image of divine justice, and the empanelled jury had decided that they did not wish to meddle further in the matter.

Thomas Gunter made his way through the press of people in order to view the body; and, when he examined the face for signs of injury, he experienced the faintest tremor of recollection. Where had he seen this poor boy? In what previous scene had he played a part? And then the physician noticed five small circles painted above his left breast. They had in fact been placed there by William Exmewe who, on the discovery of the body, had pretended to share in the feverish joy of the people; he had also feigned the same delight in daubing the corpse with the devil's emblems. Thomas Gunter drew back at the sight of the circles. He had not expected this sudden confirmation of Bogo's claims, and was shocked by it. There was some sorrowful mystery here. He had the ghostly impression of many human lives crowding around this corpse. Darkness was calling to darkness.

He walked towards the altar of saints Cosmos and Damian. It had been badly damaged by fire, and a small child carved out of lead was lying upon the blackened tiles. He knelt down to retrieve it, when he glimpsed a strange white marking standing out upon the floor; he brushed away ash and debris, and there in calcined form was the circle which Exmewe had carved with his knife.

"God be merciful." In his surprise the physician had spoken out loud. He picked up the lead image of the child, and placed it gently upon the altar. He had no doubt now about the summoner's suspicions; there was some deep plot concerning this device of the circles, but how could he proceed? In the mayor's court or the bishop's court he might be derided as a jangler; he might have carved the circle with his own hand. Yet Bogo himself had suggested one way through the maze. In five days' time Gunter would be eating supper with Miles Vavasour, on the anniversary of his *fistula in ano*, and he might break his mind to him on that occasion. Vavasour was of high degree and pleaded before the king's bench; he was familiar with the great ones of the city, and would know how to fare forward with this matter.

*

On the following morning the body of Hamo Fulberd was carried in triumph up Snow Hill and across Holborn Bridge. Having been judged corrupt and abominable to the human race, it was taken to the area beyond the walls known as "Nomanneslond" where it was buried in a pit of lime.

Five days later Thomas Gunter rode out towards Scropes Inn, where Miles Vavasour had his chambers.

"Welcome, master leech." Vavasour spoke as one who enjoyed speaking. "For three years now I have sat without flinching."

"I have brought you some fresh ointment, to curb any effusions of blood."

"No blood, God willing."

They were standing in a small parlour overlooking Trivet Lane, as one of the servants brought them Rhenish wine in cups.

"What is new?" Thomas Gunter asked the sergeant.

"You mean, what is new concerning the king? These are days of bale and bitterness, Master Gunter."

Henry Bolingbroke was moving from Chester, with King Richard in his keeping; Henry's forces had already made their way from Nantwich to Stafford, and were soon expected in Coventry. Henry had issued a summons, in the king's name, for a parliament at the end of September. Miles Vavasour was a burgess of London and would have to travel to Westminster Hall for that assembly. "I would rather be a world away from the parliament house," he confided to Gunter. "It is no easy thing to rid the realm of its lawful king. Yet I am Henry's servant. I have worked for him in the courts –" He broke off. "Well, I stand in doubt whether I may say yeah or nay." In this, of course, the sergeant spoke less than the truth; he had long been set against the king. "Can we wash away the name of Richard?"

"Surely it may not come to that?"

"It will come as certainly as tomorrow."

"But will Henry not maintain the king, and rule beneath the cloth?"

"One swan is enough to fill a charger. Only one man can govern."

"But the duke is a subtle man."

"Subtle, yes. Sub telaris. Under the heel. Henry will have Richard under his heel."

"And the nun has been ringing like a bell."

"Oh? How so?"

"She says that the crop dwells beneath the root. That the world is changed overall."

"That woman is a flyter," Vavasour said. "A baratour. She will provoke the people into madness. Set her on the ducking stool and plunge her."

"Oh no. Sister Clarice has become Christ's darling. The common people follow her with open mouths."

"The stink!" Suddenly the sergeant changed the subject; it was a habit he practised in the courtroom. "Now that I have you, leech, I find that I need you. I have the bone-shave."

"The sciatica?"

"It is the pain of lightning. It travels down my leg."

Gunter believed this condition to be the token of a melancholy or nervous complexion, to be cured by rest and easefulness rather than powders or mixtures; but he knew, also, that those in his charge required the consolation of herbs. "It is a full heavy and sharp pain, Sir Miles —"

"I know that well enough."

"In a first case I would give you the herb water-pepper or skin-smart."

"It is not the first. It is an old malady."

"Then a sovereign remedy may be the juice of the feverfew mingled with honey. I will send it by messenger. Are you wakeful by night?"

"Very wakeful."

"Great nightshade will make you sleep."

"You mean banewort?"

"It can be known as that."

"It is a plant full of malice to humankind, is it not?" One of the sergeant's techniques, when engaged in cross-examination, was to pretend to more knowledge than he actually possessed.

"Just a little. A very little. You will not be disparkled."

"So I need fear nothing from your hands, leech. Is that right?" He drank off the rest of the wine with a flourish. "Do you see this ring, Master Gunter?" He held out the fingers of his right hand.

"Indeed."

"Its jewel has been taken from the head of a toad."

"I know it well. It is known as the borax or chelonitis."

"It is a preservative against poison. Its power leaps to my heart from my ring finger."

At that moment the green jewel caught the light of a candle, and in that sudden flash Gunter glimpsed a great bonfire like that which gives the alarm. He blinked. It was gone. Yet he believed in the efficacy of dreams and visions. Some revelation concerning Miles Vavasour had been granted to him.

"Shall we go to eat?" The sergeant led his guest into the hall; on a dais, covered in a cloth of estate, was a large table with a chair at either end. Along one side of the hall was Vavasour's livery cupboard, with all his plate displayed in the torchlight and candlelight. There was a low oak chest on the opposite side of the hall, with papers lying upon it; above it was a tapestry portraying the history of the King of Love. On his summons a servant entered, did obeisance, and then proceeded to serve the meats. The meal was soon over and, after their toast to the fistula, Gunter observed in passing that he had seen the body of one Hamo Fulberd lying in St. Sepulchre. Vavasour replied that he had marvelled that one young man could nourish such hatred against God's church. The physician wondered out loud whether any more heretics would be found as a result of Hamo's death. They are as mad as wild bullocks, Vavasour replied, and God would send them such worship as they deserved. So there were more of them? Gunter noticed the slightest unease cross the sergeant's face as he claimed that he had not meddled in the matter.

"But some, Sir Miles, talk of a secret confederacy. A coivin of unknown men."

"I know a good name for its leader then." The sergeant's eyes widened slowly as he spoke. "It should be John Destroy All."

"I was hugely astonished to learn . . ." the physician continued, looking steadily at his host across the gleaming oak table, ". . . I was astonished that these troubles and commotions may be governed by the sign of five."

"Who told you this?" The question came rapidly and suspiciously.

"I see wonder on your countenance, sir."

"Wonder only at such horrible and abominable deeds. What is this about the five?"

"It was rumoured to me."

"In the old books it is a sign of the ancient church. But in these new times –"

"It does not signify?"

"Not at all."

The subject was then changed; the two men discussed the bad harvest and the price of bread, the new law restraining the length of shoes, the recent birth of a child with an eye in the middle of its forehead, until the conversation touched once more upon the miseries of the king.

Vavasour excused himself for a moment, to visit the latrine in his yard, and Gunter took that opportunity to walk over to the chest. There were two small parchments left there accidentally or hastily by the sergeant, and they concerned a court case at Westminster; Gunter could read the sentence, "In cuius rei testimonium presentibus sigillum meum apposui," but the rest was obscure. But then he noticed some words scrawled in ink on the back of one of the documents. They comprised a list, or table, one entry after the other:

Oratorium. St. J.

Powles.

St. Sep.

St. M Le Q.
Giles.

The oratory in St. John's Street had been fired. So had St. Sepulchre. There had been a killing in Paul's. Would St. Michael le Querne follow? And Giles. Could that be St. Giles in the Fields?

Thomas Gunter was already in his seat when the sergeant returned. They were served more wine but parted soon after, at the time of the curfew bell. The sergeant apologised for the fact that he still had urgent business to conduct.

As the physician left, he could hear Vavasour calling for his horse.

Gunter now knew that his host was better acquainted with recent events than he had been prepared to admit. His list was of the churches. The conclusion was clear. Vavasour had a counterfeit face. He was disguised in manners. And where was he riding after curfew? Thomas Gunter determined to follow him on horseback.

Under cover of night and darkness, ducking under the overhanging signs, keeping his horse to the straw and the mud, whispering gently in its ear to guide it, he kept Vavasour in sight. The sergeant was a great man, and would not be hindered or questioned by the watch; Gunter was a known apothecary, on his way to administer to someone's pain, and would pass unmolested. They were two figures enclosed by the darkness of the city. Vavasour rode south-eastward along Fetter Lane and Fleet Street, down Addle Hill with its deserted porters' stalls like great bulks in the shadows.

Gunter stopped at the corner of Addle Hill and Berkley's Inn, dismounted, and tethered his horse to a weather-beaten gate by the side of a tenter-yard; he had seen Vavasour ride up to the round tower north of Castle Baynard. Gunter concealed himself behind the ruin of an old postern gate, just as Vavasour knocked upon the door of the stone tower and was admitted.

A few moments later Gunter observed two cresset lights

approaching, attached to spear-headed poles; a hooded figure came up to the door and, by the light of the torches, Gunter could plainly see the visage of Sir Geoffrey de Calis. Then a chair, pulled by two horses, emerged from the darkness; Gunter recognised William Swinderby, the canon of Paul's, being helped from the vehicle. He was followed by an under-sheriff. Here was a wonder indeed, a wonder to pass all wonders. Why had the high men of the city come to this place by night? What had Bogo said of those who stayed in concealment and who walked in evil ways? "They use quaint craft," he had told Gunter. "The world is brittle."

Gunter found himself gazing at the round tower. He knew it to be of great antiquity; in the torchlight he could see the blocks of rough stone in the mortar at its base. If Brutus had founded London after the fall of Troy, as all the historians suggested, could this be an emblem of New Troy lingering into the present with its own baleful history? The physician was filled with sensations of power and of purpose as he looked upon it; it had already completed its destiny, and now persisted in time through its indomitable will. So it attracted secret men like Miles Vavasour and Geoffrey de Calis. A rotten nut is called a deaf nut. Barren corn is known as deaf corn. This was deaf stone. Whatever dark business was conducted within its walls, it would never be whispered abroad.

Gunter stayed by his hidden point of vantage, while an hour passed. The under-sheriff was the first to leave, entering his chair in the flare of many torches. Geoffrey de Calis followed, in the company of a man whom Gunter did not recognise. Behind them walked Miles Vavasour who turned and waited for his horse beside the great wooden door. He had about him an air of expectancy, and he mounted lightly. Gunter quietly untethered his horse and decided to go after him. Vavasour turned up Addle Hill, and Gunter realised that he was not riding home when he turned eastward into Carter Lane. The gates of the city were closed but he seemed to be making his way towards Aldersgate; the streets were very quiet, and Gunter made sure that he kept his distance. He had thought of tying rags to his horse's hooves, but he was content now to avoid cobbles and loose stones. He looked up at the universe of light which guided his way; he could see the stars in the highest celestial sphere, and was comforted by their brightness. There was one order which did not decay.

Vavasour had ridden down St. Martin's towards the gate; it was closed, of course, and barred with chains which were fixed across the road. So he turned east down St. Anne's Lane and then north into Noble Street at the corner of which, as Gunter could see, a section of the wall was being reconstructed. The workmen removed the ladders and scaffolding each night, for fear of thieves, so there was a narrow gap or rent in the structure. Vavasour had settled his horse for a moment, whispering in its ear, and then had leapt beyond the wall. Gunter murmured to himself the hunter's cry, "So! Ho!" and followed him. He rode over the wall just as the sergeant was making his way down Little Britain towards Smithfield.

There was a wide path there between the priory church and the hospital, where sand had been laid for the easy conveyance of wagons and carts; it glowed in the moonlight, with the turrets and eaves of the surrounding buildings casting strange shadows across it. The posts by each side of the road, where the horses were tethered in daylight, seemed like stakes for the condemned. The physician always associated Smithfield with death – the animals being led to slaughter, the guilty men riding to the rope, the sick approaching their end in the hospital itself. But he knew that each part of the city had its own trouble and its own tainted air.

Vavasour was riding across the open market towards Cow Lane and Clerkenwell and, by the time he had reached the Fleet, Gunter knew his destination. Turnmill Street was a notorious stew haunted by gestours and lechours, roarers and bawds. By the time Gunter rode down the narrow thoroughfare, Vavasour's horse was being kept by an old huckster who sold second-hand clothing by day.

Gunter dismounted and gave the man a groat. "Where has he gone?"

"To see the Wife of Bath."

Dame Alice, familiarly known as the Wife of Bath, was the most notorious procuratrix in the city. She ran a tavern in Turnmill Street called the Broken Fiddle; it was known by everyone as the Broken Filly, however, because of the nature of its trade. The physician had been visited by some of Alice's clients, who had contracted the pox known otherwise as the brand of Venus or the love-lick.

Dame Alice greeted Miles Vavasour in her usual fashion. "What! Are you here? Sir Robert Run-About?" She wore a kirtle of red velvet, with a girdle of gold-work around her waist; she had a caul over her hair embroidered with jewels, and a red hood behind her neck. "You have come for a sweet hole, have you, sir? Are you wanting a scabbard for your dagger?"

Dame Alice had pursued her trade for many years, despite manifold punishments and injuries. She had been placed in the compter; she had been exhibited in the stocks and on the stool; she had been paraded through the streets in a striped hood and beaver hat as tokens of her profession. In more recent times, however, she had been permitted to establish her tavern, or her "shop" as she called it, outside the walls; in any case she now had too many secrets to be prosecuted in open court. It was said that the monasteries and the nunneries would be emptied if she told all she knew.

"You old fetart, you lusk, what will it be with you tonight? What raging damsel will be your delight?"

Dame Alice had acquired a reputation for the contempt which she showed to her customers; they accepted it as part of their humiliation. She had many words for men like Miles Vavasour who came in search of young women – lorrel, loricart, lowt, slow-back, hedge-creeper, looby, lobcock, crafty Jack, long lubber, hopharlot – each with its own range of allusion and association.

"You are in high kick, I see, Miles Rakehell. You lift your leg like a dunghill dog. Well, I have a young fair one for you." Dame Alice knew his tastes very well. "Eleven summers. Rose. I call her Rose-a-ruby because she smells like camomile." She was standing on an old wooden staircase, much rubbed and discoloured with the tread of a thousand shoes, and she beckoned him upward. "She is still a maid."

"I am glad to hear it, ma dame."

She laughed, and a necklace suddenly appeared from beneath her chin. "I see your meat-wand is stirring in your hose, Sir Trindle-Tail."

"Love is in season, Alice."

"Love is hot in summer, then. Fall to work with a will."

"If you will show me the way."

Dame Alice never jangled about love, as she put it. Hers was a more practical humour. "I may not stop the evil that blows about the world," she had told one of the priests who frequented her tavern. "But I may help men to forget it."

"We are all frail," the priest had replied. "We come of sinful stock."

"By Christ's cross it is the truth."

She knew of what she spoke. Her mother had followed the same trade, from an undercroft in an alley off Turnmill Street. As a very young girl she had seen all the corners of lust. At the age of twelve she had conceived a child by Coke Bateman, the old miller's son, whose dwelling was a few hundred yards to the north, but her mother had persuaded her to drown the newborn baby in the Fleet. Many infants had already floated down that river into the Thames, where they were "taken up" by watermen as a danger to nets. She had met Coke Bateman in a pudding shop, the following week, but he had not spoken of his child; they had sat side by side, but they had said nothing to one another. And she had thought then – what is all this feigning of love? It is a mere mock of the mouth.

After her mother's death Alice had opened up a *balneolum* or small bath-house in St. John's Street; that is how she had acquired her name. When she had purchased the lease rent on a tenement in Turnmill Street, however, she was surprised to learn that her landlord was the convent of St. Mary. But then she began to profit from her fame. "The Wife of Bath" became synonymous with bawdiness. A sermon was preached against her by the priest of St.

Mary Abchurch, during which he had declared that "a fair woman that is foul of her body is like to a ring of gold in the snout of a sow." She had heard the phrase a few days later, and ever afterwards she called him "the priest of Apechurch." She compared him to the loathsome toad which cannot endure the sweet smell of the vine. He returned the insult, one evening in the pulpit, when he spoke against certain bawds or lenos who are like the painted beetle which, flying in the hot sun of May, has no liking for fair flowers but loves to alight on the filth of any beast wherein alone is its delight. It became known as "The Wife of Bath sermon," and her fame in London was assured.

Dame Alice took Miles Vavasour into a small room warmed by a brazier. "We have no crowders tonight, Sir Piss-Pot."

She had hired no musicians since, as she had said, lewdness needs no tunes. In truth the last night of music had ended in disorder, when one of the musicians had insulted an elderly courtier. The old man had put his hand in his hose in order to scratch himself, and the musician had noticed the movement. "They should have taught you at Westminster," he said to general laughter, "never to touch meat with your right hand." The courtier had drawn his baselard and a scuffle ensued which, as always in London, ended as suddenly and as abruptly as it had begun. Dame Alice had ordered the musicians to leave her tavern – or, as she put it, "hitch your stained buttocks!" – and swore never to hire them again. So there was no music on the night of Miles Vavasour's visit.

"She is a maid," she said again, "but I swear that she will jet up and down for you. You will sweat well tonight."

"Does she frisk about?"

"She is a giglet. A fisgig."

"Then I will have her."

"But you must pay. Empty fists retain no hawks." Miles Vavasour had a reputation for meanness. He was known as a scrapegood or, as Dame Alice said, "a dry fellow who will not lose the droppings of his nose."

"Well, ma dame, what is the reckoning?"

"Two shillings."

"What?"

"You look more sour than wormwood. I said two shillings."

"My doublet cost me the same!"

"It will not warm you so well, Sir Pox."

"I can have a roast pig for eightpence, dame."

"You may pay a penny a night for a bed with blankets and sheets, in any hostelry. Is that why you are here?"

"But two shillings!"

"If you do not like her, I have a remedy for lust. It can be put away by smelling the savour of your own shoes when they are taken off. Is that what you wish?"

The deal was done, and the child was brought into Miles's chamber; she was wearing a blue robe trimmed with fur, and nothing else. "Well, girl," he said, "it is not with your estate to wear such fine furs."

"Dame Alice has been good to me, sir."

The Wife of Bath had been listening at the door but now, with a candle in her hand, she made her way quietly down the staircase. Then she saw Thomas Gunter leaning against a small prie-dieu by the door; he was examining its wooden carvings of grotesques. She knew him very well. "Is it you, leech? We have no need of you tonight, you carcass bird."

"At least, ma dame, I am no screech owl." They both enjoyed the play of insults, in which neither ever triumphed.

"How do you, nurrit?" She had a wealth of words to express his littleness – knurl, nirb, murch, nurg – and never refrained from using them.

"Well, thank God." He lifted his eyes to the top of the staircase. "And how does Miles?"

"Hold your tongue and say the best." It was an ancient proverb. "And let your neighbour lie in rest."

"I am not a carry tale, Alice. I will not nick anyone's name. Sir Miles is under my charge, and I have a great care for him –"

"Is it so? Well, have no care at all. This smith is good. Can you hear him beating with his hammer?" She laughed. "He has a young tutty. A tuzziemuzzie."

"A maid girl, then?"

"Rose le Pilcherer. Of this parish."

"I warrant she is too young to be found in the catch-poll book."

"Not too young to be fisked and ramped. Eleven years. I found her in the clipping house. Sweeping hair."

"And you stalked her like a crane."

"I spoke with her, and she followed me. She wants coin."

"It is no wisdom to want a thing that is not honest."

"How! Trolli-lolli, Master Gunter. A fool will always be teaching and never be taught. There are girls who will go behind a hedge for twopence or a sheaf of wheat. Rose will have shillings in her purse. Am I to be blamed for doing good works? Truss up your gear, and ride away."

The Wife of Bath was as hard as London, some said, and as merry. You could no more rail against her than against the city itself. So Gunter bade farewell to her with the kiss of peace. It was not returned.

Chapter Sixteen

The Cook's Tale

The coquina on Nuncheon Street was the largest in London; its principal chamber could hold one hundred people, and there were several rooms or "messes" where a smaller number could eat together. It was familiarly known as "Roger's" after Roger of Ware, the cook who owned it and who still supervised the preparation of the food. He was a slim man with a small and neatly cut beard, who wore the white pie-shaped hat which was the symbol of his trade. "Everything must be scrubbed fair!" He was walking around the great kitchen beside the principal chamber. "Fair! Fair! Fair! Do you hear me, Walter?" He approached a young servant. "Let me see your hands. Have you been touching turds? Go wash! John, this skimmer needs rinsing. Do you see the scum upon it? It is not good. Not good!"

There were two fireplaces facing each other on opposite sides of the kitchen, a fish fire and a meat fire, and the combined heat of their flames was so intense that most of the workers had taken off their shirts and were working in their under-linen. So the smell of human sweat mixed with the other odours. Roger walked among them in a richly embroidered jacket, with his hose attached to it by latchets known as gadlings or harlots; he wore long and pointed shoes fashionably curved at the tip and known as cracows. His pie-shaped hat, however, turned him into what he called a "mixed medley."

"There is white grease in the base of this skillet! Do I need to scrub everything with my own hands?" He inspected the pots and flesh-hooks, the ladles and the pestles, the plates and pans, hanging against the plastered walls. "Simkin, have you sent to the spicer's shop?" He loved to shout over the general noise. "There is no more saffron here than in a nun's arse!" Simkin was one of the three cooks who tended to the meats, an ill-favoured man who was said by his colleagues to have a trick of curdling milk by belching into it. He was pounding larks and pigeons in a platter bowl and paid no attention to Roger. "God forbid, Simkin, that you should hear me." Roger wiped his fingers across the rim of a wooden bowl containing pig grease. "They say that evil manners follow the likeness of an ugly man. Is that so, Simkin?"

Simkin studied him for a moment. "I have too much business here, Master Roger, to run after saffron like some pannier woman."

"Oh, tra-la. She answers back." Roger was known privately by those who worked for him as Dame Durden or Old Mother Trot; he had the same sharpness of tongue, and the same ribald humour, as those old ladies from the interludes. With his pinched features and exaggeratedly mincing gait, he also resembled them.

On one long table were laid out pheasant, goose, wild fowl, brawn, pork, bacon and tripe; some meats were already turning on the spit, together with the head of a boar and a side of venison. A large cauldron stood over one part of the fire, its three legs planted firmly in the burning embers. An elderly man was drawing out pieces of meat with a flesh-hook, as he had done for thirty years; he had worked in this kitchen long before Roger had come here. There had been a cookshop on this site for more than a hundred years, testifying if nothing else to the fixed habits of the London population.

Thick waves of smell, meat upon meat, were mingled with the

sharper savours of pike and of tench; the musty odour of eel was mixed with the tang of pig's flesh, the quickness of herring with the slowness of oxen. It was point and counterpoint taken out of a songbook of smell. The kitchen was a little city of smells. There was not one person who passed the cookshop who did not perceive the differences between them, who did not distinguish between the savour of beam and of perch, of leeks and of beans, of green figs and of cabbage. The savour of cooked food, fish or flesh, permeated the stones of the neighbourhood; the area was haunted by dogs of every description, which were sometimes killed by the arrows or slingshots of the apprentices and flung into the ditch at the end of the street. The name of the street itself, "nuncheon," signified a meal or repast taken in the afternoon.

"This is the man who started to build and could not finish!" Roger was watching one of his cooks, who was trying unsuccessfully to blend chopped pigs' livers, milk, hard-boiled eggs and ginger. "God may send a man good meat, but the devil may send an evil cook to destroy it. Is that not so, Myttok?"

The young cook did not look up from his board, but he cut a little more deeply into the ginger. "These livers, Master Roger, are so hard that I might play ball with them. When did you go to market?"

"I see that it must be my own fault. Bless me, Mary, for I have sinned." The heat and the noise of the kitchen always infected their words; anyone coming upon them, from the street, would believe them to be engaged in continual ferocious argument.

"Well, master, fair words will only fatten your head."

"You should know, whoreson. Your arse is as big as two barrels."

Walter, the knave of the kitchen, ran through the passage and put his hand to his mouth in order to make the sound of a bugle. "They are come! They are come!" The first customers had arrived for their noon meat, and had pulled off their caps. Walter had already set the tables. The places had been prepared with trencher, napkin and wooden spoon; every man had his own loaf of bread and cup laid out before him, together with a bowl of salt for each pair. On each table was a small iron lantern with horn windows, to be lit on dark days, although the coquina itself was bright enough. Its walls had been plastered and decorated with scenes of hunting and hawking; there were words coming out of the mouths of the huntsmen, such as "sa cy avaunt!," "so ho!" and "ware! ware!" The red clay floor was strewn with fresh rushes.

As Roger walked into the chamber to welcome the first arrivals, he was surrounded by the familiar and friendly language of greeting. "What do you?" "How is it with you?" "How do you fare?" "God give you good day." These phrases were a form of perpetual renewal, so that each day was joined to others in the line of harmony. Roger took their cloaks and gowns from them, nodding to strangers and addressing familiar acquaintances as "sir gully-gut" or "sir lick-dish" or "sir glutton." As the bells of St. Denis rang twelve the room was filled with calls for boiled beef in cloves and fried almonds, mussels in pike broth, pigs' ears boiled in wine, partridges roasted with ginger, fried eels in sugar and mackerel in mint sauce. In the kitchen the cooks were making plates of fruit and vegetables, all boiled or stewed; it was considered unhealthy to eat anything which had not been cooked. The customers ate with their own knives off plates of pewter; they drank out of cups made of leather or wood or tin. There was also a voider on each table, for all the slops and crumbs which would be distributed by Roger to the beggars outside the door.

The conversation was loud and coarse and animated. Who had heard news of the king? There were many rumours and false reports exchanged between the tables, as well as laments about the condition of the time. It was known for certain only that Henry Bolingbroke, with Richard II as his prisoner, had recently arrived in Dunstable. He had proclaimed to the crowd from the clock tower there that he would arrive in London on the first day of the new month. The first of September was the Feast of the Twelve Martyrs, and the customers in Roger's coquina spoke of a thirteenth. Henry had a violent ambition for the throne. "The change of season may make us all sad and sick," Hanekyn Fytheler said to Hugyn Richokson.

"I pray God send us a merry world," Hugyn replied.

"I do not say to the contrary. How does your sister do?"

"Well. Never better."

At the next table Roger of Ware himself was examining a jewelled box handed to him by Henry Huttescrane. "What is it worth?"

"You shall have it cheap, Roger."

"I smell a beard."

"No, I swear not. It is out of Afric."

The physician, Thomas Gunter, was eating with Emnot Hallyng, the clerk; they were both members of the Ancient Order of Men Who Like to Stroke Cats. The title may have had some literal connotation but "to stroke a cat" meant also to approach a problem or conundrum in a quiet and amicable spirit. The question they had been discussing the previous evening had been, "If Adam had never known Eve, would all humankind be male?" During the course of these proceedings Gunter had asked Hallyng to eat with him on the following day. He did not know that the clerk was one of the predestined men, but he enjoyed both his company and his conversation on abstruse matters. In fact he had been telling Gunter about his cousin's encounter with certain supposed spirits in Camomile Street; to which the physician had replied, it were possible that shapes, whether corporeal or incorporeal, might be conjured forth from powers which were neither earth nor water, fire nor air, nor any creature made from them. He recalled the words of the monk, Gervase of Winchester, before his sudden death, which were, "Who is there knocking?" There were many deep in mawmettrie who cast plots and said the night-spells. "Well enough, master clerk. There are so many subtle passings and dissimulations that I say no more. How is your cheese?"

"Too dry," Emnot replied. "I like Essex cheese, not this Sussex cheese."

"Have no more then. Dry cheese stops the liver and engenders the stone. If it lies long enough it makes a stinking breath and a scurvy skin."

"But I am hungry."

"Take some butter instead. You know the sentence. Butter is gold in the morning, silver at noon and lead at night. Try some silver."

"You never leave off your trade, Thomas Gunter. You are bound to the stake."

"It is for your good. Butter is best for children while they are growing and old men when they are declining. You are in the middle way. Eat butter first and eat it last, and live till a hundred years be past. Have you heard that verse?"

"I have heard that a good cook is half a physician. That seems to be your theme."

"And a good physician is half a cook. I cook essences and qualities over the fire. As no one will eat night-old vegetables, so no one will trust a cure that has not lately been mixed. Why, the other day –"

"Stint your clap, leech." Emnot said this in good humour; it was the licence of the coquina. "My ears ache with your drasty speech."

"For the earache I have a very good ointment."

"No more."

"Better unfed than untaught, master clerk."

"I said, no more. Do you have any news that does not come by rote?"

The physician leaned forward. "Only that the nun is about to be challenged."

"For what?"

"For prophesying against the king."

"Everyone now prophesies against him, Thomas. She will not be so wrong if she fears his ending."

"The city will take her, be sure of it. They wish to keep her silent until they know what will befall. They are for Henry, if Henry wishes to be king. They will roll their dice with the winner. But you know, Emnot, I have more news than that." The physician sat closer, and savoured the odour of the clerk's breath. "May I speak in secrecy?"

"You may."

"You know of the five wounds?"

"Of our Saviour?"

"No. Of our city."

It had begun to rain, and Emnot Hallyng allowed his eyes to settle upon the open doorway; the rain slanted across the prospect of a horse and cart standing idly by the side of the road.

"I think," Gunter said, "there will be wild fire at St. Michael le Querne. And then later at St. Giles in the Fields."

Emnot pretended to cough upon the piece of Sussex cheese, which gave him the opportunity to put a cloth up to his face. How could Gunter know about the preparations of the predestined men? He was no part of their assembly and, as far as Emnot Hallyng knew, was acquainted with no other member. Could it be some black art that had given him the skill to peer into their conventicles in Paternoster Row?

"How is all this known to you? How?"

"A poor summoner spoke to me of some arrow pointed into the heart of the city. Of secret men and hidden ways. Then I learned further from one much more exalted."

"Who was this?"

Gunter looked around at those eating in the coquina, to ensure that no one could overhear him. "What I say, Emnot, must be declared to nobody in life." He then informed the clerk of his dinner with Miles Vavasour, and of the notes he had found scrawled on the back of a legal parchment; he described, too, the clandestine meeting of the London notables in the round tower.

Emnot Hallyng had no need to feign surprise. He was alarmed, and horrified, by what Gunter had told him. How could these meetings – of alderman and under-sheriff, knight and sergeant – be connected with the actions of the predestined men? Miles Vavasour was not one of the foreknown, and yet he had written down something about the fire soon to visit the church in Bladder Street. How could such a high man of law have foreknowledge of a great crime – that is, of felony and sacrilege – without making any attempt to forestall it? Thomas Gunter had whispered of secret bands and concealed associates, but the physician had no knowledge of the predestined men. Gunter knew only that the guardians of the city were meeting in private conclave under cover of night and darkness. Then Emnot repeated the question to himself. How did any outsider know of Exmewe's preparations? Emnot Hallyng felt himself to be in a maze, and he suspected that great danger was already lurking there. He believed that he and his companions were free in every sense, and that they carried within themselves the seeds of divine life, but that vision had acquired the darker vestures of human fear and suspicion.

Now the meal was over. The clerk and the physician took cardamom seeds, from a bowl, to sweeten their breath. Then they walked over to Roger's stables. "I am afraid," Gunter was saying as he shielded himself with his cloak from the rain, "that ignorance, the mother of error, has blinded and deceived certain persons."

"It seems so, Master Gunter. God keep you in His care."

"I commend you to God, Emnot Hallyng. Ride hard through this wind and rain."

Roger of Ware was standing at the door of his coquina, murmuring "God give you good day" or "May God be with you" to each departing guest.

"It was fine meat, Roger."

"Sir, by God, you are welcome." Hanekyn Fytheler had drunk too much, and Roger helped him across the cobbles to his horse. Then he went back into the cookshop, wiping his hands. "God save this fair company and its farts! God give them good turds!" He began to inspect the premises. "Who is this that has thrown his bones under the table? Who was at this table, Walter?"

"Four velvet hoods from the Swithin guild."

"When men are fools, four is three too many. Did you belch in their faces, Walter? Did you blow your nose on their napkins? Did you pick your putrefied teeth?"

"No, sir."

"More the pity." The servers were putting the stale bread trenchers and the leavings into the alms-dishes. "Did you see Goodman Rochford? His hose was so tight that I could see his horrible member. It was like some swollen hernia. I almost fainted away."

"In his hind part," Walter added, "all the guns were blasting. It made a terrible stink in this part of the room."

"It is a foul world, Walter. There are some ox-tongues left here. Take them up for supper. And sponge your jacket. I spy fat upon it." He stopped and bent down in a corner. "Jesus, someone has pissed here. Fetch a bucket. May God's curse be upon him!"

Walter laughed, and went out whistling "Double me this burden."

Roger sighed, and took from the pocket of his jacket the small jewelled box. It had come from Africa, according to Henry Huttescrane, where men dwell in trees and eat the flesh of great white worms, where women have the heads of hounds, and all the people have eight toes upon each foot. In truth it was a world of wonders.

Chapter Seventeen

The Squire's Tale

Some children were singing at the foot of the Cross in Cheapside; they came from the neighbouring streets and by unspoken consent gathered here in the late afternoon, where they played top and penny-prick. They engaged in tugs of war and in the game of pig on the back. Some would pull their hoods over their faces to take part in "I Tell On Who Strikes Me." Others would bring their toy horses, or their lead images of knights in armour. They formed a circle, holding hands, and chanted the old verse:

> "A cow has stolen a calf away
> And put her in the sack.
> Forsooth, I sell no puddings today.
> Masters, what do you lack?"

The sun was slowly descending, on this last day of August, casting long shadows of the Cross over the cobbled stones.

"How many miles to Babylon?
Eight, eight, and another eight.
Might I come there by candlelight?
Yes, by God, if your horse be light."

Their voices rose into the air and travelled through the spheres towards the fixed stars, brightness mingling with brightness.

And then there was commotion. The sound of horses' hooves drowned their singing, amid cries of "Haste! Make haste!" Two heralds mounted the lower steps of the Cheapside Cross and shouted out "Oy! Oy! Oy!" until a crowd had assembled. The sheriff of London climbed to the highest step, from which the proclamations of the city were made, and declared himself bound to the Bishop of London, mayor, under-sheriffs, aldermen with all other spiritual lords and gentles as well as commoners of the city of London. "For as much as full great and sorrowful malice, trespass and wicked conjectures have been procured and done by the nun of Clerkenwell known as Clarice, to the great and perpetual confusion and reproof to the said evil-doer, and the great villainy and shame of all those maintaining her in her said malice, wherefore the nun deserves hard and wicked chastisement and punishment."

Sister Clarice had been arrested by the officers of the Guildhall and sent to the prison of the Bishop of London; she was accused of starting vexatious reports against the king, and of inciting the citizens of London against the spiritual lords of the city.

It was a dangerous and uncertain time. Henry Bolingbroke had halted with his army in Acton, the king closely guarded, only a half day's ride from the city. It was widely believed that King Richard's next home would be the Tower. In fact the aldermen were not particularly concerned with the nun's prophecies against the king; only a few days before a group of citizens had travelled to St. Albans in order to offer submission to Henry Bolingbroke. They were, however, deeply fearful of her power to incite popular riot and discontent at this time of general instability.

The night before the announcement of her imprisonment, Clarice addressed the citizens and their wives from the site of London Stone. "I am right poor," she said. "I have ugly sights in my sleep. Now I stand a deadly creature, and every day my body draws to the earth as a child to its mother. Yet I must live to warn you. They say that this is a fair city but among fair herbs creep adders, snails, and other venomous worms. There are nests of these worms among you. You know that I set so little by myself that I have become a finger of the right hand of God, pointing to you the way. Take weapons and shields, therefore, and rise in help to me." It was not clear, from her sometimes confused syntax, who or what needed to be attacked with weapons and with shields. But the mayor and under-sheriffs believed that it was a call to some general revolt – against the city, against the Church, or both equally. So, on the following morning, she was arrested and taken under guard to the bishop's prison by Paul's Bars.

By the time the sheriff was making his proclamation by the Great Cross of Cheapside, however, Sister Clarice was already being questioned in the main hall in the keep-tower of the bishop's palace; the cells were immediately below. Her interrogators were the bishop himself and a squire, Gybon Maghfeld; he was present by virtue of his position as judge of the county of Middlesex, in which Clerkenwell was deemed to be, and as a member of the parliament house for the same county. His interest lay in maintaining order at all costs.

She stood barefoot upon the flagstones before them.

"I must ask you first," the bishop began, "if you have any stone of virtue upon you, or herb of virtue, or charm, or any other enchantment by you or for you?"

"I am no conjuror or quack-salver, my lord bishop."

Gybon interjected, his eyes surveying the wall just above Clarice's head. "But it is said that you hold nightly conferences with spirits."

"So a poor woman who speaks the word of God is to be condemned as an enchantress."

"Let us say, rather," the squire replied, "that you are a troublous woman who has caused much clattering among the common people."

"Is it clattering to ask them to confess their sins and to pray for mercy at the fast approaching day of doom?"

"What doom?" The bishop was putting on gloves of white kid, in ritual acknowledgement of his role as *disputator*. "You are out of your wit, girl."

"I tell you this, lord bishop. Cleanse your sheep from the scab lest they infect others."

"You will throw words at me, will you?"

"It is the hurling time."

The bishop spat upon the cold floor. "I see that your sore is full of matter, nun."

"My words are fit for a sick body, then."

Gybon Maghfeld had been watching her carefully. Was she inspired or simply feigning inspiration? But for what purpose? Was she genuinely possessed by prophetic utterance, or was it some Christmas game for children? It was not to be expected that a young nun could stand against the Bishop of London without some inward power, whether of mischief or of bonchief it was impossible to tell. The squire had a further interest in the nun. His senior aunt, Amicia, had claimed prophetic powers in the reign of Edward III. She had worn a white tunic with a black hood, and each week she wore new shoes; she called herself "The Woman Clothed with the Star of the Sea," and she had specifically foretold the defeat of the French at Poitiers and English control of Aquitaine four years later. Her family had at first been embarrassed and even horrified by her claims to divine grace, but the king himself had congratulated her on her fervour in the national cause. Her brother, Gybon's father, had taken her into his house at Hosier Lane where, against all the laws and ordinances of the Church, she preached before the women of the ward. "We are all moving towards the light," she had said, "but we do not know what it is." Her conduct grew ever stranger. She popped, painted and plucked her face; on Fridays and Sundays she ate only grass and drank only brook water; she was wheeled through the streets in a dung-cart, crying out that the wounds of her sins had rotted within her. Eventually she was judged to be distracted and she was consigned to Bethlem Hospital where she died from an internal tumour.

Now the young nun stood before Gybon Maghfeld, her arms crossed upon her breast as a token of resignation.

"You are as quiet as a girl, Clarice."

"I must suffer as I have done in time past, sir, and so I will do for God's sake."

"Straw for your gentleness." The bishop scraped his left cheek with one of the fingers of his glove. "Put her in irons. Let her not see her feet for seven years. She has blasphemed."

"If it is blasphemy to speak God's word, then I admit it. You may hang me by the heels, but it is your world that will be turned upside down."

"Is your bile not broken yet? What are the causes of your murmuring?"

"What else is there to do but weep in this mortal life? Oh lord bishop, you mock the misery of this world when you say 'Over the fields of Babylon we sat and wept when we thought of you, Sion.' I have heard you babbling this in the pulpit."

"You will be whipped for this insolence, nun."

"God loves chastisement. God liveth, and I will play before Him in my prison. The Lord has already disciplined me with a loving rod, and my cry is a liking song to Him."

"You speak of your prison but in these latter days, Clarice, you have moved around the city like a thief in the night."

"The teachers of truth must be prudent where they speak."

"Harlotry of the mouth."

"Take heed, lord bishop, you are of unpower. Yet you cannot

weep because you are so barren and sorrowless. The old, foul and thick sins of London surround you. You must be turned to God."

The bishop moved forward as if to strike her, but Gybon Maghfeld made a sign to him.

"Take off your veil, Clarice." The squire asked her this very gently. "Show your face."

Reluctantly she obeyed his request.

As she lifted the veil they could see that her face was almond white, her eyes wide, her lips slightly parted.

"You can make good cheer, if you wish, with your countenance. Come now. Be merry."

"Merry?" She replaced her veil, and once more crossed her arms in an attitude which now resembled defiance rather than resignation. "You are about my death. Why should I not be in great heaviness?"

The bishop laughed out loud. "She has imagined against the king, and she claims to be woebegone! Lay her on a roasting iron and turn her. She will cast out oil and grease rather than words."

"I have said that the king shall die. And so must it be."

"Clarice," Gybon murmured. "You should file your tongue."

"When I am silent, sir, my bones grow old."

"This is strange English, nun." The bishop again took a step towards her, but she did not move. "Your words are full dark. You need exposition."

"I will give you *dispositio, expositio* and *conclusio —*"

"Let be! It is an evil thing to see a schoolman in a nun's habit."

"You mistake me. Not all the words in the world can paint you the image of my soul."

The bishop seemed to be growing impatient with her testimony. "Some say that you are inspired with the Holy Ghost, and some say that you are inspired by the spirits of the cellar."

"It makes no matter what 'some say.'"

"You are a gaud and a trifle. A geegaw. A whimwham."

The squire interrupted the bishop's invective. "Clarice, can I tell you thus. You say that you have had a vision of the Holy Church of

God in sad ruin, after the death of the king. You have stirred the folk. Much of what you say is perverted and turned into malice. Those who were once your friends have become your enemies. They are like huntsmen blowing your death."

"I do not know how. Who are these who use such subtle craft against me?"

"The enemies of all good order. Who long for the doom of this world."

"Yes. I have heard some say, is the world to end at long last?"

"You play on both the hands," the bishop said. "You hear some say this or say that. You are the spotless lamb born for the sacrifice. Is that your song? You are more like my father's old mare. You will not go until you are pricked. No one in England can blear eyes better than you can."

"I open eyes. Some engrave on trees, and some on stone walls. I engrave on hearts."

"Oh such subtle lookings and dissimulations, nun. You are a limb of the fiend."

She was silent for a moment, her head cast down as if in prayer. "If I consented to do your will and abjure all that I have said, then indeed I were worthy to be cursed of God."

"Wherefore abjure?" asked Gybon. "We require only silence and public penance."

"To carry a wax candle down Cheapside? It is the same as abjuration."

"You deserve more than the candle, nun. You are worthy to be blotted and spotted, fouled and defouled. I think, Gybon, our work is accomplished here for the time."

"You have done me wrong, sirs. My tale is not finished. For, sirs, take it not badly that it may not all go as you wish." The nun unclasped her arms, and held them out before her in an attitude of supplication. She seemed to the squire to become like some statue, wreathed in flowers and incense. Then she began chanting a verse of her own invention:

"Leave your reason and believe in the wonder,
For faith is above and reason is under."

The squire still watched her carefully. Sometimes she constrained and shrank herself to the common measure of men, and sometimes it seemed that she touched heaven with the height of her head; like that of his aunt, her voice had wings.

"You know, nun," the bishop was saying, "that it is within my power to exclude you from the threshold of Holy Mother Church?"

"I know it."

"You are one who has knowingly and willingly sworn falsely by those things most sacred. May the one God curse you. May the Holy Mother of God curse you. May the patriarchs and prophets curse you. May the martyrs and the virgin saints curse you –"

"The virgin saints will lift my heaviness –"

"Oh, do you think you can hop into heaven?"

There was a rapping upon the great door. A messenger came in with a blazing torch, walked over to Gybon Maghfeld, and whispered in his ear. The squire turned to the bishop, knelt and kissed his ring. "Pardon, my lord bishop. I am summoned without delay to the guild hall."

The messenger had informed him that Henry Bolingbroke had arrived at Westminster two hours before; he had despatched the king to the Tower for his own "safety" against the supposed wrath of the London populace – or, as Henry's representative would later tell the parliament, "for the great cruelty that he beforetime has used unto the city." The mayor and the aldermen were now gathering to consider their policy for this unsettled time. They were meeting in the guild hall close to the bishop's palace, and Gybon walked there with the messenger through the darkening streets.

It was the hour before curfew, and the wardens of the gates were blowing their horns; the people beyond the walls were being warned to bring in their animals. Six hundred armed men had been called this night to keep peace in the streets, and there were many guards at the gates of the city; Gybon Maghfeld could sense an air of excitement and of impending change. It was as if the city were bracing itself for a fever. There were citizens moving about from street to street, or from lane to lane, with intense looks of fear and amazement. He observed their faces as he passed them, but he recognised none of them. He was then struck by a curious possibility. What if these figures were created out of panic fear, out of the anger and excitement of the city itself? They might emerge at times of fire or of the death, a visible group of walkers in the night. They might appear on the same London streets through all of the city's history.

As the squire passed, wondering, along Silver Street and Addle Street, the bishop of London and the nun of Clerkenwell were raising cups of wine and congratulating one another on a drama well staged.

Chapter Eighteen

The Man of Law's Tale

"Say me where was God when he made heaven and earth?"

"I say, sir, in the farther end of the wind."

"Whereof was Adam made?"

"Of eight things: the first of earth, the second of fire, the third of wind, the fourth of clouds, the fifth of air whereby he speaks and thinks, the sixth of dew whereby he sweats, the seventh of flowers whereby Adam has his eyes, the eighth is salt whereof Adam has salt tears."

"That is good. Very good. Whereof was found the name of Adam?"

"Of four stars by the name of Arcax, Dux, Arostolym and Momfumbres."

"Of what state was Adam when he was made?"

"A man of thirty winters."

Miles Vavasour was catechising his young man of law, Martin, on their way into Westminster Hall; he had explained, to all his pupils, that a thorough knowledge of biblical matters was a necessary accompaniment to the study of all codes and constitutions. He was, in appearance, a pious man. "And what length was Adam?"

"Of eight feet and six inches."

"How long did Adam live in this world?"

"One hundred and thirty winters, and afterwards in hell till the Passion of our Lord God."

"And tell me this, Martin. Why is the sun red at evening?"

"He goes towards hell."

"Hell. Yes. Never trust a red-faced man, Martin. Now draw on my gear. It is more than time."

So the man of law dressed his teacher and employer in a mantle of green cloth furred with black lamb; this ceremonial coat was embroidered with vertical stripes of mulberry and blue, so that it could be distinguished from the mantle of diagonal stripes granted to the outer barristers who were there to examine but not to plead. Miles also wore the round cap of white silk, or coif, as a token of his rank as sergeant-at-law. He was led from the chamber of the robes to the court of the king's bench by an official holding a wooden staff tipped with horn at either end, and he stood behind the Bar in his appointed place. This was God's world. Three courts were being conducted simultaneously in the Great Hall. The court of the king's bench sat at the dais in the south end of the hall, close to the court of chancery, while the court of common pleas met against the west wall. So at once Miles was surrounded by the familiar mist of voices variously rising and falling, calling and pleading, chattering and whispering.

"Furthermore I marvel that you have not come to the point." The judge on the king's bench was addressing a barrister.

"The point, sir, is like a quintain. Hard to hit."

The judge acknowledged Miles's bow before continuing in the same peremptory manner. "No more. That dance is done." The barrister then whispered to him, to which the judge replied, "God forbid that it should so follow. As David says in the psalms, Omnis homo mendax. Every man is a liar."

"You will quote David, will you?" Miles murmured under his breath.

The sergeant-at-law did not admire this judge, who was now shouting to the prisoner at the other end of the Bar. "It is lex talionis! Like for like! I am not contented with you, I promise you!"

Miles turned to his man of law, who was standing on his right side. "The learned judge will soon be finished with his prey. Bring on our witnesses in all haste, Martin."

Miles Vavasour was putting the case against the apprentice of St. John's Street, Janekin, for *murdrum voluntarium* with *odii meditatione*, or wilful homicide of one Radulf Strago, merchant, done in contemplation of hatred. Janekin was also accused of unlawful marriage – a marriage *conscientia mala* – under the second Statute of Westminster. It was alleged by Miles that Janekin had conceived a violent affection for Anne Strago, the wife of the wealthy merchant to whom he had been indentured; in the throes of his passion he had determined to use arsenic upon her husband, the said Strago. Since he had lived with his master in St. John's Street, it was not difficult for him to administer the poison; a bag of arsenic had indeed been found concealed in his private chest. It was then charged that he had prevailed upon the said Anne to marry him – which was, as Miles Vavasour put it, no better than rape and abduction under a feigned name. Anne Strago was subsequently questioned in the house, where she accused Janekin of the several crimes for which he was being tried. She confessed that she had suspected poison, when her husband had complained of a "wambling" in the stomach and a "whipping" in the bowels, but had been too afraid of Janekin to pursue the matter any further. Janekin denied all knowledge of the killing, however, and insisted that Anne Strago had come willingly to his bed even before the death of Strago; he claimed that she had fabricated these charges in order to conceal her own scandalous conduct in consorting with him. He said that he did not know who had murdered the merchant. He offered to do trial by battle, to prove his innocence, but the request was denied; he was not of the right estate.

Martin had been closely observing the judge in this case who, in his scarlet robe and cap of gold silk, seemed to him like some figure who had stepped out of a stained-glass window. He had already become acquainted with the rituals of the court. He had learned law French in order to read the year books and had studied the abridgements as well as the register of writs; he had proceeded from apprentice to inner barrister, but he would not be allowed to practise law for another five years. He possessed a good court hand, however, and Miles Vavasour employed him to complete the appropriate writs and conduct his general business. For Martin, it offered a very practical education in which he learned what no law book could have taught him. He learned that both judge and sergeant believed that any juror who followed his conscience was surrendering to the voice of God; yet a jury which acquitted a prisoner was deemed to be responsible for his future good conduct. In addition anyone found guilty by a jury, who was later proved to be innocent, could bring an action of conspiracy against its members. Cases were heard in groups of three or four at a time, but an individual prisoner might pay to have more jurors assembled if he felt that they might help his cause. If a thief were convicted, the stolen goods were given to the crown; if he were acquitted, he kept them. There were very few cases when restitution was made to the victim of a crime; that is why there were many private bargains struck between the accuser and the accused, so that the former would not give evidence if the latter would restore some of the stolen property.

Martin had been despatched by Miles Vavasour to find two of his most significant witnesses. The beadle of the ward of Farringdon Without, and the overseer of the parish of West Smithfield, were waiting for the man of law by a pillar that was reserved for witnesses and was known as "the tree of truth." He took off his cap and saluted them. "We have the letter," the beadle of Farringdon Without told Martin. "It was found in the merchant's house."

"Very good. This will please Sir Miles somewhat." He looked

back at the court, and saw Janekin being brought to the Bar. "We must run, not walk," he said. "The case begins."

Janekin had been consigned to Newgate, and he looked as if he had contracted the gaol fever; he stank terribly, and Vavasour kept a scented cloth to his nose. The floor of Westminster Hall was covered with rushes containing sweet herbs, to curb the odours of the prisoners, but nothing could remove the stench of the London prisons. All the judges carried with them a ball of linen soaked in aniseed and camomile; before they began their work they drank a posset of hogs' feet and barley water, too, in order to ward off infection. As Martin came up with the two witnesses, the judge was ordering that a proclamation be made; anyone who had reason to suspect the said Janekin should come forward on the day following.

The overseer of West Smithfield, who had questioned Anne Strago, was then called to give his testimony. He named the prisoner as the felon, outlined the circumstances of the discovery, and recounted Anne's subsequent charges against Janekin. He was then, according to custom, asked to address the prisoner directly to prove that he did not level his accusations out of malice. "I know you well enough," he said to Janekin. "You robbed one Blaise White in Long Lane. You beat him. You took his horse and purse from him." He looked across to Miles Vavasour, who made a sign to continue. "You are a hog who would rather run to turds than to flowers. I have collected three good men of the ward who will bear witness that you are a go-by-ditch, a steal-away, a late at home, a grass-biter, a wild wood-cat, a skulker –"

"Let your lips cover your teeth." The judge had grown tired of the overseer's diatribe. "You sing neither good tenor nor good treble, man. Let the sergeant plead the writ of murder." Martin passed to Miles Vavasour the necessary formulae for pleading the writ; the plaints were confirmed, so that the process could continue. The sergeant turned at once to the act of poisoning. He recounted the circumstances in great detail; as the sergeants were trained to do, he imitated the gestures and expressions both of the murderer and the man who was slain. "Noctanter," he repeated. It happened by night. He did not know this, but he knew that juries were particularly susceptible to crimes committed under cover of darkness. "I have this letter in my keeping, taken up in the unlucky merchant's house. It is addressed to the poor afflicted wife. In this letter –" he held it up before the court. "In this letter Janekin confesses his heinous crime and pleads in redress his love for the said Anne."

"What is this letter? Who wrote it?" The judge took a particular pleasure in interruption. "Tell me in plain words. One may see daylight through a small hole."

Miles Vavasour then recited the letter of passion, which had in fact been fabricated by Anne Strago who had tired of her young lover. He concluded his reading with a flourish of his voice. "Written in no heart's ease at London, the fourth day of July."

"I am hugely astounded." The judge had decided to intervene once more. "Is there any proof that the prisoner Janekin wrote this?"

"I suppose it to be his work, my lord."

"Suppose? That is theory only. A great friend is Plato, Sir Miles, but a greater friend is truth. Wherefore suppose?"

Martin had been following this interchange closely, but his attention was distracted by a small man wearing the garb of a physician, who had entered the bounds of the court and was looking intently at Miles Vavasour. Miles, however, was being berated by the judge. "Will you stand angling to catch a few flies? Let the prisoner be unbound and stand forward."

Janekin was led towards a wide table, laid with green cloth and covered by volumes and parchments, which separated the judge's high seat and the desk of the sergeant-at-law. He seemed scarcely able to stand upright, and the tipstaff who had brought him from the gaol pleaded that he might be allowed to sit; the judge refused the request, and peremptorily began to question Janekin. The prisoner denied everything. He called himself "the woeful boy," and complained that he had suffered grievously in Newgate through want of food and lack of physic; furthermore, no one had ever explained the charges against him until that moment.

"So you make your moan, do you?" The judge was very firm. "You make much sullen cheer with your countenance, as I see. But be merry, man. The truth will out. God give grace and all will be well." Then, quite suddenly, he adjourned the case until the next day under the formula of *inquisicio capta*. He was fond of surprise in his court, which was the strangest mixture of order with confusion, of strict and binding rules of procedure with sudden tirades or arguments, of spectacle and colour with stench and disease.

Martin was about to accompany the sergeant-at-law out of the court, when Miles was stopped by the small man in the physician's robe. "How do you fare, sir?"

"It is rare to see a leech in the house of the law, Master Gunter. What is your business here?"

"My business is with you. May I?" He took the sergeant's arm, and they walked towards the pillar known as the tree of truth.

"These are unquiet times, Sir Miles."

"Yes. The world will turn. Henry will be king." Only the day before, Henry Bolingbroke had asked a committee to consider "the matter of setting aside King Richard, and of choosing the duke of Lancaster in his stead, and how it was to be done." It was not by chance, as Miles knew, that several members of Dominus sat upon this committee.

"You are well acquainted with the world, Sir Miles. I have seen it."

"What have you seen?"

"I have seen how the world is set. But these are close matters, I believe."

"Matters?"

"They are known only to you and other secret men."

"Will you break your mind to me, leech?" The sergeant-at-law was becoming impatient. "I am in a maze."

"No, Sir Miles, I believe you to be in a labyrinth. But it is one of your own making." Thomas Gunter quickly wiped his mouth with his hand. "Who entered the round tower but William Swinderby? Who but Geoffrey de Calis and an alderman? Who but an under-sheriff of London? Who entered but you, Miles Vavasour? I followed you that night. I saw all."

Miles Vavasour instinctively put his hand to the dagger beneath his belt.

Thomas Gunter noticed the gesture and immediately became pugnacious. He raised his chin, and for a moment stood on tip-toe. "I have given you language not to your pleasure."

"I said nothing to you, sir. I pray God make you a good man."

The sergeant-at-law turned to walk away, but the physician clutched as him. "Tell me, Sir Miles, do you know how to make gunpowder?"

"What?"

"Did you know that its light is so hot that it cannot be quenched with water but only with urine or sand?"

"I hold you to be mad, Thomas Gunter."

"No. You are the stark fool. I believe that you have caused wild fire in abundance through London. You have fired two churches, and desecrated Paul's."

"I have done no such matter!"

"There are two other churches in your sight."

Miles Vavasour laughed, but there was no laughter in his countenance. "Yours is a vain imagination."

"I believe that you have met under cover of night with these high men and have machined some plot to bring all into disorder. There are five circles in your litany of death. You are part of some secret coivin."

"You say on like a child."

"You must confess, Sir Miles. There is death in the plot."

"Confess?"

"You must go to Bolingbroke before it is too late to be pitied."

"Must me no musts." Miles Vavasour was a tall man, and at the mention of Bolingbroke he seemed to loom over Gunter. "What, leech? Will you be lord? Am I to serve at your behest? You will play bo-peep through a pillory before long. Your trade will not save you. Greater leeches than you have hanged."

"I have other news of you, Sir Miles, which may change your mind. You have known Rose le Pilcherer. A child." Vavasour blushed, the colour staining his cheeks, and at once he knew that he had betrayed himself. "You have been seen in a crooked street. In a master street of sin. Turnmill."

"Kiss the devil's arse."

"Dame Alice knows you well. The Wife of Bath believes you to be an old man rotted in sin. Is this not yet vouchsafed to the world?"

"You threaten me, do you?"

"The judges in this hall will commit to prison any person that has been detected in carnal riot with a child."

"I am hard, Master Gunter. The sun melts the wax on which it shines, but it hardens clay."

"But then the clay may be broken into pieces. God keep you and serve you, sir."

Thomas Gunter bowed to the sergeant and walked out of the hall through the exchequer door. He was elated. He had faced down this man and, small though he was, had defeated him in word combat.

Miles Vavasour took out a linen cloth and wiped his face with it; some of the powder with which he had painted his cheeks, for his appearance in court, became smeared upon it. What is the best thing and the worst thing among men? Word is both best and worst. What thing is it that some love and some hate? It is judgement.

Martin left Westminster Hall with a law abridgement tucked under his arm. It was the third day of September, St. Helen's day, and a procession in the saint's honour was moving slowly towards the west door of the abbey. Two elderly men were standing upon a pageant wagon drawn by a horse; one held a crucifix, and the other a spade, as a token of the unearthing and finding of the Holy Cross. A young man with them was dressed as St. Helen but, in a most unsaintly fashion, he blew kisses to those assembled along the path. But then he shrank back in alarm. There was a sudden disturbance in the crowd. A group of citizens brought out swords and staffs, and began calling for the nun of Clerkenwell; for the last four days she had been imprisoned in the bishop's dungeon, according to popular report, and her confinement had incensed a large part of the city. It was somehow associated with the imprisonment of Richard II in the Tower, and some of the crowd now began to shout, "With whom hold you? With King Richard and the true commons!"

Martin watched as two men mounted the pageant wagon and started to drive it towards the crowd. The horse reared up and the wagon was turned upon its side, throwing St. Helen and her entourage upon the pavement. "They are full wild," Martin said to an apprentice who had come out of the hall to watch the affray.

"Wild men, yes. Vagabonds. They have not a rag to cover their arses. Their mouths are well wet and their sleeves are threadbare."

"Their force cannot last. They will yield to the king's peace."

"Which king?" The apprentice laughed aloud at his own question. "Your man will not hang."

"Janekin?"

"Miles has hoist himself. If Janekin wrote that letter, then he can read." Anyone who could prove himself to be literate could plead benefit of clergy before sentence was passed; he would be asked to read a passage from the Bible, commonly known as a "neck verse," and if his reading was successful he could not be hanged.

"But if he did not write the letter –" Martin hesitated.

"Then he is not in guilt."

Martin remained at some distance from the commotion, as the men of the watch marched in formation down King's Street with pikes and guns and pans of fire; they fell upon the "wild men" and quickly dispersed the crowd. Many of those who started the disturbance took to the water, in boats that had been moored by the Thames bank for that purpose, and by nightfall all was quiet.

*

On the following morning Miles Vavasour visited William Exmewe at St. Bartholomew; they sat in the chapter-house, with the central palm-tree pillar of stone spreading its boughs and branches along the stone ribs of the vault above their heads.

"All is altered upside down," the sergeant-at-law said. "A man may not stop evil air." Vavasour was prone to *timor anxius*, the daughter of melancholy; he had a vivid fantasy and saw manifold images of possible harm. That was why he was a good lawyer: he envisaged all manner of difficulties, and resolved them in advance. But, when they touched his own life, he was helpless. "He has seen us," he said, "and divined our purpose."

"Pause a moment, Sir Miles, and recover yourself." William Exmewe was cautious; like all men who love power, he was deliberate and watchful, subjugating his feelings to the matter in hand. "Who has seen us?"

"The doctor of physic. Gunter. He saw us coming to the round tower. He knows of the five circles. He knows of Dominus. He will rumble over our heads!"

"He is not of the number of Dominus. How may he know of our purpose, if he is not one of us?"

"How can I tell? In the whirling of the world, I do not know what to think or what to do."

Exmewe pondered. Had the physician traced the connection between Dominus and the predestined men? Had the sergeant given the physician a list of the five churches? "Tell me the remnant of your thoughts, Miles."

"What?"

"You have not given all. You have left something behind."

What the sergeant had not disclosed, of course, was his weakness in Turnmill Street. "I have nothing more to speak. I have knit up the matter, as far as my poor wit allows."

He looked away as he said this. Exmewe did not believe him and, from that moment, considered the sergeant's death. "Listen, Miles, I will instruct you in the way you must go. Shadow yourself for a while. Be silent. I will visit this Gunter."

"It makes no matter which saying we use in manner of a threat. Not all the words in the world –"

"Who said a saying? Mark well, Miles. 'Timor domini sanctus.' The fear of God is holy."

"I would be glad to deal with him, William, but the man is of so diverse mind that there is no hold at him."

"Hush. Go in peace. I will never disclose your coming. God save you." Exmewe watched Miles Vavasour as he left the chapter-house. Then he looked up at the palm-tree vault, and admired its beauty. "I am sure, friend Vavasour," he said out loud, "that these are your last days."

Chapter Nineteen

The Pardoner's Tale

On the corner of Wood Street and Cheapside there grew an ancient oak tree known as the Canute Tree. Small charms were hung upon it, both to placate the tree itself and to bless its benefactors with the gift of old age. The London birds loved this tree and would cluster among its branches; they were safe here because no child would stone them or trap them, not even with nooses of horsehair in the winter snow. It was popularly believed that the birds sang in Latin and in Greek, and that their songs lasted no longer than the saying of an Ave Maria.[17]

A few yards from this tree stood the pardoner of St. Anthony's Hospital, Umbald of Arderne; he was also known as a quaestor or public inquirer, but his principal role was to sell papal pardons or indulgences for money. The indulgence was a remittance of punishment in the fires of purgatory, and was therefore much prized. He also carried with him relics for sale, as well as phials of holy water and cures for various ailments; he was a true merchant of the Church.

Although he had not visited a shrine for many years, he always wore the garment of a pilgrim. He stood beneath the tree in a shaggy woollen robe, decorated with small wooden crosses; over his hood he wore a large round felt hat, upon the brim of which were tied phials of holy oil, scallop shells, the lead tokens or badges of various holy sites, and a miniature representation of the keys of Rome. He clutched a staff tipped with iron, with a red cloth wound about it, and he carried a bag and bowl by his side. The bag held his "patent" for trade in the area, as well as a testimonial from St. Anthony's Hospital that he was licensed to work on its behalf. There were small bells fixed to his hood, which jingled as he cried out on the corner of the street. "You may see by the signs on my hat that I know Rome and Jerusalem, Canterbury and Compostela. O Jerusalem! Jerusalem! I have seen the place where Our Lord was scourged. It is known as the Shadow of God. And there beside it are four pillars of stone that always drop water, and some men say that they weep for Our Lord's death. In the place called Golgotha was found Adam's head after Noah's flood, a token that the sins of Adam should be bought in that same place. I have seen the tomb where Joseph of Arimathea laid the body of Our Lord when he had taken him down from the Cross, and men say that it is the middle of the world. Nearby is a well that comes from the river of Paradise. O Jerusalem! All those who cannot weep can learn from me! Our old world is now at his last ending, as in his last age."

It was the thirtieth day of September, the morrow of St. Michael the Archangel; Londoners had already heard that Henry Bolingbroke had visited Richard in the Tower and had there compelled him to abdicate his throne. One party asserted that he had been forced with threat of torture or of death to forfeit sovereignty; another party declared that he had done so willingly to spare his country further blood and war. Whatever the circumstances, Umbald of Arderne was determined to take advantage of the unsettled time. "God does not sleep," he called out. "When the hills smoke, then Babylon shall have an end."

A priest of St. Alban, at the other end of Wood Street, had crossed the road in order to confront him. "Pardoners may not preach. They do evil through their manifest deceptions!"

Umbald glanced at him briefly. "You are an old fool. Your garb is heavy, but your tongue is light. If you had said nothing, you would have been mistaken for a philosopher. Let me be."

St. Anthony's Hospital in Threadneedle Street, to which the pardoner was attached, was an ancient institution. It consisted of an empty church which had been converted into a pillared hall, with rows of beds in the nave and aisles; there was a chapel at one end, with a refectory and dormitory for the priests arranged around a courtyard. It was known in the immediate neighbourhood as "the house of dying." That was the true name for the hospital, where care for the soul was considered to be more important than treatment of the body. It benefited from many gifts and bequests, of course, but the proceeds of the pardoner were eagerly received.

"If a man full penitent come to me and pay for his sin," he was saying, "I will assoil him. Here is the authority granted me." The pardoner held up a sheet of vellum decorated with a great initial "I" in which monkeys clambered among vines. "If anyone gives seven shillings to Anthony's, I will bestow upon him an indulgence of seven hundred years. I am entrusted to do this by the pope himself." He rolled up the papal bull and carefully placed it within his bag; then he took out a small piece of bone. "Here is a holy relic of the Eleven Thousand Virgins of Cologne. Wash this bone in any well, and the water from that well will make you whole." An old woman selling pasties made the sign of the cross, but Umbald ignored her; she would not have seven groats, let alone shillings. "Make any sheep or cow swelling with the worm drink it, and he will be healed. Sores and scabs will be washed clean." Two or three passers-by had stopped, curious to see the object which possessed all these miraculous properties, but Umbald had replaced the bone in his satchel. It was his way of drawing a crowd.

As he began his new oration, he saw someone whom he knew.

The sub-prior of St. Bartholomew had crossed the street and turned the corner; Umbald recognised William Exmewe at once, from the great feasts held upon the love-days of the London hospitals. He considered him to be an enemy, too, since it was Exmewe who had instituted a review of the alms gathered by the pardoners for the sake of their foundations; Exmewe himself had insisted upon a scheme of proper accounting. Umbald was now obliged to keep a tally of all those to whom he distributed indulgences, which afforded him less chance of private gain.

Exmewe was waiting on the corner; he was glancing up and down Cheapside, continually folding and refolding the sleeves of his habit. He had come, as Umbald supposed, at an appointed time. Who should approach him, then, but Emnot Hallyng? Umbald knew the clerk by sight, as he knew all the noted ones of the city; Hallyng was reputed to practise the black arts and to work his cunning against the good of the Church. Why was he now in company with the sub-prior?

Umbald took his hat, saluted the few who had gathered around him and, with a "God give you grace and a good death," walked slowly towards the corner of the street. The pardoner stopped beneath the Canute Tree, and listened.

"Why did you wish to see me in this open place?" Exmewe had not even waited for the greeting of "God is here!"

"No notice will be taken of us here," Emnot Hallyng replied. "And I have much to impart to you."

"Of what?"

"Of one Thomas Gunter."

"Gunter?" Exmewe was astonished by this further mention of the leech, but he feigned ignorance. "Who is Gunter?"

"He practises physic in Bucklersbury. I have spoken to him as a convivial man. But he knows all." Then Emnot Hallyng informed William Exmewe of the conversation in Roger of Ware's cookshop.

"Whom did the physician name?" Exmewe asked him.

"The law-man. Vavasour."

With this, Exmewe became alarmed, but he managed once more to conceal his feelings. "The leech, Gunter, is a rattler. A scare-bug."

"In the cookshop he spoke to me of the five circles."

"You should keep well your tongue and be still, Emnot Hallyng."

"I said nothing to him. But he knew of the fire at St. Michael le Querne, even though it has yet to be achieved. How did he come by this knowledge? He is not predestined."

"Soft, soft." Exmewe was considering the matter carefully. "Take heed. Think of what this Gunter's intent might be. His will is not rightful."

"Meaning?"

"He is about our deaths."

"But we cannot die."

"Not in a ghostly sense, no. But our work is not yet accomplished on this earth. His murmuring must cease. His bile must be broken."

"He has always been merry with me."

"He drives dust in your eyes, Emnot. Believe me. His are the snares that spell death."

They began walking along Cheapside towards the stocks; the pardoner could not follow them without being seen.

"You know, Emnot, that if anyone hinders us then God's curse is upon him?"

"There is no need for God to curse him. He is cursed enough already." There was an uneasy silence between them. "So what are we to do?"

"You are to do nothing as yet. I have another task for you."

"Concerning?"

"Miles Vavasour. He troubles me. He has discovered our holy faith. He squats by holes. He lies close to the ground like a dying lark or a frightened fowl. He is a law man. If you are born of such a nest, you will never be dumb from lack of words. He gabbles. He whispers. His open mouth must be stopped. His murmuring must be restrained. You are a clerk. You know your French. Vous estes sa morte. You must not only bridle the horse. You must curb him for ever."

Emnot was on his guard. "For whom should I quake? For him or for me?"

"To kill is to be free. We are far above the law. We are the realm of love. When love is strong, love knows no law." It was a settled doctrine of the foreknown men that they could kill with impunity as long as their instinct or humour suggested the occasion to them; they were then filled with the divine breath of all being and had become sacred. God killed His creation at every moment. But the pre-destined men could not kill for profit or with deliberate malice; the case of Miles Vavasour, then, was an ambiguous one. "I know, Emnot, that you are as true as stone. Do you know of any secret and close poison?"

"I have the means whereby I might –"

"I pray you put them in full expedition. God be with you." Exmewe scratched his arm savagely. "I rely upon God. But I rely upon you more."

"Is this your wish?"

"Turn up his halter and let him go."

"I must bring death to him then?"

"God is here." Exmewe looked up at the sky. "Come. The day passes fast."

They walked off in the direction of the cathedral, wrapping their cloaks around them as the wind rose in the wide street.

The pardoner wandered down Wood Street, starting up his familiar lament. "O Jerusalem! Jerusalem! Where is pity? Where is meekness?" But, to Emnot Hallyng and William Exmewe, it was no more than wailing in the wind.

As soon as Exmewe returned to his chamber in St. Bartholomew he took out pen and parchment; in the fitful light of a tallow candle, he scratched out a letter which was addressed to Thomas Gunter at the sign of the Pestle at Bucklersbury by the church of St. Stephen in

Walbrook. "Right trusty and well beloved friend, I greet you well."
He asked Gunter to meet the writer of this letter in the woods near
Kentystone, at the break of day, "for diverse great matters reaching
you, item: the churches of London in some peril of burning. There
you shall hear from one who is a friend who will break his mind to
you on an affair concerning your interest and your safety. I will write
no more but I purpose to write again after our meeting with true
evidences of what I will impart to you. Jesus keep you. Nota bene: I
choose the woods of Kentystone since we can be assured that no one
will be near us or with us. When you see me you will know me."

He called for a carrier and gave him a penny for this letter's
delivery, on strict instruction that he should say it had been sent by a
stranger.

Chapter Twenty

The Shipman's Tale

The shipman, Gilbert Rosseler, lodged in a hostel for travellers; although he now lived in London, he enjoyed the constant change of companions with their own stories and adventures. He had once sailed as far north as Iceland; he had journeyed to Germany and to Portugal; he had sailed to Genoa, and from there to the island of Corfu; he had taken ship at various times to Cyprus, to the island of Rhodes, and to Jaffa. But, in his talk with his bedfellows, he ranged wider into unknown regions of the earth.

His hostel stood in St. Lawrence Lane, with the customary sign of a bush hanging over its door; it had a common dormitory, containing seven truckle beds on wheels in which travellers slept two by two. It was, for Gilbert Rosseler, as close to being in a ship's cabin as was possible on land; he called his bed his "berth," and his companions were his "mates." They slept naked, according to custom. Nakedness was no cause of shame or embarrassment, and indeed it was said that a serpent fled from the sight of a naked man. Yet nakedness was also associated with punishment and poverty. It was as if all the travellers were willingly engaged in the experience of shared and bare humanity. A bed could be hired by the night, for a penny, or by the week for sixpence. The hosteler, Dame Magga, also had three private rooms – with their own bolt and key – which could be occupied for a shilling a week.

Magga was terrified of fire, like many householders of London. Since its most common cause was a candle igniting straw, she kept all candles in her possession; she would light them each night, and then extinguish them one hour after darkness had fallen. Some months before she had asked the shipman to perform that office in the dormitory, modesty forbidding her to walk among the naked men. In return she charged him only two shillings per week for his board at the high table in the hall of the hostel. Gilbert paid for his lodging and his food by taking Newcastle sea-coal up the Fleet by barge; he navigated his boat from Sea-Coal Lane, near the mouth of the Fleet, as far north as the woods of Kentystone or Kentish Town where a colony of metal-workers had set up a communal foundry.

On one afternoon, at the beginning of October, Gilbert had invited Magga on to his boat. She had expressed interest in "going up the river," and had never been as far north as Kentystone. As a girl she had been taken to the church of St. Pancras for the festive day of Mary the Child, when she and the other children had danced around a tree decorated with images of the Virgin, but she hardly recalled that part of the countryside. This first day of the month was the eve of the Holy Guardian Angels. On the morning before, the members of the parliament house in Westminster Hall had accepted the resignation of Richard II as sovereign. The Archbishop of Canterbury had asked them if they approved "the points given as reasons for the king's deposition," and they had replied with cries of "Yes, yes, yes!" When Henry Bolingbroke then asked whether they welcomed his reign "with their hearts as well as their mouths," they again shouted out "Yes, yes, yes!" Gilbert and Magga had received the news of this great change in English history with a resignation bordering on indifference; they were not intrigued by the adventures of princes.

Magga was settled on a little stool near the prow of the barge; standing beside her, Gilbert used a long pole to move them against the current. At the stern a young boy, the shipman's assistant, worked with his oar. From the wharf at Sea-Coal Lane they passed the great bulk of the Fleet prison; it was moated by a ditch, and Magga put the sleeve of her gown up to her nose as the barge passed it. Two prisoners were soliciting alms by the riverside, putting out a box and saucer to the boatmen as they passed; the barge came so close to the bank that Magga noticed the image of a spiked door impressed upon their pewter dish. From the vantage of the water she could see the valley in front of her through which the river flowed, with the steeper slopes upon the eastern side where there were houses and barns; by the bank here the tanners had set up a row of sheds, and the Fleet had become dyed deep with red. It might have been a river of blood. The air, too, was stained with odours compounded by the entrails and refuse which were carted down from the Shambles and thrown into the water.

Gilbert leaned over his pole and spoke softly to Magga. "I was afraid to tell you where we were, in case you lost heart."

"Never in this world."

They passed under a double-arched stone bridge; there was a windmill, just beyond a row of tenements and hostels which Magga recognised to be Turnmill Street. The Wife of Bath was walking there with Rose; Dame Alice pointed towards the boat gliding gently across the water.

Gilbert resumed his labour. "What is the broadest water and the least danger to walk over?" Magga shook her head. "The dew. And tell me this. What is it that never freezes?"

"I cannot tell. How can I tell?"

"Hot water." This was the game known as "Puzzled Balthasar," in which the shipman delighted.

"What is the cleanest leaf among all other leaves?"

Magga did not reply, but she guessed the answer.

"It is the holly leaf, for nobody will wipe his arse with it."

"I shall stop my ears, Gilbert. Whatever next?"

"How many calves' tails can reach from the earth to the sky?"

"Gilbert!"

"No more than one, if it is long enough."

The water became cleaner, and the air fresher, as they passed through Smithfield and came up to the fields belonging to the House of Mary at Clerkenwell. The reeve, Oswald Koo, was wheeling a cart filled with sacks. Magga pointed to the range of buildings behind him. "That is where the nun comes from." She crossed herself. "The Holy Spirit protect her."

"She has prophesied Richard's death."

"She has been drawn into kings' games. They are not made to meddle with."

"Unless she would be queen."

"No. Not her. She is a good maid. She is one of God's."

The river curved westward here, following the line of the valley, and had become slower in its course. In the fields beside it boards and shields had been set up for archery practice, and there were fixed stone marks for sessions of javelin throwing. "I have seen in Sweden," the shipman was saying, "a river that is called I know not what, but it exists still. On the Saturday it runs fast, and all the week after it stands still or runs but little. There is another river in the same country that at the night freezes, but upon the day no frost is seen." Magga delighted in his tales of the distant world. He had told her of the men who have only one foot but that foot is so large that, when they lie and rest, it shadows all the body against the sun. He had described to her the children of Ethiopia whose hair is white, and the inhabitants of Ormuz where it is so hot that their bollocks hang down to their knees. Gilbert had seen the mountain, seven miles high, where Noah's ark had come to rest. There was a well by the coast of India which changed its odour, and its taste, from hour to hour. In Sumatra there was a market for fresh children to be bought and sold, as food, which they say is the best flesh and the sweetest of all the world.

They had come up now to the pleasant mount, and in the neighbouring fields the beasts of the village were still grazing on the stubble. The wheat and the rye had been sown, and a large wooden statue of the Virgin placed in the fields in order to invoke a good harvest. Coke Bateman, the miller, was kneeling before it. "Tell me," said Magga, "of the strange folk of the earth."

He was distracted for a moment by a bend in the river, which now turned north-westward towards the woods. "The men of Caffolos hang their friends, when they be dying, upon trees. They say that it is better that the birds, who are the angels of God, should eat them rather than the foul worms of the earth." Magga was listening intently. "On another island, Tracoda by name, the men eat the flesh of serpents. They live in caves and do not speak, but hiss as serpents do."

"Is it possible?"

"All things are possible under the moon."

"As Hendyng says."

They laughed at this. The phrase "as Hendyng says" or "quoth Hendyng" was current in London, as a way of concluding some line of wit or wisdom. "Friendless are the dead, quoth Hendyng" was a favourite expression, together with "Never tell your foe that your foot aches, quod Hendyng" and "Hendyng says, better to give an apple than to eat an apple." Magga had been trailing her hand in the water. "Do you know how to catch a fish in your fingers?" the shipman asked her. She took out her hand quickly, as if she had been caught in some act of trespass. "You take saffron and frankincense, and mix them together. Then put the powder on your finger which has the gold ring."

"This one?"

"Yus. Wash your finger beside both banks of the river. Then the fishes will come into your hand."

"Is that so, Gilbert?"

"Who learns when young never forgets."

"Quoth Hendyng."

The shipman began to sing, as the barge passed under a wooden bridge that seemed to be of ancient construction:

"I am an hare, I am no hart,
Once I flee I let a fart.
You can see by my hood
My heart is naught, my head is wood."

He stopped singing, and began humming the tune. They passed another windmill, on the western bank; a small pond had been created there, and the bright beaks of the ducks were darting in and out of the water. Drago, the canon's yeoman, was lying there asleep. Gilbert began to tell Magga of the men without heads, whose eyes and mouths grew from their backs; he told her of a race of people with ears so big that they brushed the ground. There was a tribe of dwarves in Africa who gathered all their nourishment from the smell of wild apples; if they travel, and lose the smell of them, they die. In the land of Prester John there was a sea of gravel and of salt without any drop of water; it ebbs and flows in great waves, as other seas do, and it is never still. There was a faraway land entirely shrouded in darkness; its neighbours dare not enter it, for fear of its night, but they can hear from within this shadowland the voices of men as well as the sound of bells pealing and of horses neighing. "But they do not know what kind of folk they may be who dwell within it."

"London folk. If it be dark enough. There was a mist yesternight which I could not see through."

They had come up to the holy well of Chad; various pilgrims were going in and out of the little stone chapel, and Gilbert waved to them. Some of them waved back, and one young woman raised her crutch in greeting. Jolland, the monk of Bermondsey, was reciting his rosary behind her. "It is a hard road to Paradise," Gilbert said.

"It marvels me that you have not sailed there."

"Oh no. No man that is mortal can approach it, although many have tried. Its rivers run so rudely and so sharply, and come down from such high places, that no ship may row or sail against them. The water roars so and makes such a huge noise that no man can be heard, even if he is in the same ship. Many men have died for weariness of rowing against the strong waves. Many have become deaf from the noise of the water. Some have been lost overboard and have perished."

"A good life will bear them there the quicker."

"So it is said, Magga. But who can be good upon this troubled earth?"

They were passing the church of St. Pancras, where the altar of Augustine had been laid, and were coming close to the remains of the ancient woodland of the region; wild service, herb paris and wood anemone grew in abundance. The citizens of London still came for timber here, where areas of wood survived in the northern heights. There seemed to be a log floating in the water but, as the shipman drew close to it, he let out a loud "Halloo!" It was a man floating two or three yards from the barge. With his pole he steered it closer, and then bent down to haul the body on to the deck. The boy at the stern jumped quickly over the sacks of coal to view this unexpected find. Magga and Gilbert peered closely at the face. Then she crossed herself and began to pray, "We beg thee, O Lord, to receive the soul of your servant."

Earlier that day, just as dawn had washed the woods of Kentystone in red, Thomas Gunter had ridden among the trees. He was curious about the letter which had suggested so much without stating any particular thing. Could it have been sent by Miles Vavasour himself? Or was it Bogo the summoner, ready to divulge more? Gunter ducked beneath the spreading branches as the hooves of his horse made a hollow sound upon the earthen floor. It had begun to rain, and the drops pattered down upon the leaves and fern as he rode beneath the canopy of sequestered light. There were patches of mist, in the groves and glades within this great wood, and the liquid notes of the birds created for Gunter what his favourite poet called "the bower of bliss." William Exmewe was waiting for him, huddled beside an ancient oak. He had his dagger beneath his cloak. He had grasped its handle tightly as soon as he heard the horse approaching. Just as it was about to pass he sprang out, shrieking "Ho!" The horse reared, and threw Gunter to the ground. Exmewe stabbed its flank, and with a bellow it galloped away.

"When you see me you know me," Exmewe shouted.

Gunter was too shaken to reply; he had bruised his left thigh, and injured his wrist, in the fall.

"Do you know me?" Exmewe shouted again.

"I have never seen you in life." Gunter wept for pain in the green shade.

"Oh I have seen you. Or I have smelled you. I know your devices, leech."

"What have I done to you, man?"

"What is that you leeches say? Cure or kill? Make or mar? Heal or harm? Well, you were close to harming all."

"I cannot –"

"I am with Henry, soon to be highest of all. In his name Dominus has done its work."

"Work?"

"You jangled about the churches. You jangled about the circles. You did not make. You marred."

Gunter now understood. "Bogo saw the circles."

"Do you not know from Holy Scripture that chaos must come before creation?" Exmewe laughed out loud. "With Richard gone, we can begin anew." He leant over Gunter with his dagger. "And yet, for some, the day of doom is close at hand. This is for your curiosity, leech." With one movement he slit Gunter's throat. He wiped the dagger upon his cloak, and put it back in its scabbard. Then he dragged the body of the little physician through the moss and the bracken towards the Fleet which, in this place, was deep and fast-running.[18] He rolled it down the bank. Very gently, it slipped into the water. When Magga and Gilbert found Thomas Gunter, a few hours later, his features were still fresh.

Chapter Twenty-one

The Parson's Tale

John Ferrour was telling his beads in the chapel of Westminster Palace. He was a devout man, now grave in middle age, who for eighteen years had been Henry Bolingbroke's priest and private confessor. He had been a priest of the Tower in 1381, at the time of the Peasants' Revolt, and had then saved young Henry's life.

The fifteen-year-old Bolingbroke had taken refuge in the Beauchamp Tower, in one of the stone "apartments" which were generally given to noble prisoners, and Ferrour had been asked to comfort and advise him. "And David thereof bears witness," he told him, "where he says, Laqueum paraverunt pedibus meis. They have delivered a snare for my feet. You must walk carefully through this trouble. David also says, I am turned in my anguish while the thorn is fastened in me. But the thorn can be plucked out."

"Why all this talk of David when you see before you suffering Henry?"

From the narrow windows, no more than slits for arrows, priest and fugitive could see the rebels running up to the Tower. Some clandestine elements within the fortress were even then drawing down the bridge, but many of the rioters were so eager to enter the building that they swam across its moat. There were cries of alarm within, and then screams for help. The boy king, Richard, had already ridden out to Mile End in order to parley with the main company of rebels; in his absence from the Tower, the disaffected mob had come to plunder and kill those who remained. Ferrour could hear heavy footsteps mounting the circular stairway of the Beauchamp Tower. He took off Bolingbroke's richly embroidered doublet, and with his knife ripped it to shreds. Then with a piece of charcoal he made dirty marks upon the boy's throat and arms. Bolingbroke wailed and put his hands across his face as if he might blot out his own image. There was a straw mattress on the floor of the cell; Ferrour asked him to lie upon it and pray. "Rely upon the bounty of God," was all he said, before opening the thick wooden door and stepping out on to the stone landing. From the stairway came the sound of roaring, with no distinguishable words, and within a few seconds there appeared a tall man in a threadbare doublet wielding a sword.

Ferrour put out his arms. "Christ keep you in His holy keeping. We look for deliverance."

"Who do you hold in there?" Two other rioters had joined him, and peered at Bolingbroke lying very still upon the mattress. "What little mouse is this?"

"The son of a poor prisoner immured on the orders of the king himself. The father is but lately fled, leaving behind his child who is sick. Come closer. Look at the tokens of that sickness."

They did not move. "The death?"

"The very same. The pestilence."

"To kill him would be to cure him."

"Oh, my masters —" This was a happy choice of phrase, which seemed to cheer the ragged men. "Consider well. Reflect what horrible peril there is in the sin of murder, what an abominable sin it is in the sight of heaven. It is the very full forsaking of God. Come." The priest put out his hand, but they stepped back. "Approach the bed. Kill the lamb. Heap up in your hearts a dunghill of sin. Then kill me, for I will not shrive you. The blood will be too hot upon your hands. And remember this. You may send your soul out naked to Him no man can tell how soon."

His eloquence disturbed them. They spat upon the floor, looked at one another, and then retreated down the stairway.

Thus John Ferrour entered the service of young Bolingbroke as his confessor.

He had listened to the voice of Henry's conscience through intrigue and rebellion, peace and war. He had heard him whispering of avarice and of lust, of pride and of envy. He had raped a young girl; he had stabbed in anger a bedfellow. Nothing, however, had prepared Ferrour for this moment. Only two hours before, his master had been acclaimed king of England in the parliament house.

He had heard the cheering as Henry left Westminster Hall. At that moment Ferrour had clutched his rosary to his chest, pinching the wooden beads until the tips of his fingers burned. Henry had acquired his throne by rebellion and conquest, not through divine right. He had not confessed as much, but had murmured to the parson about the realm's undoing and Richard's bad laws. He had told his confessor about his duty, but he had never once mentioned the promptings of avarice or ambition. But Ferrour could see into his heart. He knew the depths of sinfulness to be found there. Would he himself be caught in the snares of mortal sin, if he remained silent about these matters? Was he giving the new king his tacit blessing, and blinding them both to God's law?

Someone knelt down beside him. He sensed unease and sin. What man was this, for whom Henry's guards had made way? He turned, and recognised Miles Vavasour; the sergeant-at-law had worked on behalf of Bolingbroke in several pressing matters of feoffment and jointure.

"I am in great heaviness, father. I am alone as I was born."

"Do you wish to give me words *in secreta confessione?*"

"Yes. May my last hour be my best hour."

"Benedicite fili mi Domine." Before he heard his confession, he pulled his hood over his eyes. "Is your repentance unfeigned?"

"It is, father."

"Are you consumed with sorrowfulness that you are such a damnable sinner?"

"I am."

"Do you believe that Christ will forgive you and receive you into mercy?"

"I do."

"And furthermore do you promise to offer satisfaction and make amends by doing holy works unto God?"

"Yes, father."

"Then confess, my son, with contrite heart."

"Oh most holy and devout father," Vavasour bowed his head, "I have been homely and familiar with evil men." The sergeant then told the parson about the activities of the predestined men. He told him of their leader, William Exmewe, the sub-prior of St. Bartholomew. He claimed that he had previously said nothing, for the sake of his friendship with Exmewe. He made no allusion, however, to the assembly known as Dominus, which had stirred up unrest and sacrilege to snatch the new king's victory.

When he had travelled to Westminster Hall that morning, to take part in the debate, Vavasour had no intention of confessing. But he had been stopped outside the chapter-house by the clerk, Emnot Hallyng, who had run beside his horse and shouted to him, "You are taken with enemies you cannot see."

He reined in his horse. "How is this?"

"I swear that the matter of this information is true, Sir Miles. One man is casting a plot against you."

"Are you in earnest or in game?"

"In deathly earnest."

"Which man is it you speak of?"

"William Exmewe."

"Exmewe? He is –"

"One of your confederacy? I suspected so."

As the sergeant dismounted, Emnot Hallyng silently made the connection between Exmewe and the men who met in the round tower.

"Companionship is no vice," Vavasour was saying. "And in every proof there must be two witnesses at the least."

"You are deep in law, I know, but the truth is deeper. Exmewe has asked me to encompass your death with poison. He does not trust you to keep his *secreta secretorum*."

"The lion always sits in ambush."

"He is no lion. He is the smiler with the knife under his cloak. He has dark imaginings. I know him."

"Tell me this. Are you one of the foreknown men?"

"Do you know about us?" The sergeant-at-law nodded very quickly. "This is all Exmewe's contriving. He has played both the hands."

Emnot Hallyng now knew what he had before suspected: Exmewe had been leading the predestined men into a trap, at the behest of certain high men, and he would very soon betray them. The clerk feared for himself, too. Exmewe was no doubt planning to have him taken up after the murder of Vavasour. Exmewe himself would play checkmate.

"Answer me another question." Vavasour was very grim. "Why does Exmewe contrive my death?"

"He suspects some bond between you and one Gunter, a leech and a gabbler."

"But the leech is dead."

"What? How so?"

"He was found within the Fleet. Stabbed foully."

"His spirit has changed house?"

"Is that what your new men say?" The sergeant did not wait for an answer. "The one who maimed him has fled. There is no trace."

"Believe me, sir, this is Exmewe's doing. He will try to attach this stabbing to you. You have five wits. Use them. He plans to destroy you, and this death will continue his purpose marvellously."

It was then that the sergeant, fearful for his life, decided to betray Exmewe to Henry Bolingbroke's confessor.

He could not expect an audience with Henry himself, so soon after his seizure of power; but Ferrour could be asked to pass on his report by word of mouth. William Exmewe would then be arrested, with the other predestined men. Vavasour might even earn merit from the new king by uncovering the confederacy of the foreknown; thus Dominus would remain hidden under the leaf, in which secure place the king would no doubt prefer it to be kept.

"Wherefore I pray you as heartily as I can," the sergeant murmured to Ferrour, who had just heard his confession, "that you will diligently take heed of my words, and send to our good lord Henry my plain sayings. I trust to God in the great confusion and shame of all these false judging and miscreant persons."

"I shall share your information with my good lord, and with God's grace he will so deal with them that they shall not all be well pleased. At such a time a king must know his friends and his foes asunder."

"Surely."

"These things I will to no man utter but to him. But what of you, Miles Vavasour?"

"I end it thus, since I can do no more. I give it up for now and evermore."

"And do you repent?"

"I repent me heartily that in times past I have groped after a wrong way, dark, crooked, hard and endless."

"Do you speak as a true and faithful man?"

"You may hang me by the heels if it be not so."

"So may you still reach the everlasting bliss of heaven."

"That is worth more than a penny." The sergeant was greatly relieved, and with some difficulty rose from his knees.

"Yet it may well be likened to a penny for the roundness that betokens everlastingness, and for the blessed sight of the king's face that is upon the penny." He stopped for a moment. "Our coming king, at the least."

"How does his grace?"

"I have not seen him since he was acclaimed. But be comfortable. After I have talked with him, I will send you word how the world is set." The parson seemed to sigh at the way of that world as he, too, rose from his knees. "Beware how you walk in the city. And have fellowship with you when you do walk out. Exmewe is not yet found. This corruption may linger. A fog cannot be dispersed with a fan. Remember, for the passion of God, that these predestined ones are also troublous men. They might turn you towards great harm."

"Then, father, I pray you, let me have the thing I came for. Absolution."

Ferrour sighed again, and lifted up his hood. They stood face to face. He stared at Vavasour for a moment, and moved his lips as if he were thirsty and wished to drink. In a low voice he imposed the penance, at which Vavasour sobbed aloud. Then he made a rough sign of the cross upon the sergeant's forehead. "Ego te absolvo," he began as Vavasour whispered his act of contrition. When it was completed the parson took his arm. "God give grace all will be well. Come out into the air."

They left the chapel, and walked into a paved courtyard.

"The moon is huge tonight, God bless her."

The sergeant made no reply. He was already contemplating the nature of his penance which would take him beyond this familiar sky. John Ferrour had commanded him to go on pilgrimage to Jerusalem, leaving all his goods and possessions behind; he would be obliged to beg for his sustenance during the long journey, since he must proceed only with robe, stick and empty sack. He had kept silence while all good authority was set in doubt, and must pay the forfeit.

Ferrour had heard of the predestined men, since these arch-heretics had been reported in Antwerp and Cologne. But he had not known of their presence in London itself. No doubt, among the citizens, they had won converts whose names and numbers remained unknown. This Exmewe was a limb of the fiend. How could God permit heretics to work their will? Was all preordinate by Him? But if the time was prefixed, there could be no remedy through the agency of grace. Man was doomed perpetually. The parson had once told Henry Bolingbroke that the star which led the three kings towards Jesus from the east might well have been their belief which they acquired first at baptism. "The sacrament of baptism is called the east, where the sun first arises," he had said, "for there sprang first to them the day of grace after the night of original sin." But now all seemed to be in twilight. It was hard to see clearly in this world. What if sin came from God, the maker of all things? The predestined men might then have issued from the hand of God. God might have created damned souls. "Lord, in thy wildness," he murmured to the cold air, "do not undermine my faith."

The first fog of autumn was gathering in the courtyard of the palace. Westminster had once been marsh ground, and the palace itself had been built upon an island "*in loco terribili.*" It was terrible still, filled with the passions and envies of men fighting for power; the atmosphere of fog and gloom had never left it. As John Ferrour walked across the courtyard he encountered one of Henry's men, Perkin Woodroffe, who had that day threatened Richard with sudden death. "The breaking time is over," Perkin said to the parson after they had exchanged greetings. "We must begin to build."

"Until the end of time shall undo it all."

"Why, Sir John, you speak darkly. Be cheerful. Tomorrow is not born."

"But then tomorrow becomes yesterday."

"Your wit is marred, good parson. This fog has entered your

head." He stepped closer to him. "Be sure that it does not enter Henry's. His will must be rightful and strong. A man who borrows hot coals to start his fire must run with leaps and bounds over all obstacles."

"I will assist him as much as I may, Perkin. Christ keep you."

Yet the parson secretly believed that Henry Bolingbroke was cumbered with corrupt humours. When the snuff obscures the light so that it cannot burn clear, then there is more smoke to add to the vapouring mass. He slipped upon a loose cobble, and fell heavily to the ground where he lay for a moment in severe pain. "Why, you have fallen like humankind." It was Henry Bolingbroke himself, who helped him to his feet. "You should beware where you walk."

"You represent grace, sir, after the fall."

"They say that all mist is decaying cloud. But I believe that this fog issues from the earth."

"It is decay, certainly. For me it is an allegory of sin."

"Well said." Henry clapped his confessor on the back. "We must always remember our frailty." His hot breath mingled with the fog. "You stand at the door of my conscience. On this day of triumph, let us talk of things spiritual."

"I must first talk of other matters, sir, which may concern you deeply. We have dark tidings to digest."

The fog had now spread along the river, and had entered the walled city.[19]

Chapter Twenty-two

The Second Nun's Tale

Ten days after Henry Bolingbroke had learned of the predestined men, Sister Bridget was standing beside the nun of Clerkenwell in a gallery of Westminster Abbey. Sister Clarice was peering through a squint at the ceremony in the chancel below. By the high altar sat Henry, wrapped in cloth of gold; his throne was of alabaster richly decorated with jewels, and the tapestry at his feet had been embroidered with gold and silver thread to represent the story of Samuel and Saul.

"I see the crown," Clarice whispered to Bridget. "It has arches in the shape of a cross. A wondrous work to put on an unhallowed head. They have broken the temple, and stolen the vessel of grace." The voice of Henry could be heard, reciting the coronation oath in English. Clarice was whispering fiercely once more, but she was no longer addressing Bridget. "He will sell the souls of the lambs to the wolf that strangles them. He will never have part of the pasture of lambs, that is the bliss of heaven. No holy oil will lift him there." Clarice knew that the oil for the new king's anointing had come from a miraculous phial which the Virgin Mary, in apparition, had given to Thomas Becket. It had been discovered by King Richard two years before, while he had been searching in the garderobe of the Tower for a necklace worn by King John. The nun knew this because Richard himself had told her so.

She had visited the broken king three days previously, in the company of Bridget. Richard had been informed of her prophecies concerning his deposition and death, and had asked to see her. When she was taken to him, however, she knew that he was not in his rightful mind. He was dressed in a white gown which touched his bare feet; on his head he wore a black skullcap, and he held out some papers as she approached him. "Be of good cheer, Dame Clarice," he said. "Be of comfort. I am God's fool." He was sitting within a stone alcove, cut into one of the walls of his cell. "You prophesied my end, but you cannot prophesy my beginning."

"Your grace?"

"You must get eight miles of moonlight and knit them in a bladder. You must take eight Welshmen's songs, and hang them on a ladder. You must mingle the left foot of an eel with the creaking of a cart wheel. Is this more impossible than deposing a king? God's anointed one?"

"To make a mirror bright, you must first cover it with black soap."

"You are madder than me, maid. Or do you tell me that the holiness of the sanctified one will one day shine again?" He stood up, and then genuflected before Bridget. "How do you find me, nun?"

"I find that you are poor, sir."

"Poverty is the eye-glass through which we see our friends." He turned to Clarice. "I have come to love weeping. The tears trill down my cheeks. I am the fount of all waters. When do they crown this bug?"

"The thirteenth day of this month. The feast of St. Edward."

"The feast of the good king who built the abbey. The stones shall smite and hurtle together. There will be a trembling of the earth."

"If he is God's foe, then –"

"The rain will fall upon the altars. That is my prophecy, nun." He paced rapidly around the confines of his stone cell. There was another alcove, where he could sit, and from its slit window the Thames could just be seen. "Read my dream, and I will say that you are God's fellow. I dreamed that a king made a great feast, and he had three kings at the feast, and these three kings ate but out of one gruel dish. They ate so much that their balls burst, and out of their balls came four and twenty oxen playing at the sword and buckler, and there were left alive only three white herrings. And these three herrings bled nine days and nine nights, as if they had been the remnants of horse shoes. What is this dream?"

Clarice was confounded, but kept her composure. "It passes my wit, sir."

"And mine." He still paced about, his bare feet upon the cold stone. "They say that you have scrolls, and that you are an enchanter."

"They say untruth. The only scrolls I carry are prayers to God."

He stared at her for a few moments, but she remained demure; as modesty demanded, she looked away. "Do you bind your breasts with lace, ma dame?" She did not answer, but made the sign of the cross. "You do not blush. You are deeper than a well, Sister Clarice. In ghost and in body." They spoke a little more, and Richard informed them of the holy phial. "This feigned king is but a painted image," he told them. "The oil upon him will smell rank. It will reek to heaven." He sighed, and sat down once more in the stone alcove. "Delightable to me are ghostly songs, releasing my travails in this wretched life. Sing one for me."

So in a clear, calm voice Clarice began to sing "Jesus, mercy! mercy, I cry."

When they left him, singing to himself in his chamber, Clarice murmured to the second nun that "his death is shaped before him."

In this prophecy, as in so many others, she was proved correct. She also told Bridget that, if an unhallowed king such as Bolingbroke came to rule, then others must hold the power until an anointed one returned to the throne. She did not say who those "others" might be.

"What I have done," she told her, "I have done for the sake of Holy Mother Church. If the rulers are unclean, then Mary must be queen. We will lead, and others will follow."

Four months after the interview in the Tower, the unhappy Richard was starved to death in Pontefract Castle.

Between the day of this encounter in the Tower and the day of the coronation in the abbey, there had been reports circulating through the city of arrests and imprisonments. William Exmewe had been taken up for treason and forced to abjure the realm. In a solemn ceremony at Paul's Cross he was dressed in a long white robe, his shoes were taken from him, and a large wooden crucifix placed in his hand. Roger of Ware, Bogo the summoner, and Martin the law clerk were among the crowd taunting him. It was ordained that he should walk barefoot to Dover carrying the cross before him.

Among the dignitaries on the scaffold were Sir Geoffrey de Calis and the Bishop of London; William Exmewe looked at them both, and then nodded at the knight almost imperceptibly. It was enough. Exmewe had fulfilled his destiny. Dominus had not been, and never would be, revealed to the world.

The sentence was then read out to him. "You, William Exmewe, cannot stray from the high road and you may not spend more than one night in the same place. Your path is to Dover, where you will remain upon the shore. Each day you must walk up to your knees in the sea, until a boat is ready to take you away from this realm. Before embarking you are ordered to proclaim, 'Oyez! Oyez! Oyez! I, William Exmewe, for the foul sacrilege which I have committed, will quit this land of England never more to return, except by leave of the Kings of England or their heirs, so help me God and all His saints.' "

And so it came to pass. When Exmewe arrived in France, however, he was taken secretly to a small castle outside Avignon where he was closely guarded for the rest of his life.

After his departure the citizens marvelled that, on the same day, Sir Miles Vavasour had gone on pilgrimage. There had been rumours, too, that a conventicle of heretics had been detected and destroyed; they were described as the "new men," and nothing more was known about them.

Sister Bridget had informed the nun of these startling events; Brank Mongorray had been sent away, and Clarice spent most of her time in her chamber at the House of Mary. Bridget slept at the foot of her bed, and joined in her prayers. She trusted the nun of Clerkenwell, and never doubted for a moment that her intentions were holy. She was perturbed, however, on those occasions when Clarice ventured from the convent alone. She was absent for four or five hours, and would return without a word of explanation. When she had been imprisoned by the Bishop of London, Bridget naturally feared for her safety, but Clarice had been freed by Robert Braybroke after three days without incurring any noticeable harm; indeed she seemed refreshed by her ordeal, and had told the second nun that there was much spiritual comfort to be found in confinement.

She had now become so popular with Londoners that any further attempt to arrest or to silence her would be met with an immediate and violent reaction. The prioress, Agnes de Mordaunt, had given up any attempt to restrain or discipline her. "Mark well your bedfellow," Dame Agnes had warned Bridget. "Be sure that she does not stray into the path of temptation and sin. Certain people may be injured or bewitched by immoderate praise. It is known as forspeaking, Bridget. I pray that Sister Clarice does not rely upon fickle fame."

"I am sure that she does not, ma dame."

"An hour's cold will suck out seven years of heat. The wheel may turn for her. What was whole may be bruised."

"I will tell her that you have spoken, ma dame."

That is why, perhaps, Sister Clarice formally asked the permission of the prioress to attend Henry's coronation; her presence had been requested by the senior clergy of the abbey, but she had agreed to arrive secretly and to remain in the upper gallery.

She was still looking through the squint. "Now, Bridget, the crown is upon his head. He holds the orb and sceptre. He sits very still for a condemned soul." The sound of the choir, singing the anthem of jubilation "Illa iuventus," surrounded the two nuns. "The archbishop has raised his right hand to heaven. Now he has extended it to the image of the Virgin on the north side of the altar. Now he genuflects. Henry rises." She laughed. "A foul person richly dight seems fair by candlelight. Now Henry processes before the earls and all others." Lessiez les aler et fair leur devoir de par dieu. They should do their duty before God, she had whispered fiercely to the second nun.

That evening, long after the ceremonies were over, Bridget was startled out of her slumber. Clarice was shaking her arm. "Bridget, come. Come with me. It is the time."

"Time?"

"Follow me."

The two nuns left their chamber, and walked quietly through the cloister. Clarice insisted upon silence and secrecy. A chariot, pulled by two horses, was waiting for them by one of the side doors of the convent; as soon as they had entered it the horseman raised his whip.

"Where do we go?" Bridget asked. She could smell the new straw laid at the bottom of the vehicle, and for some reason it instilled in her a profound unease.

"Not far, but a great distance."

They were travelling south, across Smithfield, along Little Britain and down St. Martin's; as a girl Bridget had walked through these streets with her nurse and companion, Beldame Patience, and their perpetual activity never failed to reassure her. She knew every shop and shack, every stall and tenement, but she was always surprised by the city's endless life. Then she had been obliged to enter the convent.

"You need say nothing," Clarice was telling her. "What you see, lay up in your heart for the fullness of time." They were coming close to the riverside, and the chariot stopped by the round tower of Roman stone.

Two servants with torches came out of the great porch to greet them and Clarice, leading the way, entered the tower. Bridget noticed three men in sumptuous attire waiting in a passage, and, much to her amazement, they made obeisance to the nun. They followed her down a turning stair of stone, into a large vaulted room where others were waiting. Bridget recognised Robert Braybroke, the Bishop of London, who had imprisoned Clarice a few weeks before. And was not that the archbishop himself? They were wearing cloaks of blue striped cloth. Why had they assembled in this place on the evening after the coronation?

Sister Clarice stood in the middle of them. "You know my name," she said to them. "It has come to pass as we have wished. Exmewe has been expelled, and will not speak. He plotted with heretics, and he has gone out with the winds. The predestined men have been scattered, and nothing further will be known concerning them. Yet they have left a comfortable inheritance. This new king is not holy. He is a usurper. God is with us and now, through us, He will guide the destiny of this kingdom."

"King Henry will argue –" the bishop began to say.

"There is many a man who begins language with a woman and cannot end it.[20] No. We are the holy ones now. We are truly anointed. We will rule behind the king. So be of good heart. Dominus rises."[21]

Chapter Twenty-three

The Author's Tale

1. By the time of Agnes de Mordaunt, the citizens of London insisted upon holding three days of mystery plays here, enacting the sacred history of the world from Creation to Judgement.

2. There remains no trace or memorial of the convent in Clerkenwell except for one public house, the Three Kings, which stands on the ancient site of its hostelry. Its underground tunnels can still be seen, however, in the basement of the Marx Memorial Library at 37a, Clerkenwell Green.

3. It was said that the Virgin had once appeared in this cloister to William Rahere, the founder of the priory, but at Rahere's insistence no statue or altar had been erected; the Virgin's words to him had not been recorded, but he had cried afterwards of the bush with red flames burning.

4. Every Londoner was accustomed to the smell of faeces, and there were still parts of the city that were shunned for fear of contagion – shunned, that is, except for the snufflers and the gongers or rakers who collected the dung to spread upon the fields beyond the walls.

5. On the site of the yard and privy where Radulf's spirit left his body, singing, the bar and café of St. John's Restaurant now stand.

6. That area of Camomile Street is, to this day, reputed to be haunted.

7. In some respects the stated beliefs of the Lollards have been considered by modern historians to be close to those of the predestined men or foreknown ones; but the Lollards were quite without the apocalyptic and messianic tendencies of that much smaller sect.

8. In a sermon composed during this period, collected in *Sermones Londonii* (London, 1864), Swinderby inveighed against "the men commonly known as Lollards who for long time have laboured for the subversion of the whole Catholic faith and of Holy Church, for the lessening of public worship, the destruction of the realm, and very many other enormities."

9. In 1378 certain cardinals had proclaimed the election of Pope Urban IX invalid, whereupon the new pope excommunicated the complainants. The errant cardinals then retreated to Avignon, where they elected one of their own number as the "true" pope. Thus there began the division which brought forth two popes, one in Rome and one in Avignon; there were two sets of cardinals, and in certain monasteries there were two abbots with contrary allegiances. The schism was maintained by

personal jealousies and political ambitions, but also by ecclesiastical corruption and national rivalry. The Avignon popes were supported by France and by her allies, Scotland and Naples; the Rome popes were maintained by Germany, Flanders, Italy and, less enthusiastically, by England.

10. A hundred years before an artist known only as "Peter the Painter" had been requested to delineate "the plain figures of death's dance" and had succeeded in impressing and terrifying generations of Londoners.

11. The Eighteen Conclusions have been found in a manuscript now kept in the British Library, under the reference Add.14.3405. It has been transcribed by Dr. Skinner thus:

"Item. Churches are dens and habitations of fiends. They are places of sin and occasions for sinning.

"Item. The pope is father Anti-Christ and its head, the prelates are its members, and the friars its tail.

"Item. The holiest man in the world is the true pope.

"Item. The place hallows not the man. The man hallows the place.

"Item. The needy man is the image of God, in more perfect similitude than wood or stone.

"Item. Confession should be made unto no priest, for no priest has the power to assoil a man of sin.

"Item. It is lawful for priests to take wives and for nuns to take husbands, since love is more commendable than chastity.

"Item. After the sacramental words said of a priest, there remains a cake of material bread on the altar which a mouse may nibble at.

"Item. The water hallowed by a priest is of no more effect than the water of a river or a well, since God blessed all things that He made.

"Item. It is not lawful for any man to fight or to do battle for any realm or country, nor should he plead in law for any right or wrong.

"Item. It is lawful and right to do all bodily works on a Sunday and all other days which have been commanded by the Church to be had holy.

"Item. Those who are saved can commit no sin.

"Item. The ringing of bells availeth nothing but to get money into priests' purses.

"Item. Those who are saved make up the true church, in heaven and in earth.

"Item. The sacrament of baptism is a trifle, and not to be pondered.

"Item. It is no sin to do the contrary of the precepts of the Church.

"Item. It is as well to pray in a field as in a church.

"Item. It is no better for laymen to say the pater noster than to say 'bibull babull.' "

12. The husting of the citizens assembled at a stone amphitheatre a few hundred yards from St. Paul's Cathedral. This was the ruin of the Roman building which had also been used for similar communal activities and been preserved by the citizens as an evident token of London's ancient origins; it still contained the rows of seats for any great assembly. The guild halls of the eleventh and fifteenth centuries were built upon the same site. The present Guildhall can now be found there.

13. Historians harbour conflicting opinions about the persistence of the secret group known as Dominus. In the events related here it became clear that Dominus was dominated by one faction, serving the interests of Henry Bolingbroke and using the predestined men to achieve its purpose; but it is not at all clear that it maintained its partisan stance in the subsequent affairs of the nation. Some believe it to have been dissolved at the time of

the Civil War in the seventeenth century, when it could no longer manage the scale of religious conflict; but others trace its existence in the Gordon Riots of 1780 and in the Oxford Movement of the 1830s. Some historians believe that Dominus persists to this day, and they cite the events in Northern Ireland as evidence of its malign conspiracy.

14. Haukyn's Field is now a grass mound, to be seen a few yards south of Whitechapel High Street. It is not much visited by night.

15. It has been argued that the festival of Midsummer Eve is of ancient origin, and that its drinking and its violent games had once been part of certain religious ceremonies which had never lost their power or efficacy over the populace; the bonfires and the sports represented some atavistic recollection of the time before Christian worship. The feast of Midsummer Eve was discontinued in the period of the Reformation, in the mid-sixteenth century; nevertheless, even now, public houses customarily display garlands or baskets of flowers by their doors.

16. The place where he died can still be seen in what remains of the church of St. Bartholomew.

17. At the corner of Wood Street and Cheapside, a tree still grows out of the soil and rubble of the city. It is a plane tree, rather than the oak, but it also prospers in the London air.

18. The course of this part of the Fleet river can still be traced in the curve and flow of the London streets in that neighbourhood. Thomas Gunter was murdered by William Exmewe at the turning of the river where Pancras Road now flows into Pancras Way.

19. The same fog is mentioned by Strabo, in his account of London in the first century; he reported that the sun could only be seen for three or four hours each day. It was also invoked by Herodian two centuries later, when he described "a thick mist rising from the marshes." On certain nights, in Westminster, that fog still returns in gusts of darkness.

20. The role of the nun has been much studied in histories of late fourteenth- and early fifteenth-century England. She has been compared to other "turbulent women" such as Elizabeth Barton, the sixteenth-century "Mad Nun of Kent," and the eighteenth-century duchess of Newcastle. Others have seen her as an integral part of the Church in schism, representing what has been called the "matriarchal" tendency. It is clear, however, that she maintained the supremacy of the universal Church opposed to national sovereignties. Whether she took part in the plots of Dominus, to sow discontent and thereby to discredit the rule of Richard II, remains an open question. Her subsequent control of the organisation continued until her death in 1427 – by which time she had become prioress of the House of Mary in Clerkenwell. During the period of her leadership Dominus became a recognisable group, albeit a clandestine one.

21. Only in recent years has the connection between Dominus and the predestined men been discovered. For more than five centuries the activities of the predestined men were described by historians as a brief, if unique, episode in the anti-clerical activity of the period. In 1927, however, a letter from William Exmewe was found within a bundle of ecclesiastical documents in the library of Louvain Cathedral. It had been written in Avignon, but apparently had never reached its destination. Its recipient was addressed simply as "Dear father in Christ." In this letter, Exmewe confesses to his association with the predestined men,

and claims that "Dominus me festinavit" – which might mean either that Dominus [the organisation] or Dominus [the Lord] hastened me forward. But Exmewe then goes on to list those who were members of Dominus before the coronation of Henry Bolingbroke, as well as the names of the predestined men. Without the assistance of his letter, this narrative could not have been written.

Peter Ackroyd, 2003

ALSO BY PETER ACKROYD

THE PLATO PAPERS

At the turn of the thirty-eighth century, London's greatest orator, Plato, lectures on the obscure and confusing era that began in A.D. 1500, called the Age of Mouldwarp. Basing his work on an incomplete archeological record, he pieces scraps of evidence together into a semicoherent whole. His subjects include Sigmund Freud's comic masterpiece *Jokes and Their Relation to the Subconscious*, and Charles D.'s greatest novel, *The Origin of Species*.

Fiction/Literature/0-385-49769-5

ALBION
The History of the British Imagination

In *Albion*, Ackroyd ranges across literature and painting, philosophy and science, architecture and music, from Anglo-Saxon times to the twentieth century. Considering what is most English about artists as diverse as Chaucer, William Hogarth, Benjamin Britten, and Virginia Woolf, he identifies sometimes contradictory elements: pragmatism and whimsy, blood and gore, a passion for the past, a delight in eccentricity, and much more.

History/0-385-49773-3

LONDON
The Biography

Here are two thousand years of London's history and folklore, its chroniclers and criminals and plain citizens, its food and drink and countless pleasures. Blackfriar's and Charing Cross, Paddington and Bedlam. Westminster Abbey and St. Martin in the Fields. Cockneys and vagrants. Immigrants, peasants, and punks. The Plague, the Great Fire, the Blitz. Through a unique thematic tour of the physical city and its inimitable soul, London comes alive.

History/0-385-49771-7

ALSO AVAILABLE:
The Life of Thomas More, 0-385-49693-1

ANCHOR BOOKS
Available at your local bookstore, or call toll-free to order:
1-800-793-2665 (credit cards only).